QUEST MASTER

The Boy Who Would Be

Prequel to the Fabled Quest Chronicles

AUSTIN DRAGON

Published by Well-Tailored Books, California

Quest Master: The Boy Who Would Be
(Prequel to the Fabled Quest Chronicles)

978-1-946590-08-4 (paperback)
978-1-946590-03-9 (ebook)

http://www.austindragon.com

Book cover design by Rena Hoberman

Printed in the United States of America

CONTENTS

INTRODUCTION

Once upon a time...before there was the Kings' Caravan...

The known world of Pan-Earth, or the Lands of Man, was divided into the major continental regions of Larentia, Gondwana, Oceania, Laurasia, Baltica, Avalonia, and the uninhabited Borea. Of all the Seven Empires, however, it was only Avalonia, at its northernmost tip, that possessed the sole legendary gateway to the realm of the Magical Lands. Men had passed through the gateway in the millennia since its discovery in search of adventure and, later, riches—a gateway created by the ancient Titans themselves.

Long ago, before the dawn of man, fae, and beasts of light and darkness, was the Age of the Titans. They were gigantic humanoid beings of such size that their heads reached high above the clouds into the heavens. According to myth, a Titan known as the Maker of All Mountains was so devastated by the death of his beloved, he walked the entire circumference of Pan-Earth, dragging his fabled weapon, the Star Slayer, upon the earth. He inadvertently carved a massive valley, before he killed himself by leaping off the world to disappear into the void of space. This valley, cut through not only the known world, but every other realm, was known as Titan's Trail, and the Avalonia gateway was its entrance.

Every year, the northwestern lands of Avalonia attracted men—royals, nobles, and commoners, farmers and knights, apprentices and warriors, rogues and ruffians, human wizards and their apprentices, mercenaries and thieves—from every corner of the Lands of Man. All sought passage—a year-long or more journey—like no other through unimaginable dangers, mortal and magical, by day and night, to obtain the limitless riches of its final destination—a magical kingdom named Atlantea. The odds of success for any human, even those gifted with magic, guile, and wealth, were rare. However, despite a venture filled with likely death, there were always plenty of men glad to gamble with their lives.

There were many cities and towns that naturally became a last stop within the Lands of Man before crossing the threshold to the Magical Lands. The rural town of Hopeshire soon became the most popular of them all.

We know him as Quest Master. You know him as the man called Traveler. But when it all began, he was merely a small boy. One unremarkable day, he arrived for the first time, but far from the last, in the town of Hopeshire.

The following takes place many years before the events of ***Through Titan's Trail (Fabled Quest Chronicles: Book One)***.

PART ONE

THE LANDS OF MAN

The Seven Empires of Humans

CHAPTER ONE

A Boy

Young Traveler was nine years old.

He had been walking all along the Row for days. That was what the wide, dirt road was called that wound through the territory connecting the many towns but the best of them all—Hopeshire. He was a boy of normal height for his age. He kept the hood of his cloak snug on his head, he gripped his walking stick firmly, and walked with purpose as he had always heard his elders instruct the young men of his city. He had years to go before he was even a "young man" but that was why he had set out on the small journey. He knew he would return to this place when he was a young man, so he had to prepare. His mother said he had a sickness when it came to thinking, organizing, and preparing and was proud of him for it. His father always laughed at him and said, "Real men do, they do not plan or think their life away."

They both were right. This small journey was so that he could plan as he grew to be a man, and then he would "do"—travel into the magical lands themselves.

The boy had to force himself not to smile. "Walking with purpose" meant he wanted to give the appearance that he knew where he was going and he was not a stranger. In fact, he had never been on the Row; he had never been outside his home city before. But had heard the many stories of men of the Seven Empires. While he was typical of men of his region—dark hair and eyes, olive skin, the men of Pan-Earth were vast in their variety—fat and skinny, tall and short, smooth-faced or fully bearded, long, fair hair to their shoulders or bald. From stories, languages, and dialects he could pick out whether men were from Baltica or Avalonia. From the darker skin and features whether men were from Laurasia or Gondwana. One would not see a man from Laurentia or Oceania; they were as rare as a wild unicorn, but he would know them too if he saw them.

As he watched the men—commoners, knights, warriors, merchants move in all directions along the Row, he wished he could spend time with each group to learn more of their lands. However, that was not his purpose. He could do that at a later time. The town of Hopeshire had been visible for more than an hour. The Row descended down from the hills so the view was unobstructed for many miles. Hopeshire was a merchant town that survived and thrived based on the many visitors that passed through it. The town welcomed strangers no matter who they were, because without them the town would fade away. The Row was evidence that Hopeshire had been a fixture of this region for ages. Looking down at the road, he wondered what kings or queens, or maybe even wizards, had passed years, decades or centuries ago.

His eye caught sight of them. Every city had them—dirty, unkempt men who stood watch at the entrances or main roads of large towns and cities. Most were looking for handouts of food or a stray coin; ready to look upon gullible strangers with the saddest of eyes, begging without saying a word. However, there were more sinister men also watching. They were the professional thieves and the murdering kind. He watched them and gave a smirk to show that there was no fear in him despite his age and continued on.

Bravery was a good trait for one to have, but so was wisdom. He shot a glance back and he saw a couple of the men staring. Traveler smiled and pointed to his eyes, then at them. The two men laughed. He returned his attention ahead as he was about to step into the busy town of Hopeshire.

It was as he was told. Inside the main market area was an endless gathering of parties buying or trading for supplies and provisions. Not all of them would be traveling into the magical lands. In fact, few if any would be. It was something that many talked about, but few had the means or courage to do so. As he looked at the different groups with horses and wagons, he realized that none of them were large or impressive enough for a year-long journey.

"Excuse me, sir," Traveler asked a man who wore the bright colors typical for an Avalonian royal.

"What is it, boy?" the silver-haired man replied.

"Sir, where might the parties preparing for the journey to the magical lands be?"

"Why? What services do you have to offer a royal caravan to the magical lands?"

"I do not know, sir. That is what I am here to find out. I have no intention of joining any caravan today. But years from today, I will be ready."

"Ah. You are a reasoned thinker. Where are you from, boy?"

"I am from the lands of Baltica bordering Laurasia, sir."

"You certainly are not. Look at your shoes. They would be far worse for wear if you walked on foot from the outer borders of Baltica to here. Also, you do not speak like a

Baltican, nor any region of Laurasia. You are Avalonia. What kingdom are you from?"

"No kingdom, sir. I am a commoner."

"Boy, you are not very good at this. If you were a commoner, you would not be here. No commoner mother or father would let their young son freely stroll into strange lands unaccompanied. And if they were a commoner, they would not have the money to send someone to accompany you and they surely would do so themselves. No work, no food is the life of a commoner. No. I had suspected you might be a noble but now I think you may be a royal. Only, a typical lazy royal would be too self-absorbed to know their own son left their court days ago. So how many servants do they have to raise you?"

"I am not raised by servants," Traveler said with a hint of anger under his breath. "I am not of nobility."

"Yet in a market square of dozens of men you freely approach the one that is identifiable as nobility. Even hardened knights steer clear of royals and nobles, never quite sure how to act or what to say. But not you. It is common practice for you even at your young age."

A young Traveler turned his head to mentally kick himself for such a mistake.

The royal laughed. "Boy, if you are going to pretend to be a commoner, maybe you should actually spend some time with commoners, so you can learn how they talk, think and act."

The boy stopped himself from responding and simply sighed.

"I know why you have set your mind on this ruse, but you have not thought it through. You should pretend to be a noble. You think commoners will respect a commoner but not a royal. You think this because the commoners of your home do not respect the royals of your court. No. Outside of your home, everyone respects a noble. Royals, I agree with you, not always. Commoners, definitely not. No royal or noble will take you seriously. You must be a noble. Does my analysis of you meet with your approval?" The royal held in his chuckling.

The boy's eyes darted away.

"Observation, boy, observation. It is not one of the better traits of nobility—being able to size up a man's life from their clothes, grooming, and posture. However, there is nothing preventing you from elevating such a petty pursuit to one that would instead appear as if the work of a wizard who can see what is not visible to the mere commoner. Understanding the art of observation will then give you the ability to outsmart other practitioners of the art. You received two lessons today, boy, and I did not even ask for payment. So, again, does my analysis of you meet with your approval?"

"I will do better next time, sir," Traveler said.

"Yes, I suppose you will, but I shall not be here to see that progress. Ah, your request."

The man extended his arm and pointed far into the distance within the town.

"Thank you, sir."

"Do not thank me yet, boy. But you are welcome. Though you do not know why yet either."

The royal had already turned his attention to his own men and horses as a young Traveler continued on.

The horses were beautiful. In much of Lands of Men, people would save a horse before they would save even another human being. For a simple family, a good horse meant a better life, whether for farm work or transport. For kingdoms, horses—ridden by knights and other warriors--were what extended the power of kings and queens to every corner of their domain. Traveler could not help himself, rubbing the necks and sides of the animals as he passed. They were kept close by their masters, who waited. Others were hooked to long wagons as servants filled them with supplies.

"What do you want, boy?" a gruff warrior asked him.

"Are you going to the magical lands, sir?" Traveler asked.

"Why? I am not taking you. Look at you. My sword weighs more than you." Other men began to laugh.

"Yes, sir, I am young now, but I will grow up. When I do, what tasks do caravans most need when they take on men?"

The warrior watched him as he thought. One of his companions stepped forward. "What do you think, boy? If you are not a fighter, caravans need bearers and sentries and cooks and such. A caravan is a moving city of men. Whatever a city needs to function, so does a caravan."

Traveler nodded. "Yes, sir, but..."

"But what?"

"But competition will be stiff. All the young lads will say they want to be a bearer, sentry, or domestic."

"So?" the men asked.

"I should offer services most will not want, sirs."

"You are looking to cheat," one of the said.

"Cheat, sir? No. I am looking to offer a needed service that is hard to come by but is in high demand."

"You are looking for an edge to ensure your acceptance by some caravan steward."

"No different than you, sir. You offer the service of the sword."

"Then learn to use a sword then, boy."

"Anyone can do that, sir."

"If you cannot wield a sword then you have no business being on any caravan, let alone to the magic lands."

"I hear, sir, that even the best human with a sword is no match for an elf or any other fae."

"True. So what are you saying? Enter their lands without any means at all to defend yourself? Then why go, young boy?"

"I hear, sir, that the good caravans have elves or other fae, like sprites or dwarves join them for safe passage."

"That is not true, boy. They do not join good caravans. Good caravans join them. Elves do not need men to move about their own lands."

Another man appeared and threw a shovel to the boy's feet. A young Traveler looked up from the instrument.

"There is something you can do," the new man said. "You can dig the graves from all the men who die along the way."

"I think not, sir."

"Is that a task beneath you?"

"No, sir. I would think that the whole caravan would join in such a task."

The man shook his head. "No. Every caravan has a group to tend to dead bodies, whether human or animal.

In real caravans, everyone has their task that they are solely responsible for. That is how good caravans run. You can be the gravedigger, boy."

Traveler knelt to pick up the shovel. "Thank you, sir."

"Are you stealing my shovel, boy?"

"Are you the caravan's gravedigger, sir?"

"I am and stop calling me 'sir.'"

Traveler dropped the shovel back to the ground.

"We do not like you, boy," said another man.

The boy noticed that other men were watching him, glaring.

"Have I done something wrong, sir? I am only trying to learn so when I am old enough, I can be ready to join a caravan."

"No good caravan would take on some royal little boy."

"I am not a royal and I am not a noble..."

"You are a liar, boy."

Traveler held his tongue.

"You pretend to be one of us. Do you think we are stupid? Is that what you think? We are so stupid that we cannot recognize the way a royal talks down to men."

Traveler was about to respond but said nothing. He began to back away from the men, now realizing that a crowd of men had formed up.

One of the men pointed. "There is a man worthy of respect by royal, noble, and commoner alike."

Traveler turned to see a tall knight approaching.

The boy had seen knights before but the one nearing him was clad in exquisite silver armor. He had no helmet—his light brown shoulder length hair moved as he moved, he had a full beard and mustache, his blue eyes were locked on his. Strapped to his back was a large broadsword, its hilt glistening in the daylight. It was the style of the modern times—the main weapon strapped to one's back rather than clumsily hanging on one's waist in the days of old.

The knight picked up Traveler with one arm and threw him!

The boy's body smashed again the establishment's wall and fell to the ground. Instantly, Traveler realized he was crying. His body was trembling with shock. He noticed there was some blood smeared on the wall and jumped to his feet. The crowd of men were laughing as the boy rubbed his hands over his face. He was bleeding badly.

Before the boy could react, he was suspended in the air. The knight held him up with one arm.

"I will teach you a lesson today, little boy. It will be a lesson you will remember today and all the years after."

The knight threw the boy with such force into the wall of another establishment.

There was no laughter. The pain was so severe that Traveler lay on the ground. He had cried all his tears away already. The trembling had stopped but his body could not move at all. He closed his eyes then opened them. He knew he had been knocked unconscious but he did not know for how long. Standing all around him were dozens of men. The knight came into view and towered over him.

"If I wanted to pick you up again and throw you over one of these buildings could you stop me?" The knight lunged down at the boy. Traveler closed his eyes, crying, unable to move.

"I did not think so," he heard the knight say and opened his eyes to stare up him. The knight knelt beside him.

"See how quickly life can change. In the snap of lightning, a man can be smiling one moment, then dead the next. Men are frightened of journeys into the magical lands because there are things to be frightened of, and far more fearsome than I. Go home, boy.

The knight stood up straight, never taking his gaze off the boy. "You are a foolish boy. And hopefully I have done my part to keep a foolish boy from growing into a foolish man. Caravans are not for foolish boys or foolish men.

Men die on caravans. I have seen many die coming to join a caravan, on the caravan, and many more still in the magical lands. You probably think I am quite frightening. In the magical lands, I am nothing. Lie still on that ground, boy. Let the pain and fear, the helplessness echo in your mind. When you are able to rise to your feet, take yourself home and never come back to this place. You think you are the first to do what you are doing? My friend the gravedigger, here, has buried many such foolish boys and foolish men who left the safety and sanity of the Lands of Man because they had the insane notion in their heads that they must see fairies, gnomes, unicorns and flying white horses, or a singing mermaid. Instead they found death at the hands of man-eating spiders, giant ogres in the day, and giant trolls at night, eaten whole by any manner of evil beasts, pulled into the center of the earth by a mammoth wurm. You have no idea what nightmares are. The magical lands are a land of death for humans. Nothing more. Lie there, boy, for a good long while and think of what I said and feel what I did. I, Tymond the Defiant, did this to you, little boy. Do not ever let me see you again in these parts again. I am always in these parts as I am a caravan master. Should I ever see you again, I will slam your body into the wall ten times, one hundred times, a thousand times, however many times it takes for your body to be in bloody pieces and you to be dead."

The shock of the words froze Traveler's eyes wide open. Tymond reached down to his right boot and pulled a dagger from it. The knight stared at the boy. Traveler tried with all his might to keep from whimpering. Tymond returned the dagger to his boot.

The knight walked away from him with all his men following. In quarter of an hour, their entire caravan was mounted and off. Traveler heard the riders gallop away with their wagons in tow. All he could see was the blue sky above from his prone position on the ground.

It would not be until nightfall that a local tavern owner and his wife had pity on him and fetched Hopeshire's local healer to attend to a battered, broken, and utterly demoralized young boy.

CHAPTER TWO

The First Caravan

Young Traveler was nearly fourteen years old.

Hopeshire was different than before. Many more people traveled the road to and from the town, if that's what it could be called. Dotting the green countryside were many tiny establishments and wagons used for both legitimate and criminal purposes. Most visitors knew what was safe and what not to go near, but there was always the naive, destitute, and depraved. There were more than enough passersby for everyone to sell and trade their goods and services.

While the outer establishments were not as presentable, Hopeshire proper maintained its charm. As Traveler passed into the town's market square, he noticed that royals and nobles were far more prominent with their knights and mercenaries for hire. A large man sat on a wooden throne to one side of the main road with a small army of knights and ruffs as bodyguard. The man was a royal of some kind, likely a prince or duke, and watched him. Traveler ignored him and continued by.

He was taller and bigger than five years ago. The hood of his cloak snuggly clung to his head, his cape was draped to hide any possible weapons he might have. He had one satchel of belongings hidden away and strapped over one shoulder underneath. He may not have been big enough to fend off thieves, but they would not try to steal something they were unaware of.

'Thick with thieves' was the phrase that came to his mind as he walked deeper into town. The dirty and shifty men mulling around one section of the road made no attempts to hide their ill intent. They hung together as a pack to distract one passerby with a prank while another brashly tried to steal something. There was a playfulness to it all and all victims felt comfortable in fighting back the thieves. No one would get killed for the simple reason that not too far away were real knights. One swing of a knight's blade would fell several thieves at one time. The thieves could be rowdy but not murderous as they were clearly capable of being.

"Lads! Step on up! The Caravan of the Kingdom of White Tower sets out within the hour!" The man calling out to everyone's attention with hands held high was a noble in lavender clothes and feathered princely hat. If he did not have brutish, toothless guards encircling him with swords many would have laughed at the ridiculous sight of the man.

"We need bearers with strong backs. Sentries, cooks, fire-lighters, trappers and hunters and scouts. Men for the quartering parties. Men to mind the horse and livestock. Men to mind our hunting hounds. Step up and be counted. The Caravan of the Kingdom of the White Tower travels from these Lands of Man across to the lands of fairies, elves, and sprites. You will see fantastic wonders and be protected from all its dangers by one thousand of our kingdom's best knights and war horsemen."

"What will be our payment?" a man's voice rang out in the crowd.

"Your payment, sir, will be the all the riches you can carry from the magical lands back to your home wherever it may be in the Seven Empires!" the steward replied.

Men responded with applause and laughter.

"Are you joining the caravan?" another boy about Traveler's age asked him. He had a large bag over his back and held a sheathed dagger tightly in his hand.

"No. Not this time," Traveler answered.

"If you do not join them, it may be years before another passes by," the boy said.

"A new caravan sets out every week or so."

"Is that true?"

"Yes."

The boy thought for a moment. "Well, I am not waiting. One thousand men. We could defeat any man-eating giant."

"You must be right."

Traveler moved past him. Men of all ages were queuing up in front of the caravan's steward for inspection. The lavender dressed man was accepting everyone who stepped in front of him. Past the forming caravan was what Traveler was looking for.

Quietly off to the side waited a large group of men. Some wore armor, others chainmail tops, others thick leather jackets. Every eye watched Traveler as he neared them.

"May I wait here?" he asked them.

"Why?" a man asked sitting on the ground with a large wolf-dog.

"There are two kinds of men in the world—smart ones and dumb ones. The dumb ones are joining that caravan. The smart ones are waiting here for the next, real caravan."

The man started to laugh and so did others. He pointed to the boy and to a spot next to him. "Sit."

Traveler did so and was happy to be off his feet for the first time since last night.

"How old are you, lad?"

"Fourteen."

"A boy."

"I am at the age of maturity."

"That means a boy."

Traveler heard muffled laughter behind him. He focused his attention on the assembling caravan. He felt a nudge and noticed that the man's wolf-dog wanted his attention. The boy rubbed the dog's forehead. In a moment, the animal was lying on his belly next to him, resting his head on the boy's leg.

"Men, we have a thief amongst us. He has been here barely a minute and he has already gotten my lifelong companion to abandon me. If you are going to steal my dog, lad, I should know your name."

"Traveler, sir."

"Traveler?"

"Yes."

"My name is Gut-Cutter."

"Nice to meet you, sir."

The man shook his head, stifling a laugh.

"I suppose out here one can call himself whatever he wants. So tell me, Traveler, why are you not jumping at the chance to join the Caravan of the Great White Tower?"

"Men can have any name they want outside their homeland, sir, but kingdoms cannot. If a caravan has to make up a name for itself, then it means that its true name is unimpressive. Such a kingdom could not afford a thousand-man army of knights and horsemen. Such a kingdom probably spent all the money they did have on the ridiculous lavender outfit of their steward. Look at their wagons—empty. Look at their horses—hardly capable of lasting a month's journey, let alone a year. Look at their weapons—dull, worn, unimpressive. They freely admit anyone who wants to join because without them they are nothing."

The man nodded. "Good. You did say there are two kinds of men in the world. We know now which group you are from. How long will you wait for the proper caravan?"

"Until the right one comes along. I am in no hurry. I am not old like you." Traveler grinned as he looked at the man; the man returned the grin.

"I have a question for our young visitor," said a knight standing with his body braced against the wall of an establishment.

Traveler turned. "Yes, sir?"

"You will learn that proper caravans do not freely accept anyone who appears before them. They accept very few in fact, and only those who provide value to the caravan. What value do you bring to a caravan? Because if you say bearer or sentry or such you will be turned away. A proper caravan has those roles filled well before it sets out. It passes through towns and cities for men who can fight and kill. You do not seem like you ever killed a chicken to eat for a morning meal."

Traveler could see the smiles from the men waiting for his response.

"I am a healer's assistant."

"Healer?" the man sitting next to him asked.

"Yes, sir. I am the one person you wish to see on the battlefield, if wounded, to keep you from the last person you ever wish to see."

"What last person?" the knight asked.

"The gravedigger, of course, sir."

Taverns were the center of nightlife for any lively town and Hopeshire was no different; it had a dozen of them. Traveler had been adopted by the men, who informally called themselves the Atlanteans.

He was not supposed to but after spending every day together for the last week, the men allowed the boy to drink as much alcohol as they.

"What does an Atlantean look like?" Traveler asked.

Their leader with the wolfdog leaned to him with large mug, sloshing its alcoholic contents everywhere, much of it lapped up by his dog. "They are a people made of pure magic."

"Are they fish people? I heard they are fish people."

"No, boy, they are certainly not fish people. Fish people live there but the Atlanteans are from the stars."

"Stars, sir?"

"They are not of this world. They came here when the Titans and dragons roamed the earth. Legend has it that they are part-Titan themselves."

"But what do they look like, sir?"

"When we get there, you will see."

Traveler grinned.

"Lad. You are drunk."

"I think so, sir."

"I hope you can hold your drink because there will be no sleeping in for any of us. The men that is. However, for lads..."

"Sir, I am with the men. I can hold my drink."

"Good." Esis patted him on the back. "In fact, I think I am going to sleep right here in the tavern."

"Here, sir."

"Yes. It is the safest place for us. Who knows how many thieves and cut-throats hide in the shadows outside waiting for drunkards like us?"

"But to stay on the tavern we have to keep drinking, sir?"

Esis smiled widely. "Yes, indeed, lad!" He patted Traveler on the back. "And you too!" He patted his wolf-dog on the back.

"Want to stay alive in the lands of magic and monsters?" Esis asked Traveler. "The team!"

Traveler so enjoyed the days he spent in Hopeshire with Esis and his men, learning and hearing their stories.

"The team of men, sir," Traveler said, nodding.

"No, it's more than that, lad. A caravan is a community of men who assemble for the dangers of the trek, often across lands no man alone would travel. Every man must be able to rely on each other. Most caravans believe it's about simply the knights and warriors and their weapons but fighters fight. They do not manage your caravan. The master-at-arms is only one of the most important man of the caravan. The other is the steward; the man who runs non-fighters and if they are truly accomplished run the fighters and any royals or nobles too. But in the end, your caravan is only as strong as your weakest or most cowardly or youngest lad. The very fate of a caravan may rest on what that man or boy does or does not do. The caravan master must ensure that every last man is one that can be trusted, especially if the steward or man-at-arms does not possess that ability to read men. Do you understand?"

"Yes, sir. I had worried that I might be that weakest man on a caravan."

"And what did you do about it?"

"Other than grow older, I studied. I hear and understand what you mean about the non-fighters being as equal as the fighters, but that is only partly true. When attacked, it will only be the fighters defending the lives of all, not the non-fighters or even the steward."

"True, but they can defend and assist. They can warn fighters of an attacker sneaking up behind them. They can throw a spear or even a rock from the ground if it will help. My point is that every man must be willing and able to defend the caravan and its men, not that each man must be a fighter."

"I understand now, sir. All must contribute, however they can."

"Yes."

"How many journeys have you been on, sir?"

"So many that I cannot count or remember—dozens, no, hundreds by now. I began when I was a bit younger than you."

"How many into the magical lands, sir?"

"Only a few. None of them reached very far. Only one made it past Titan's Bridge."

Traveler straightened up. "Titan's Bridge, sir. I have heard the rumors."

"And they are all true. The chasm on each side of it is truly bottomless. It is a frightening experience to travel across it. A caravan must never start off across unless it is the very break of dawn, because it takes the entire day to reach the other end."

"I heard there are monsters, sir."

"No monsters are needed for Titan's Bridge. A man can conjure up more than enough within his own mind."

"It is the first...marker, sir?"

"Yes. You have been learning your legends well. Titan's Bridge is the first marker on Titan's Trail to the fabled city of Atlantea—the only one in the Lands of Man. There is Titan's Step and Titan's Arch next in the lands of fae. Then there is Titan's Walk in their magical Great Forest. Then Titan's Fall to their fae oceans. Titan's Point awaits when you reach landfall again. Titan's Gate is the last of the marker as you gaze upon...Atlantea."

Traveler could not help but smile. "You speak as if you have traveled the entire way, sir."

"That is my intention, and all my men. Maybe we will take you along...if my dog lets us."

Traveler turned to playfully rub Esis' dog's forehead then his back. "He will allow me, sir."

"Yes, I forgot. He has forsaken me for you. The ingratitude of it all. I raised him from a pup."

"It is not your fault, sir. I have a way with animals. They all like me."

"Let us hope that the ones that like to eat men and boys whole do not also like you."

Though Esis and his men waited in Hopeshire as days turned to weeks, they were never idle. They informally adopted Traveler and he too had his daily routine and chores. In the early morning, he helped prepare the meals for all the men, some three hundred. They were an impatient lot when they awoke and food had to be ready and served quickly. After the mess of eatery was attended to by only a few of the men and Traveler, the boy was off for his training. Depending on the week, he would attend instruction from their two weaponsmasters to learn all about every kind of cutting, piercing and bludgeoning weapon there was, the wounds they made, all about the metals, and the forging process. As a treat, the two men would tell him about the weapons they had seen with their own eyes wielded by fae—weapons that moved on their own, flew through the air, those that glowed with magic.

Time always went by too fast as it would soon be time for the noon meal and the return of cook and serving duty. Afterward, when chores were done, he spent time with the party's hunters to learn how to track and hunt, how to read the land, learn proper fire-lighting, and how to make weapons from sticks and rocks.

In these short weeks, while Esis became a trusted father figure to him, his second-in-command, Roth, a large brawny, but gentle grizzly bear of a man became that much older brother he never had. He was like a sibling who took on the mission to give life advice and protect him from all danger. Esis schooled Traveler in the ways of caravans, weapons, and battle. Roth schooled him in dealing with men: how to read them, motivate them, and when needed, entertain them to take their minds off the troubles around them.

He was always excused from nighttime meal duties because his lessons for the day were not over. This was when all the men gathered around to exchange the news of the day, then tell tall-tales of supposed fae or monsters they encountered in the past. News reports always took a few moments, no matter how serious. The storytelling took the whole night accompanied by much rowdiness and laughter.

"You have to learn to tell good stories, lad?" Esis told him.

"I am learning, sir."

"No, you do not understand. Storytelling in the Lands of Man is one thing, but in the magical lands, stories are like money."

"Money, sir?"

"If you learn to tell good stories in the lands of fae, you will go a long way. Fae will give you free food and drink, give you information, help you even when you do not ask. They all are enraptured by good stories—fairies, gnomes, all of them." He turned to his men. "If only I could tell good stories."

Men laughed at him. "Yes, Esis, when will you learn so we can get free food and drink and maybe dance with fair fae woman."

"Hear! Hear!" men yelled out.

"Be careful, Roth. You may think you are dancing with a fair fae female but it could be a changeling with the face of an ugly pig."

"But Esis, all pigs are ugly."

"Roth, stop speaking that way of your mother and sisters!"

Traveler was laughing as much as the men. Banter had turned to throwing food at each other.

"This is a good team of men, Mr. Esis," Traveler said.

"Yes, they are. It took me a long time to assemble them. All we need is a good caravan to join, so we can be on our way."

Esis and his men had taken over one particular livery stable in Hopeshire to use as their temporary domicile in exchange for managing the establishment and providing security day and night. The proprietor was eager to have a brief defense against the nighttime horse thieves.

Traveler had his chores and lessons but for most of the men they had much work to do and for those not working for the town, they practiced their sword fighting skills. The workday was long but ended with a good meal and entertainment. However, when it was over and time for sleep that's what the men did. The men crowded into different empty pens of the livery stables and slept where they could. Traveler always managed to find a space and had gotten used to the snoring of most of the men. He had also gotten accustomed to Esis' dog seeking him out to curl up and sleep beside him.

After a month, Traveler had almost forgotten that Hopeshire was not home. Every day they waited for that call to ring out. That day came.

"Caravan!"

The announcement made everyone stop what they were doing and take to the main road. Real caravans—those with horses, wagons, knights, and royals—not only meant new visitors but money and trade.

Traveler was on horse-grooming duty when the cry rang out. Esis had told him to always hold his emotions close when it came to strangers and especially caravan, but he could not contain his joy. He dropped the large brush, startling the horse he was grooming, as he burst out of the stable. But when he got outside, he stopped in his tracks. People were running and gathering. It wasn't a caravan passing through Hopeshire to the magical lands; it was one returning!

He ran through the crowds, looking for Esis and the men. He spotted the caravan master and ran to him.

"What does this mean?" Traveler asked. "I thought returning caravans are never seen, sir."

"They are not. We will soon learn what it means, lad."

"But what could it mean, sir?"

"Why ask questions? Let us go and see for ourselves."

Hopeshire was an unaffiliated town, meaning it did not have a king or queen, or any type of overseeing noble, not even its own town elders. It began as a collection of farmers ages ago and it was how it remained. So there was no royal or official welcoming party to greet the caravan.

"What cities lie beyond Hopeshire, sir?"

"There is Goodmound first, then Ironwood, and finally Last Keep—the last vestige of human civilization before crossing into the Lands Between. But you assume they came straight along Titan's Trail. Not necessarily. Titan's Trail is the best path, but not the only one."

"But Titan's Trail is the safest, is it not?"

"You are correct there, lad. I would say to leave the Trail to be an act of madness but maybe they are so powerful that they can make their own path."

As Traveler looked around, it appeared that all of Hopeshire and nearby awaited the new caravan. He stared as it became visible and his mouth hung open. It was unlike anything he could imagine; a piece of the magical lands was coming to them.

The lead rider slowly approached them on what the boy thought was a horse which was draped with a sheer whitish cloth hood, like the rider. The "horse" had a giant bird's head and a feline-like body—in fact, the body was more like a slim lion.

"It is called hieracosphinx," Esis said to him.

"Like a griffin, sir?"

"Griffins have wings and are much larger and powerful. There is also a beast called a hippogriff...and an axex. You may see them on the Trail. They are popular steeds among royal caravans."

The boy focused on the beast's human rider. He could always tell desert people—slim build, dark skin, loose, flowing clothing. Under both eyes was a white tattoo symbol. Under his whitish hooded cloak, he could see the man's chainmail vest, a glimmer of what must have been a sword or dagger on his side.

"Are there no elders to greet us?" the man asked.

People in the crowd looked at each other. No one wanted to speak.

"There are no elders in Hopeshire," Esis said. "Did your caravan not pass through here before?"

"No, we entered the magical lands from another portal. This is our first time here. Last Keep and Goodmound's Castle did not have the men and supplies we needed. Ironwood is for weapons, Goodmound is for livestock and animals, Last Keep is for information. We need none of that."

"Are you not returning from your journey?" another man in the crowd asked.

"No. We will secure more men and supplies and we will return but this time via the Trail."

"Why do you need more men, sir?"

"There was a battle between elves and goblins on the path we traveled. We lost many simply trying to escape from them both. The elves thought the goblins would get control of our magic weapons and beasts. The goblins thought we would join the side of the elves in the battle. Neither was the case but we were not in a position to discuss it with them."

"What is the name of your kingdom?" another man asked.

"We are the royal caravan of the kingdom of Dunespire," the rider declared. "We are not from this empire. We come from the desert regions of Laurasia."

"You must have come a distance I cannot even imagine," Esis said.

"We began ten years ago," the rider revealed. "It will probably take another five for us to reach Atlantea and return to our homeland, but it is well worth the time and risk for our mighty king."

The rider stood up in his saddle, glancing back, gesturing with a hand. Another rider on a similar beast rode up to stop at his side.

"My name is Tahelm and this is our wizard Thas."

The new rider, the wizard, leaned down. "Who has a piece of fruit to treat a nimble wizard?" he asked.

Esis reached out his hand with an apple. The wizard smiled and reached out for it. He did not take it but touched it with his finger. Esis and everyone were aghast; the apple turned to gold.

"We will pay handsomely for men and supplies," Thas said.

"How did he do that, sir?" Traveler asked.

Tahelm smiled, and so did his wizard. "My wizard is a midas wizard. He can change anything he wishes with a touch to gold."

"Magic, huh?" Esis said skeptically. "That means it is not real. Spells can dissipate."

"No, sir," the wizard said. "That apple will remain as gold long after all of us have faded from this earth as dust. However, if you doubt it, we have plenty of coin."

Thas raised his hand and suddenly their entire caravan began to gallop into Hopeshire single-file.

"Where can we rest?" Tahelm asked.

"Outside the gates on the other side of the town is plenty of grazing and fields for your men," someone said to him.

"Good. We will set up camp there."

Traveler swallowed hard. The men on fantastic beasts ran by fast but what lumbered past was a seven-foot cyclops in full golden armor using a golden spear as a walking stick. Following him were the biggest and tallest humans the boy had ever seen—the shortest of them well over six feet.

The cyclops stood next to Tahelm and the wizard as the rest of the caravan moved past into the town. There were swordsmen, spearmen, shieldmen, many bearers with pull-carts, then wagons pulled by large black horses. Then came seemingly an endless stream of warriors without armor with a dagger in each hand. They all wore whitish hooded cloaks and all had the same white symbols tattooed under each eye.

Traveler could not keep from staring at the cyclops until its large single eye in the center of his forehead moved to watch him back.

Why do you stare at me, young one?

Traveler almost yelled out and stumbled back. The words were within his head—in his mind. The cyclops laughed loudly.

"What happened, lad?" Esis asked him.

"He spoke in my mind, sir!"

"Oh." Esis was unconcerned. "Is that all?" He turned his attention to Tahelm and his wizard. "Can we be of any service?"

"What service can you provide?" Tahelm asked.

"I am a caravan master by occupation but that is hardly of value since you already came from the magical lands and undoubtedly know the way to Atlantea. However, I am also an able warrior with 300 men under my command."

Tahelm nodded. "We need good men. When the sun sets bring them to our camp for our caravan master to inspect." Tahelm pointed to the wizard. "He is the caravan master of the Dunespire's Royal Caravan."

Esis nodded. "We will all be before you at nightfall then."

The wizard smiled and nodded back. Esis grabbed Traveler and pushed him along. "Back to camp, lad."

At their livery stable base, Esis and his men gathered. They had quickly put on their best armor and grabbed their best weapons. A very serious tone had overtaken them and they had no time for any "adopted" boy of theirs.

"Have any of you seen their like before?" one knight asked.

"I have never heard of Dunespire," another man said.

"The empire of Laurasia is far more vast than Avalonia. Who among us can really say if there is or is not a kingdom of Dunespire?" Esis added. "The question before us is this: is this the caravan we have awaited so long?"

"And they do have a real wizard," another man said.

"And a cyclops as an aide," another knight called out.

"Yes," Esis said. "This is what we have waited for. They have the wealth, the means, and the knowledge of the Trail. When we present ourselves to them at nightfall, I want them to see the shine in our armor and our blades from miles away. Get to work, men!"

The men all nodded and moved closer to their base or knelt where they stood to unfasten their armor or draw their weapons to buff and shine as close to perfection as they could attain. One of the men walked from man to man with a comb, quickly grooming each. There would be no time to wash properly.

Traveler looked around and realized that he might as well be invisible. He was merely a boy again to them. They had "grown men" work to attend to.

None of them saw him sneak off. While Esis and the men readied themselves, he strolled down the road to the main entrance of town. Dusk was nearing and there were very few people on the main roads, and it seemed that all the establishments along it were already closed for the day. He knew where everyone was.

Outside the main entrance were crowds of people watching. He had heard the commotion before he was in sight of them. He lots of talking, and sporadic laughter, and sounds of astonishment. The Dunespire knights were showing off their hieracosphinx beasts; Hopeshire children were especially taken by the magical animals, who were well behaved.

Traveler looked past them to the Dunespire caravan camp and found himself enthralled again. Their tents were unlike any he had seen before—whitish fabric like their hooded cloaks, and uncharacteristically tall as if each one had to entertain an eight-foot cyclops. He ignored the crowds and the show being put on for them. His mind was focused on how to sneak into the camp. He grinned to himself. Being a boy had its benefits after all.

Even if caught no harm would come to him—he was just a "little" boy.

When he reached the outer edge of the crowds, he tiptoed away then lowered himself to the ground. He crawled along the dirt and grass, closer to the Dunespire camp. Men were gathered at large campfires in front of their tents, but he saw no sentries.

A strange flash of light grabbed his attention. He looked again. It was brighter than anything he had seen and it came from one of the tents in the center of camp. His eyes focused on it and there he noticed there were not one sentry but many—maybe dozens. What was that flash of light from the tent?

He was startled. At the edge of the Dunespire Caravan was an elderly man at a small fire all alone. He stared at the man for a moment; he looked familiar. His hair was white and shoulder-length. His eyes narrowed trying to confirm the identity of the man. He stood to his feet and walked to him.

The elderly man somehow heard his movement and turned his head. Traveler could see that the man's eyes were pure white and from his mannerisms he knew the man was blind.

"Who is there?" the man asked.

"A boy from Hopeshire."

"Have you tired of the magical beasts, boy?"

"I have. Are you part of this caravan?"

"I was."

Traveler noticed that besides being blind, half the man's face was horribly mauled by some type of beast.

"I know what you are thinking, boy. How could an old, blind, mauled man be of any use? I was not always the pitiful form you see now. I was a great knight in my time."

Traveler stared at him. The man was Tymond the Defiant, but it was impossible. His encounter with the knight was only five years ago. To be the same man, he would have had to have aged many more years.

Young Traveler jumped. The cyclops stood next to him.

Tahelm stood on one side, the wizard stood on the other. Their king was a midget of a man no more than five feet. His bald head bore a gold crown. The cyclops stood behind him.

"I am King Arr, the ruler of Dunespire. Who is it that requests an audience?"

"I do, sire," Esis stood in silver armor, his helmet in his right hand. All the men behind him.

"Is that boy yours?" King Arr asked.

Esis flashed a look of anger at Traveler. The boy sat on the ground with a Dunespire knight on each side.

"If he were not a boy, we would have killed him," Arr said. "His impudence will cost you."

"The golden apple, please." The wizard reached out his hand.

Esis turned his head to one of his men, who handed them the sparkling golden apple. It flew from Esis's hand into the wizard's. Now all the men glared at the boy. Traveler bowed his head in shame.

"Enough of that," King Arr said. "Offense and payment as punishment. The matter is over. Let the boy join his people."

One of the knight's picked him up from the ground and pushed him forward. The boy slowly walked to the men, but kept his gaze down and stood to the side.

"What is that you wish?" King Arr asked. "By morning there will be thousands of men seeking to join this caravan. The Fates have smiled upon you by allowing you to be the first. My oracle, the cyclops here, tells me that you are above all the others who I will see. Is that true?"

"It is, sire. My men and I are professional caravanners and traveling knights. We protected many a caravan in the Lands of Man, now we wish to do the same in the magical lands."

"I see," said the king. "Will you swear total allegiance to me?"

"We will, sire, if you accept us onto your caravan."

"Good. My wizard is the caravan master to chart our path to Atlantea. My cyclops is my oracle to see the dangers we will face before they are upon us. My son is my master-at-arms to kill all those who oppose us."

"Yes, sire," Esis said.

"Loyalty is the trait I demand above all others."

"Yes, sire."

"I must know that the men under me will do as I command without question at all times. Our caravan once had a powerful knight as the head of our vanguard, a coveted position, but he forgot his place. He forgot that I command everything and everyone in this caravan, no one else. He forgot I commanded his men, not him anymore. So I let them walk into danger without the foreknowledge of our oracle. I kept letting him walk into danger. He lost his youth, his sight, his attractiveness. I leave him here in fact to die. Do you understand?"

"Yes, sire."

"The reward is beyond anything you can imagine...in Atlantea. It is not simply humans that covet its riches—the elves, centaurs, elementals, goblins, fairies, giants, many, many others. And there is enough treasure for us all, but so few every reach the destination. For the chance of that reward you will have to prove that you are worthy, Esis of Avalonia."

"Yes, sire."

"You will have one chance and one chance only to prove your loyalty."

"Yes, sire."

"Draw your blade."

Esis grabbed his helmet cradled in his arm with his left hand and drew his sword with right.

"Pick one of your most trusted men…and kill him now!"

When Traveler saw Esis kill his second-in-command, Roth, thrusting his blade through the man's neck, the man who he had revered was dead to him. The expression of shock on Roth's face lasted only a moment. The man was dead and dropped to the ground. All his men did nothing, but none of them looked at Esis.

"Good," King Arr said. "You and your men are worthy. You will be Dunespire's new vanguard. Retrieve your belongings and join the caravan. Thas will settle you into the routine."

"Yes, sire."

King Arr turned and disappeared into the camp with Tahelm, the wizard, cyclops and half a dozen guards following.

All of Esis's men turned and headed to the livery stables, none waiting for Esis. The caravan master stood alone, not able to look at the man, his man, that he had killed.

"We should return to our stables for the night. I am sure we will leave at dawn," Esis said.

"I will remain out here," Traveler said.

Esis looked at Traveler. The boy glared at him.

"But you should go back to the livery stables and get a shovel," Traveler said.

"This is our best chance to journey through the magical lands and successfully reach Atlantea."

"But you told me that if the situation does not feel right then—"

"Boy, life is from perfect. If a man waits for the situation to be perfect, then he will never venture past the prison of his own homelands."

"You are quoting an axiom to me to contradict the very rule you have cited to me so many times these past weeks. I will remain here and wait for the next one."

"When you have traveled as far as we have and waited here for as long as we have, you will understand."

"No, sir. I will not understand. I will simply return home."

"I have no home. This is my home...here, with my men, on this journey."

"Then when you get to Atlantea stay awhile and give me time to catch up."

Esis man smiled. "Maybe I will marry a good Atlantean woman."

"Yes, sir."

"I better fetch that shovel. Good luck to you, Traveler."

"You too, sir."

Esis was like a father to him, but no more. The Dunespire Caravan did leave at dawn the next day. Traveler watched surreptitiously from the back of the crowds. He had no interest in the caravan, its cyclops or magical beasts. He wanted to get a final glimpse of the man who was like a father to him and a group of men who had took him in and treated him with respect of an adult. They had taught him much, more than he could have learned on his own in a year. But it was all ruined. Esis marched behind the cyclops and his men marched behind him, but there was no longer any kinship between former caravan master and men. There was an underlying sadness in Esis' face; it was if he wanted to see Traveler's face in the crowd but did not. The gaze of his men were fixed downward. They would never look at Esis with respect again. Traveler suspected they would never gossip, laugh, and talk as a group again.

The Hopeshire crowds watched the Dunespire Caravan march onward the start of Titan's Trail. Traveler had seen enough and slipped away. He would likely never see Esis and his former men in his life ever again.

CHAPTER THREE

Caravan of the Doomed

Young Traveler was fourteen years old.

He could no longer bear to remain in Hopeshire. Despite its quaintness, the town and its surroundings had lost its appeal. It was the safest of the four stops on the Row to remain, but to stay would mean to relive the memories of a father-figure and older brother figure who were lost forever. He had to move on.

The second place on the Row was Ironwood. A proper city also called the City of Stone and Metal, encircled by great stone walls and every structure inside its walls were forged of solid iron or made of the same stone quarry of its great wall. Unlike Hopeshire, Ironwood did not care for strangers unless one was there for commerce and the only goods they sold were weapons. Ironwood weaponsmiths were known as the best throughout the Seven Empires. Most parties came to Ironwood not to journey further for Titan's Trail, as that in fact was rare. Most journeyed solely to Ironwood for its second-to-none weapons and armor in the Lands of Man.

As a true city, it had a royal government. The king and queen of Ironwood were known as benevolent rulers, and if they did have a vice it was considering anyone not a royal or noble as no better than livestock, even those who had money to pay for goods and services. However, Ironwood merchants did not possess that vice; anyone with money was a royal to them.

Traveler walked to Ironwood at dawn during the time that anyone traveling to Ironwood did. Safety in numbers was the reason. He walked with a large group of men and occasionally watched behind only to see other lads his age following. The bad thing about moving up the Row was that the further you went—from Hopeshire to Ironwood to Goodmound to Last Keep—the thieves and cut-throats grew more plentiful and more brash in their violence.

As they walked, a two-horse drawn open wagon passed by slowly. In the wagon were several men, a couple of boys, and...a blind elderly man with a mauled face.

"Can anyone help an honored former knight with a meal?"

The elderly man stood in front of the tavern to the side of the front entrance. Everyone who passed ignored him. There was a slight tremor to his frail body, his clothes old and worn, the bright color long since faded. He tried to remain composed as he repeated his plea from time to time.

Dusk arrived and the man now sat in front of the tavern's entrance. No one had helped and no one likely would. Nighttime was the most dangerous of times for the weak but the fact that he had nothing worth stealing made him of no interest to the many thieves that watched the roads.

Traveler stood there near the tavern. A look of disgust hung on his face. He had been fighting to leave the man and go about his business. The elderly man would die but that could take several days.

"Why should anyone help you?" he asked.

Shock came over the elderly man's face upon hearing the question. He slowly rose to his feet.

"I am a wounded knight, lad."

"What is that to me?"

"You should help those in need."

"Why?"

"Because if the tables are ever reversed you will want someone to help you."

"Maybe you deserve to sit out here and die."

"Maybe I should."

"I saw you at Hopeshire. You were cast off by that Dunespire Caravan."

"Yes, I was. They had squeezed all their use from me and cast me off to nothing."

"I will help you only because that is how I was raised. My father once said it will get me killed one day. My mother says it will bring me greater fortune than I can imagine one day. You do not look to be either."

"Is there something I can say to convince you to simply buy me a meal and drink? It might likely be my last."

"How many caravans into the magic lands have you been on?"

The elderly man's eyes began to weep as he smiled. "I was a caravan master. I journeyed many times to the magical lands."

"That is of interest."

"I will tell you any and everything you want to know."

"Though I would have no idea of knowing what is truth and what are lies. However, it seems a fair bargain. You can put your hand on my shoulder and I will lead you into the tavern to a table and a meal."

The elderly man ate and drank as if he hadn't had either in ages, or because he felt it would be his last.

Traveler watched him with an expression of disgust then turned away to observe the other patrons of the busy tavern. Most of those seated seemed to be Ironwood residents. The atmosphere was cheerful and he could hear the many stories being exchanged about the news of the day.

"Good benefactor, I feel as if we have encountered each other before. Tell me where? I can hear a familiarity in your voice."

"Do you?"

"Yes. I mean no disrespect. You have so graciously fed a starving man tonight."

"Do you not remember me, great knight?"

"The tone in your voice tells me that it may not have been a welcome encounter."

"At the time, you violently threw a little boy at the wall." Tymond's face changed and he looked at Traveler though he could not see. "More than once, I believe."

"I do remember," Tymond said.

"Do you?"

"Yes." Tymond sat up straight and pushed his plate of food away from in front of him so he could rest his clasped hand in the table. His fingers looked even more decrepit than the rest of his body. "Apparently then, I failed in my goal. Here you are again, though I suspect far less naïve than that time."

"How do you know it is who you think? Especially in your aged condition. Do you know when you last saw me?"

"Five years ago. My body may be aged far beyond that but not my memory. I remember because I remember the caravan I was with. How old were you?"

"Nine."

Tymond nodded. "You are of the age of maturity these days. Rightly, you can no longer be called a boy, not quite a man, but no longer a boy."

Traveler watched him for a moment.

"I don't need your pity," Tymond said.

"What happened to you?" Traveler asked. "You were Tymond the Defiant."

Tymond closed his eyes as he seemed overcome by a rush of emotion. There was a sigh and he opened his white, blank eyes again. He was fighting back the tears. "I was that man." He wiped his eyes with his hands. "Is this your way to be cruel?"

"Cruel? If that was my intention, I would have left you where you were to die. Food and drink are not free, and in Ironwood three times the price of the same portions in Hopeshire."

"Yes, true. I am sorry for the insult. I truly thank you for what you have done for me."

"You almost killed me that day. My broken body has long since healed, and if I had not seen you in Hopeshire with the Dunespire Caravan and here again, I would have completely forgotten, never to remember you again in my life. So, no, you will never receive any pity from me. I do not view you are worthy of such."

"Yes." Tymond lowered his head. A smile came over his face. "I probably told you about with the 'snap of lightning' how a man is smiling one moment and dead the next. In my case, I was struck by the lighting of bad luck once and then it happened over and over again. Humans must be careful in the magical lands. Fae are long-lived, we are not. I spent my time living like a king in a fae city. I lived there seemingly forever. Actually, it nearly was. The second I set foot outside the barrier of the magical lands to ours, I knew I had done something terribly wrong. I pulled my foot back but I had already aged decades within moments. Then we were traveling and...at least it was a basilisk rather than a gorgon. Blinded for life I was, however, I had already learned to see without seeing. It is the only way to defeat them and their pet basilisk. Cruelly set upon humans for sport. Then I was mauled by the king's griffin—"

"Defeat who?"

"Elves. Humans cannot fight elves because we fight through sight. But if you can learn to fight without your eyes, you can fight them as equals. You can learn to master your abilities. To our eyes, elves and other fae move faster than the blink of an eye. So don't blink." Tymond laughed.

"Elves do not behave in the manner you say. They are a noble race."

"They may be a noble race but they have plenty of ignoble members just as we humans do."

"How does one learn this trick of seeing without using one's eyes?"

"That is my secret. But I can see the shadows of shapes."

"A secret which does you little good."

"Why should I tell you? I said I would tell you of my travels as a caravan master—but secrets? The ones who could train you in those abilities live in a realm outside of Faë-Land. You could never get there."

"What is this place called, where they live?"

"I will not tell you, because, in your case, I believe you would try. The journey would kill you."

"Your choice. What happened to your face? It does not seem you were so well trained in seeing without sight if such a large creature was able to scratch off half your face."

"It was a griffin. They are beasts of magic and I did not know that some can become invisible as they guard their treasures. I was caught unaware."

"Was it all worth it, this life of yours as a caravan master? Would you do it over if you had to live it all over again?"

Tymond did not hesitate and said with a smile, "I would. I was a respected caravan master for many years. I was known for my honesty and knowledge. I was well paid for it. I saw many amazing things. I am old now so it does not matter to me that it is over."

"But your life is not over yet. What will you do?"

"I am not certain. Maybe I will throw myself off a cliff and be done with it all."

"Since you no longer can see with eyes and your eyes cannot see at all, maybe your sight should be restored so you can see to fling yourself off that cliff, which I would not mind."

"Restore my sight? The basilisk blinded me for life."

"Basilisks do not blind. They kill by turning living things to stone. Since you are not stone, I imagine you escaped its dark powers before the full effect could overtake you. By your own words you see shapes. That is not blindness. I have a theory."

"Theory?"

"If I am right, you could be made to see again."

"I do not understand." Tears were streaming down Tymond's face.

"Our eyes are covered in moisture. My theory is that the gaze of the basilisk petrified that moisture but not your eyes."

"No. It could not be so."

"You would remain elderly and mauled, but maybe you could see again."

"I—I—I do not know what to say."

"I do not care about stories of your travels. I care about secrets; knowledge is what is valuable to me. That is my offer of trade. Your choice."

Traveler had some money but he was not going to spend any more of it on Tymond. Ironwood had stables too and he convinced the owner of one to let him try his procedure on the old man. They were given a corner of an empty stable and the boy set Tymond down to lie on a bed of hay.

"I will need materials, sir," the boy said to the owner.

The owner looked on surrounded by a dozen stable lads. "What do you need, boy?" the owner asked.

"I need twelve buckets of water, a rough cloth, and twelve of your sharpest knives."

The look of shock came over all of their faces and Tymond sat up, as if he was about to run.

"Lie down, Tymond!" he yelled.

"What do you need those knives for? What are you going to do?" the owner asked.

"Are you going to cut on his eyes?" one of the stable lads asked.

"Get me the materials I need and I will show you how to defeat the ill magic of the common basilisk."

"Those reptilian chickens in the magical lands?" the owner asked.

Within the hour, everything Traveler asked for was in his possession. He had the twelve buckets of water on one side of a frightened Tymond lying prone on the hay covered ground, and on the other side he had the twelve knives lined up in order of smallest to largest.

"I do not want any blood in my stable," the owner said to him with his arms on his waist.

"There will be no blood but there will be yelling."

A look of shock came over all of their faces and Tymond sat up, as if he was about to run again. Traveler pushed him back down.

The boy pointed to three of the stable lands. "I need your help. I need one of you on each side of him, hold him down tight at the shoulder. You, the third one, you will hold him down against his chest.

"What are you about to do to me?" Tymond yelled.

"Silence!" Traveler yelled. He pointed to two other stable lads. "Each one of grab a bucket of water. Go on, do it!" The stable lads picked up a bucket, water sloshed around inside. "When I tell you, I want you to slowly pour the water into his eyes."

"What do you mean?" the owner said.

"Exactly what I said. Pour the water into his eyes."

"What are the knives for then?" he asked.

Traveler looked at the knives. "Oh, I don't need them, that is a different procedure."

"What—" the owner looked at the stable lads, none of them knowing whether to laugh.

"Pour!" Traveler yelled.

The boy took his cloth and as the stable lads poured, he forcibly rubbed the Tymond's eyes.

"Ahh!" Tymond yelled.

"Hold him down!" Traveler yelled.

The three stable boys around Tymond did so as the other two continued to pour the water. Tymond kept yelling as Traveler rubbed his eyes with the cloth.

Tymond stopped yelling and sat up throwing all three of the stable lads holding him off. They all looked at him—his blue eyes were as clear and visible as the day. Tymond sat there with his mouth handing open looking at Traveler and the others.

"You had a thin layer of petrified stone covering your eyes and face." Traveler stood and threw the cloth into Tymond face. "In the Lands of Man, it is called taking a bath you dirty, smelly animal!"

The owner and the stable lads burst out laughing. Tymond aghast mouth turned into a smile, then the laughter came.

"Much of what I will say you will likely forget, for now, or not really understand, until you do," Tymond said.

Outside the taverns, there were more than a few places along the road for men to sit and talk with.

"Is this your way of telling me you have no secrets to tell?" the boy said.

"They will not tell you, none of the fae but whatever you do you must get a circle."

"What is—?"

"Listen. There are many kinds. Some large enough to protect an entire caravan. Any real caravan master will have one or know where to get one. If they do not, then they are not genuine. But most will not, so you must get a personal one. A circle and pocket-realm."

"Pocket-realm?"

"They can fit in your pocket but they can be as vast as an entire city. Do not cross into the magical lands without either of them. Forget the weapons. Humans cannot defeat fae in hand-to-hand combat. Non-magical humans learning the ways of spell-casting only leads to darkness or worse. Circle and pocket-realm. Every fae knows of them but virtually no humans do, with few exceptions. They keep the secrets to themselves. The fae have many secrets, many tricks they do not want us to know."

"How did you learn of these things?" "A half-elf told me. I did not even know he was one. The fae were very angry with him. They said we humans like to steal things from the magical lands like we stole the inventions of arrows from the elves and centaurs."

Traveler laughed. "We invented those."

"They said a human stole it. I told him humans do not need to steal inventions of weapons to kill from others. Our minds are quite accomplished in such pursuits all on our own."

"What other secrets do you have to tell me?"

"That's it, lad, at the moment. You restored two of my eyes. I gave you two secrets."

"Do you not owe me another for almost throwing me through a solid wall for no reason."

"It was not for no reason. And you know that now. You would be dead, a slave or worse if it were not for me."

"Perhaps."

"No, doubts. A certainty."
"I still feel you owe me another secret."
"Fair enough. There are two cities of Last Keep."
"What?"

Tymond was no younger but with his eyesight restored he was like a new man—smiling and helping anyone he could. Two weeks had passed when a new caravan approached from Hopeshire. In Ironwood it was not one crier to announce their arrival but many. Traveler and Tymond had just sat down for the noon meal when the calls rang through the air.

It was a large caravan. It looked to be a joint Avalonia-Baltica party with two sets of flags and men clearly of two different kingdoms. At the head of the double columns of men on horseback, followed men on foot, dozens of armored men. People closest to the entrance spilled out in front of the castle walls, Tymond and Traveler among them. A single Ironwood agent on horseback rode out to greet—obviously all that the royals of Ironwood would spare. The men have been nobles, honorably in service of their kingdoms, but there was not a royal among them— no king, lord, duke, or prince.

"The City of Ironwood welcomes you," the Ironwood rider greeted.

"Thank you, kind sir," one of the caravan's riders responded.

"Our city is at your disposal for whatever provisions needed, but we are known for the best blacksmiths and weaponsmiths of the Seven Empires."

"Yes, thank you," another caravan rider.

"And as you can see there are plenty of men in the city who would be eager to join should you accept them."

"Yes, thank you."

"May I have the names of your kingdoms to announce you to my king?"

"The Kingdom of Griffon-Horn in South Avalonia and the Kingdom of Ru-Zantine of Baltica."

Rumors ran through Ironwood of the new caravan almost before the riders dismounted and gave orders to set up camp. Merchants quickly made their way from all corners of the city to them, as did all the men who had been waiting for the next suitable caravan.

"You will be joining them," Tymond said to Traveler.

"How do you know?"

"I see it. I can see many things now, thanks to you. Maybe it is your lucky caravan—the one you have been waiting for."

"And you?"

Tymond shook his head with a grin. "No. That life is behind me. My new life awaits back in a tiny town in East of Avalonia. My life will end where it began, where I was born, full circle, as it should be. I had hoped to return with riches, but I gladly settle for surviving with my life intact." He patted Traveler's back. "And my restored sight. I hope all my secrets I shared with you are put to good use."

"Thank you, Tymond the Defiant."

"No. I am Tymond the Grateful. I will squeeze every bit of joy from life in the days that remain."

"That could be a long time."

"Then I better start living it then. Good luck, Traveler, in all your many quests to come."

Tymond waved as he left the boy standing in the crowd and walked forth on the road towards Hopeshire. Traveler watched him until he was gone.

Men seeking to join the caravan had already formed a line—warriors and non–fighters, men and boys. Traveler had been there at the very start but by the time he fell into the line forming there were already at least a thousand or more in front of him. Fortunately, the receiving was fast in their assessment of men which meant the decision, whether good or bad, would also be quick. Men could be heard yelling out in joy or they were seen passing by dejected. Most warrior men were accepted, most others were not.

Traveler was next in line. The man in front of him was a large armored warrior with a bag of weapons in each hand. He was immediately accepted by the two inspecting men of the caravan. The shorter, fatter man with a perpetual frown waved to him to step forward.

Traveler ran forward to them. He nodded. "I am—"

"You will speak only when spoken to, boy! You are not big enough to be a bearer or brave enough to be a sentry, and we have too many domestics so we cannot use your type—"

The man hadn't finished his sentence when Traveler turned from him and walked away. He was unconcerned; he would simply wait until the next caravan.

"Boy!" It was another voice calling him. Traveler turned.

"What were you about to say?" another man in armor asked.

"I was going to say if your caravan's healer needs men, I am a healer's assistant."

"Are you now?"

"I am."

"Myles!" the man yelled. The other man stood next to him with a frown. A third man appeared. Average height and build, dark hair, unremarkable in appearance or bearing. He was without armor.

"What is it?"

"Do you need any assistants? This boy says he is a healer's assistant."

The healer stepped to him. "I do not believe that."

"It is true, sir," Traveler said. "I have studied the profession for the last few years."

"With who?"

"Other healers, some good, some not, but that is how you learn."

"Why a healer's assistant?"

"It is the only non-fighter position in the caravan that has the respect of all."

"But only if you are any good. Are you any good?"

"I am."

"We shall see." The healer looked at the two men. "I will take him. None of them ever last long. Maybe this one will do better; he is at least older than most." He turned back to the boy. "What is your name?"

"Traveler."

"Traveler is it." The healer sighed. "Get your things. You have joined the caravan of Griffin-Horn and Ru-Zantine."

"Ru-Zantine and Griffon-Horn," the frowning warrior corrected.

The healer looked him square in the eyes. "Griffin-Horn and Ru-Zantine!"

The men approached each other to fight. The other man kept between them. The boy laughed to himself as he ran off to get his few belongings.

Three days had passed before the caravan set out from Ironwood to Goodmound Castle. When they had first arrived at Ironwood, they were already five-thousand men strong, now they were over eight thousand. Traveler marched with the sole healer of the caravan, he and six other healing lads followed. He was the oldest of them. Their healer had already put him in charge of the other lads, so this caravan would also be Traveler's first chance at leadership.

The boy studied the formation during the march. They were eight-thousand strong but only a thousand of them were the true fighters. Most of the knights and warriors were at the front with a smaller contingent at the rearguard. Traveler noticed that the other healing lads were watching him study the caravan.

"Nothing is wrong," Traveler told them. "I am just looking."

They all smiled, and nodded.

The other unusual thing Traveler noticed was that the Griffin-Horn and Ru-Zantine caravan had two stewards, one from each kingdom. The two men clearly did not care for each other, and the men had observed them arguing with each other three separate times already before the caravan had even set out.

Provisions-wise, the caravan was well stocked: food, water, weapons, tents, etc., plenty of horses and wagons. They would not be wanting there. Traveler knew that the march to Goodmound's Castle would take seven to ten days. He had heard talk of the trip many times before. The lands of Ironwood were rocky and barren, but once the land changed to green, one knew that the green fields of Goodmound were near. The boy had not yet been there but looked forward to the visit.

Traveler heard a whizzing sound then one of the healing lads screamed. He looked up just as their healer was collapsing to the ground, his forehead pierced by an arrow. Screams and chaos erupted from everywhere, as did distant war-cries all around them. Arrows rained down on the caravan.

Another man dropped to the ground, hit in the chest by an arrow. Traveler grabbed his shield and braced it over him.

"Under the shield!" Traveler yelled to the other healing lads.

But the volley of arrows had already done their terrible damage. Dead men littered the ground. The blood-curling war-cries neared and the caravan could see the charging marauders. They were the roaming killers of the lands between the empires. Their appearance: matted hair down to their waists, clad in a patchwork of animal skins and rusted armor, faces of tattoos and war-paint, wielding blood-stained weapons—battle-axes, war hammers, maces, scythes, halberds, and flails.

Traveler looked to the front columns and realized that for those in the center and rear of the caravan they were completely undefended, the few warriors assigned to protect them were either dead or had run to the front.

"Grab all the quivers from the dead warrior!" Traveler commanded the lads. "Stay close and keep handing me a new arrow. Both of you will protect us with the shields, in case they throw anything. Keep a close circle around me as we move."

Traveler had already picked up a crossbow from the ground; its owner had been killed by an arrow through the eye. How he wished they had the crossbows from the magical lands, but this was the Lands of Man. Thankfully, he had used the weapons many times before.

He dropped the crossbow to the ground, put his foot in the stirrup of the bow, pulled the crossbow string back until it is cocked. One of the healing lads already had an arrow in his hand, Traveler placed it in barrel of the crossbow, aligning as he raised the weapon, aimed and fired. A marauder had been racing to them with great speed, both arms in the air, ready to smash them with a spiked mace. He fell dead to the ground with an arrow through the skull.

The healer's lads wanted to cry out in joy but their faces went white as they saw many more running to them.

"There are too many!" one boy cried.

"No, there are not," Traveler said and fired a second arrow.

He killed a second marauder. The healing lads returned their attention to Traveler, as he prepared a third arrow and fired. A third advancing marauder was killed.

"Perhaps if one of you find another crossbow, two of you can prepare it and I will be able to shoot two arrows at a time."

The healer lads looked at each other. One of them saw it and ran to another unattended weapon and returned to their fighting circle. They watched Traveler's technique, then copied him. Traveler killed another marauder, and right after, killed another.

The fighting in the caravan waged on. Traveler was the only one in the caravan firing arrows; all of the other combat was hand-to-hand. Marauders soon realized that the boy was following a strategy. He now was killing every marauder that was fighting face to face with the remaining caravan's fighters by shooting them in the back.

"Kill that boy!" one yelled out. Seconds later an arrow—from Traveler—killed him.

The healing lads had found other crossbows and Traveler was able to shoot four, then five arrows at a time. One of the caravan's surviving knights joined them. They were able to fire six arrows in succession.

After three hours, the remaining marauders had their fill and escaped into the distance. The caravan had won, many marauders had been killed but less than five hundred of their eight-thousand strong party remained alive.

The two stewards were dead. All of the caravan's leadership was dead save one of the Griffin-Horn knights who took command. The remaining men surrounded the sole knight with only anger and revenge in their eyes.

"We must bury our fallen," the knight said to them.

"What of the marauders who fled?" one of the men yelled. "We must avenge our comrades. We must chase them down to the ends of Pan-Earth if we must and kill them all."

"No, we will not!" the knight yelled back. "This is their lands. We will not be able to track them all and if we are, then it is a trap. No, it ends here."

"What do we do now?"

"We return to Ironwood and rebuild."

The men were in near-mutiny. Other cried out for revenge. The knight did not have the confidence of the men and he knew it. He saw Traveler and the healing lads standing quietly to the side, as with most of the non-fighters who had survived.

"Young man. We also lost our master-at-arms in the battle. It would appear that we are in need more of a replacement of him than of a healer."

"Sir, I am a healer not a warrior. If the caravan has to rely on my clumsy crossbow shooting skills then we are truly lost."

"Do not dismiss your bravery, lad. You performed more nobly than seasoned men twice your age."

"Thank you, sir, but as much as it pains you to admit, the journey for us is over. The marauders will return with greater numbers. We were fortunate."

"Yes, we were, lad. But all is not lost. We can rebuild our numbers at Ironwood or go back to Hopeshire, if need be."

"Sir, you must return home to Griffin-Horn and the other men to their kingdom. You must begin again, but only when replenished. One cannot be desperate with a journey such as this. It is too deadly for that. I am not that old yet, but even I know that. So do you. It is too deadly, and you did not even set foot on the magical lands."

"Yes, lad, true indeed. Too deadly indeed. We were turned back by the evil ones of our own lands, not by some troll or army of goblins in the magical lands. I wonder how many lives have been claimed on Titan's Trail. More than I am sure any of us could imagine."

"Yes, sir."

"Your counsel is sound, lad." The knight turned to the surviving warrior men of the caravan, but they had heard the conversation. "Men, we return home. This day, the Trail has beaten us. We have to bury our men so we should cease the talk and get to it."

Traveler helped in with the gravedigging. There was one patch of ground of green, a whisper of the lands of Goodmound in the miles ahead, but it was green soaked in the red. The caravan would not be seeing Goodmound Castle in the days ahead.

PART TWO

THE LANDS BETWEEN

The Path to Titan's Bridge

CHAPTER FOUR

Caravan of the Vile

Young Traveler was fourteen years old.

The life of anyone waiting for a new caravan on the Row was filled with boredom and danger. The jobs were few for so many in need. Likely one became a vagabond littering the roads between and within towns and cities, or the open fields and wooded areas. However, that meant being preyed upon by the criminal class or, worse, the savage marauders that watched for arriving caravans to plunder.

Traveler was fortunate only because he secured work being done by men taken away by the Ru-Zantine and Griffon-Horn caravan. He was back in Hopeshire working at the stables as a stable hand primarily but word spread that he was really a healer's assistant so almost on a daily basis men showed up looking for their cuts, bites, and stomach ailments to be attended to. The healing arts were one that had to be practiced all the time to maintain one's skills, and Traveler was getting plenty. The work paid well and helped distract him from the growing restlessness he felt as days became weeks of waiting.

One day shortly after dawn, the voice of one of the local town criers rang out. Such announcements made everyone stop what they were doing and many would run to see what could be seen.

Traveler could do neither at the moment.

"We need to go!" the man said, lying prone on the ground in the corner of the stable. He was on a bed of hay with Traveler kneeling to his side in the process of re-bandaging a nasty wound on his lower back.

"You can go if you must. Rip up your bandages. Begin bleeding. And die," Traveler said as he leaned back with his hands held up.

"Lad, you have a terrible bedside manner."

"Do you want bedside manner, for me to finish my work, or do you want to run outside? Please make up your mind."

"A good healer reassures his patient. A bad healer makes his patient want to strike him. You are too young to be a cranky old man."

Traveler smiled. "Sir, you are completely correct. It is this place and the constant waiting. I will bandage you up then you can walk...not run...outside to see what there is to see. I will go with you."

The men turned his head with smile. "There. The beginning of a proper bedside manner."

"I glad you approve. Now lift up your belly so I can get my hand under there and finish your bandages."

Excitement among the people always swept through the arrival of a new caravan. As their men on foot and horseback made their way down the main road, everyone had time to carefully inspect them and decide in moments if they were "worthy" or the "walking dead."

Traveler stood with his new bandaged, bare-chested patient. The man braced himself with a single walking stick. The boy had his own to use as a ready weapon if needed. However, as he watched the newly arriving caravan, he noted than they were strong and seemed to be genuinely capable fighters, but neither alone were indications of honorable men.

"How do you find them, lad?" his former patient asked.

"They look...dangerous."

His patient laughed. "That is what you want, lad. Men who can kill man or beast. I thought you wanted a real caravan."

"I do."

"You seem disappointed that they are more formidable than a boy like you. Lad, you want nothing less than scoundrels. If you await saints and holy men, you will be here until your hair is gray and all your teeth fall out."

"I am not seeking the perfect, sir. However, good men who trained and advised me said on a long journey it must be of men who can trust each other with their lives. If they are not, they are not worthy."

"Well, I cannot argue with that, lad. Me of all people. Considering the fact that one of the men of my own party was the one who stabbed me in the back to take my possessions."

"You did not tell me that."

"You did not ask."

Traveler grinned, then said, "I should find out if this caravan are back-stabbers or not."

"You should, lad. But do not look at me. My caravan seeking days are over. I am content with living all my days in the Lands of Man. You foolhardy ones should go."

"We should."

"Good luck to you, healer lad."

"I have not been accepted by the caravan yet."

"They will. You do not have that look of desperation in your eyes like all the men queuing up now. And you have that presence about you, the bearing. Young but knows what he's doing. They will accept you. If I say so, then it must be true."

Traveler laughed. "Yes, then it must be true."

The man towered above him with his long dark hair resting on silver armor. Everything about the man seemed to be larger than any warrior he had seen: the breadth of his chest, his neck, his hands covered in black leather gloves, all except for one thing—his voice. It was but a mere whisper. But Traveler doubted anyone every had trouble hearing the man when he spoke.

"A healer's assistant?" the man asked.

"Yes, sir," the boy answered.

"Well, you at least have good manners." The man turned to the armored warrior next to him. "Get the healer."

"Erl!" the other man yelled so loud that Traveler winced.

The man who was their healer appeared from within their ranks. The top of his head was bald but he had hair on the sides almost touching his shoulders. He was dressed in dirty purple clothes and his face held a perpetual smile. Traveler remember his father's warning. "Never trust a man who is always smiling. He is either simple in the head or plotting ill deeds." Traveler had encountered many good-natured men who were neither, but the warning did flash in his mind.

"This is our healer, Erl," the giant of a man who he would later learn was named Taner.

Erl stepped to the boy and looked him over. "You are a healer's lad. How do you feel about blood?"

"I am not squeamish, sir. I have assisted other healers in procedures and treatments."

"How many healers?"

"A few, sir. I consider myself to be ever training."

"That is for sure, boy," one of the other warriors said.

"What if you are assisting a healer and the patient vomits all his food on you?"

"I ignore it and continue my duties."

"What if he empties his bladder on you?"

Men started laughing.

"Same answer, sir."

"What if your healer master tells you to clean up all the filth of excrement from a dead patient?"

"Then I will do so, sir, afterward."

"After what?"

"After I properly bury the man."

Erl was caught off-guard by the Traveler's answer.

"Boy, you are hired," Taner announced.

"Master Taner, he is but a mere boy. He has said nothing that shows me he can be an able healer's assistant." The words were futile and Erl knew it but he tried anyway. "Boy! Tell us what is the last major treatment you performed."

"I cured a man of the blindness of a basilisk, sir."

"What?" Again Erl was caught off-guard. "I do not believe—"

"Shut up Erl!" Taner's real voice boomed. In a whisper he asked, "Tell us more."

Traveler had the attention of Taner and the main men of the inspecting party.

"The man was not really blind, sir. He had ventured into the lands of magic and told me of the encounter. However, he had mentioned that he was still able to perceive of shapes. I had observed the man and surmised that the evil affects had not had a chance to fully overcome the man. If so, then only the outer layers of his skin had been petrified. I guessed that maybe it would be the case with his eyes. I scrubbed off that outer layers. Fortune was with the man as it also worked with his eyes, no permanent damage."

"What healer taught you that?" Taner asked.

"None, sir. It was a theory and I was right. I could have easily been wrong."

"But the man had nothing to lose."

"Yes, sir."

"You could have killed the man!" Erl countered. "What if you scrubbed the layers of his eyes off and all that lay beneath was the man's very bloodstream. He would have horribly bled to death."

"No, sir. The instruments I used in my treatment were merely a wash cloth and plenty of water. To heal him I washed his face and eyes."

Tanner laughed and patted the Traveler on the shoulder. "Get your belongings. You have joined Good's Caravan."

Traveler smiled. He glanced at Erl who flashed a look of contempt. Then the healer's smile returned—a very false smile.

"Erl, you better get used to this boy. He is your new assistant," Taner said to him. "And I expect this one to last longer than the others."

Good's Caravan was impressive with its nearly two thousand men, including almost five hundred horsemen on some of the most beautiful warhorses Traveler had seen in a few years. The caravan did not fly under the banner of any kingdom; they were a caravan of warriors and mercenaries, most of whom had been a part of several royal or noble caravans in the past. Taner had even led a few himself though he was not the caravan master but their master-at-arms. They had come together to work for themselves, not any king, queen, or noble.

Traveler returned with his satchel of belongings to a waiting Erl. The healer led him through the camp of men sitting or standing around, talking, smoking, drinking—waiting. The caravan's horses were in the center of the camp guarded by their best warriors.

"We are here," Erl said. His camp was a collection of canvas bundles, boxes, and bags. The boy set his satchel down.

"We shall soon learn how able a healer's assistant you are," Erl said.

"Sir, I will be as able as you train me to be."

Erl stood watching him. "Yes, and as long as you remember that I am your master in this caravan, and no one else."

"Yes, sir."

"The others may be taken by you, but not I."

"Yes, sir."

"You must prove yourself to me. I am not easily taken to anyone. None of my previous healer's assistants lasted for too long. I do not expect different from you. For the moment, until the caravan is ready to leave, you are to roam through the camp and keep it clean. That is all you are to do for the day. I do not want to see you doing anything else. Understood?"

"Yes, sir."

"You will learn that there is very little healing for a healer or his assistants to do before battle. The assistants do the lowly tasks and the healer sleeps. Off to it, boy."

"Yes, sir."

"Have you ever killed a man?" Taner asked him the question sitting in front of a roaring campfire. All the warriors around him were sweating from the heat and had taken off their chest armor and tunics to be bare-chested. Taner, fully clothed and armored, sat comfortably with a large cup of ale in hand.

The boy's rounds through the camp had taken him to the lead warriors which, other than the horses, was the other most guarded section.

"No, sir," Traveler finally answered. Only after did he realize he wasn't truthful.

"Now, that does disappoint me about you."

"Why sir? I am a healer."

"Meaning what?" Taner asked. "When a marauder comes to slit your throat, who exactly are you going to heal?"

"I will defend myself, sir."

"I do not want you to defend yourself. That means you leave an enemy alive so he can come back later and kill one of my men. I want you to kill him so he will never trouble us again. You may be a healer's assistant but you are above all a member of the caravan. Every man, no matter how young, must protect it at all costs, whether that means to give up your life, or to kill to keep the caravan safe."

"Yes, sir."

"I have thrown many a man out of a caravan who did not understand those two principles. Do not think I will not do the same to you, even though I like you."

"Yes, sir. I will do my duty."

"Good. Continue on."

Traveler continued to walk through the camp, tidying as he went. He had been in unattended stables and barns less filthy than the camp. Men threw their clothes everywhere, left their weapons on the ground unattended, food was scattered all over. He would make one pass through the caravan and come back around and find the state of the camp as untidy as before.

If he hoped to learn from the men from their stray conversations, he quickly learned that was not be. These men were not Esis and his men; there was nothing noble or honorable about them. When they weren't speaking about people they killed or robbed, they spoke of their many sexual conquests, many of which were forcible. It got worse as the men began to drink more and many began to engage in nasty horseplay exposing themselves and dancing to amuse themselves, laughing hysterically.

He had seen the caravan master a few times and had not realized it until one of the men yelled, "Here, caravan master!" and threw his drink in the man's face. Their caravan master was a thoroughly unimposing and weak individual. Traveler had to stop himself from staring, wondering how such a person possessed the knowledge to safely lead them through the magical lands.

"Where are my things, sir?" Traveler asked the healer who was half-drunk sitting at his own campfire with one mug in his hand and many other strewn around him.

"What are you talking about, boy?"

"I left my satchel with my things and now it is gone."

The healer took another drink from his mug then belched. "You should have been more careful."

"I did not expect to have my possessions stolen when I joined a caravan. Men in the caravan do not steal from one another."

"Says who?"

Traveler watched him with squinted eyes. The healer's smile returned as he took another drink of his mug.

"It is no matter, sir. It is not my real satchel. Whoever the thief is will find they are only in the possession of hardened chunks of cow dung."

The healer stopped drinking and his stared back with droopy, reddened eyes. His smile was gone again.

"I will return to my duties, sir." Traveler turned his back on him walked away.

When he first encountered Good's caravan, he was impressed, and as quickly, moving amongst them, grew to loathe them. By the fourth day, after word of their arrival had spread throughout the region, their ranks of two thousand men had nearly tripled. It was time and their leadership assembled the caravan.

The caravan master was named Federic, and as Traveler watched him address the men and wondered if he attained the position because he could speak with a booming voice above all others no matter the size of the audience.

"Men, Good's Caravan will depart tomorrow at dawn. We have secured all the men and provisions we need for our great journey into the magical lands. We leave the good people of Hopeshire for the city of steel and iron, called Ironwood, to the plush, green lands of Goodmound's Castle, and finally to the Last Keep, the last vestige of civilization in the Lands of Man.

"Men, we will leave behind the Lands of Man for the legendary Titan's Bridge. All of us have heard the myth: Long ago, before the dawn of man, fae, and beasts of light and darkness, was the Age of the Titans. Gigantic humanoid beings of such size that their heads reached high above the clouds into the heavens. One among them, a Titan known as the Maker of All Mountains was so devastated by the death of his beloved, he walked the entire circumference of Pan-Earth, dragging his fabled weapon, the Star Slayer, upon the earth. By happenstance, he carved a massive valley, before he killed himself by leaping off the world to disappear into the void of space. The valley that Titan created, cut through not only the known world, but every other realm, is known as Titan's Trail, and is no myth. It is the path we travel to the magical lands not for adventure...for treasure beyond all our dreams!"

The caravan burst out in cheers, some raised fists or swords or other weapons into the air.

"Prepare men! Eat well tonight! Our quest begins at dawn!"

There was no respite for Traveler. Erl had him working for the noon meal, only allowing him a few moments for food and water before returning to his duties. When night fell, it was no different. Traveler worked during the night meal while the men ate, drank, and carried on.

Then the fighting began.

It was one caravan but contained many factions. With the alcohol flowing, insults turned to pushing, then fighting, then the killing began with one man thrusting his dagger into another. Seemingly, the entire caravan erupted into battle—with itself.

Traveler felt no sense of security as the fighting grew and he noticed unknown men from outside the camp run in. The only sentries not drunk were the ones guarding the horses, but that left everyone else without protection. He heard screams and saw men collapsing. While the inner fight raging, the camp was being plundered by murderous thieves.

"Stop!" He could not tell if it was the caravan master's voice or another. Regardless the fighting continued.

The thieves doused campfires and turned over torches to hide their assault on the camp.

Traveler looked at the dagger he held in his hand. Could he really use it to defend himself?

More screams rang throughout the darkened camp. Taner galloped through with dozens of riders, some with torches. Men jumped down from their horses to give chase and kill any fleeing thief they could catch.

"Secure the camp!" Taner yelled, as he got down from his horse too.

The caravan master came out of the darkness to stand by Taner's side. The master-at-arms glared at him.

"If we did not need you, I would run you through now!" Taner said to him.

"Why are you surprised by my behavior? I am the caravan master. I do not need to know how to fight. That is why you are here."

"You are nothing but a coward. You are a lowly guide and nothing more. You are no caravan master because you are master of nothing."

"Taner, we have had this verbal exchange before. Your anger will pass and I will lead us on. When riches fill your hefty hands all your unkind feelings will be gone."

"We shall see, guide!"

"You do the killing. I will do the guiding." Taner turned his attention to the wounded and dead in the camp. "Healer! Where is your wretched carcass?" His eyes locked on the boy. "You!"

He ran to Taner and noticed his hand with the dagger was trembling. He grabbed it with the other and slowly returned the weapon to his waist.

"Are you a coward too?" Taner asked.

Traveler looked up. "No, sir. I was overcome by the moment. However, it has passed. I am ready to attend to the wounded."

"Good. Then do your healing duties."

"Yes, sir. Can you assign a man with a torch to me, sir? So I can see what I am doing."

Taner grabbed one of the torch bearers and pulled the man to the boy. "Make sure the boy has the light he needs."

"Yes, Taner."

Traveler knelt before the first man he saw. He listened for breath, then grabbed his wrist. "This man is dead." He moved to the man, who was awake but holding a deep gash on the side of his leg.

When Erl, the healer, finally appeared, Traveler had attended to no less than a dozen men already. The boy was constructing a tourniquet.

"What are you doing?" Erl yelled and kicked the boy away from the man he was helping.

A warrior punched the healer in the nose. "The boy is saving lives, you drunken leech."

Erl held his bloodied nose.

Traveler picked himself up from the ground. "The man needs a tourniquet to stop the bleeding but I do not know how to do it properly."

Erl rushed in. "Let me." He examined the bleeding man's leg. "You will lose this leg," the healer said to the men, "but you will live. Give me the lengths of wood you gathered."

Traveler handed him the wood and watched as Erl quickly made the tourniquet, ripping the man's own tunic into the lengths of cloth he needed. Taner stood over them, watching. Healer and assistant stopped the man's bleeding then moved onto the next wounded man. Both men worked throughout the night.

Erl sat at the campfire deep in thought as he sipped from a new mug of ale. The chest of his tunic was bloodied. Across the flame Traveler sat with his white tunic covered in dirt and blood. The boy wanted to help bury the men who had died, but Taner sent him away.

"Not wise to wear white as a healer's assistant," Erl said as he sipped from the mug.

Traveler ignored him then noticed someone approaching.

It was Taner. Their master-at-arms stood at the fire. "You both did good work tonight," he said. "It is our good fortune, do you not think so, Erl?"

The healer made a grunt as he kept drinking.

"At least we know the boy has the real mettle of a true healer, and unlike you, Erl, the true mettle of a man. If we lose you in battle or to drink, at least we know we have a suitable replacement." Taner grinned at the boy and turned to walk back to his campsite.

Traveler turned his eyes to Erl. The man had the cup to his mouth, but he wasn't drinking. He glared at the boy.

Traveler could not shake the senselessness of it all. Most of the men that died that night were not because of the robbers but the deadly brawl that broke out between the factions of the camp. News of what happened spread and their numbers of over six thousand dwindled to less than a thousand—less than what they had when they took on all the new men. Newcomers abandoned them as quickly as they could. The boy was looking forward to the new men to offset the lowly men of the original party of Good's caravan. Now, the good men were gone and the wretched remained.

He felt someone staring and turned to see Erl watching him with a fiendish grin. The boy would no longer sleep anywhere near the man, camp near him, or turn his back to him. He was not allowed to stay in Taner's group but there were plenty of warriors left for him to stay close to.

At dawn they left with two-thirds less men than when their caravan master gave his speech. Traveler felt demoralized but the men of Good's Caravan acted as if nothing of concern had happened.

They reached Ironwood, the city of metal and stone. For a caravan comprised of commoners alone, they had no shortage of money. Taner replenished their weapons stock and hired a dozen weaponsmiths to join them on the journey.

Traveler had never ventured past Ironwood, but when Good's Caravan crossed from the rocky terrain that marked Ironwood's region to the green wooded lands of Goodmound's territory, he was anxious to see the castle city himself. He had wished that his Griffin-Horn and Ru-Zantine caravan had made it, but it was not to be. They reached the great castle city complete with an official royal welcoming party. Taner did the talking for the party, while their toady caravan master stood behind him.

"All the men and provisions you need," one of Goodmound's noble knights told them.

"We will need many," Taner said.

"I will have word spread throughout the city. By tomorrow morning you will have more men than you could possibly use lined up before you for your magical journey." The noble smiled and reached out his hand.

Taner smirked and placed a large pouch of coin in the noble's hand.

"Your caravan will have the blessing of the king and queen themselves."

It was as the noble had said. Thousands of men showed up the next day seeking to join their caravan. Thousands of men were accepted. To the boy's dismay, those chosen were not the best and brightest. The many new men to join their ranks were the most brutish, fearsome, and violent.

They had not even left the fields of Goodmound's Castle. Two men were already killed in fights between factions over the merest of slights.

"What is wrong with you, boy?" Erl the healer stood over him. Traveler was burying the second man in makeshift graves in a section east of the city.

As he often did, Traveler kept an eye on the man but ignored most of anything he said.

"This is not a caravan of the noble class or royal blood. We are a caravan of the common man, the real men of the world. We will travel through the magical lands to find our riches not because we have the best manners but because we are willing to kill any who stand in our way. We will not hesitate and will show no fear because we have none."

Traveler watched him, holding his shovel.

"Do you have something to say, boy?"

"I heard an elf in the magical lands can fall one hundred men in the blink of an eye. So, we may be murderous and fearsome here in the Lands of Man, but I do not think we will be viewed as such by those elves and sprites when we get to their lands."

"You know nothing, boy."

"I know that you know even less about the magical lands than I do."

"I know considerably more than you."

Traveler began to pat the ground with his shovel again. "Yes, about getting drunk and sleeping."

"What did you say, boy?" Erl snarled.

Traveler held his shovel, ready to strike the healer. The man stepped back. "I said nothing at all. Did you say something, sir?"

Erl smiled as he walked backwards. "Poor, poor boy. I am liking my caravan very much. It is men of my own heart, but sadly not of yours. What is a poor boy to do?" Erl laughed as he turned and strode away.

Good's Caravan left Goodmound's Castle with as many men as they could enlist, but few of them were good in character or in skill. The lands around the castle city were beautiful, lush and green reminding Traveler of his own home land, but that was the past. Ahead of them lay the last city within the Lands of Man before the crossing the threshold to the magical lands. He felt both fear and exhilaration at the prospect but the more he thought of the fabled Titan's Bridge, the more fearful he became. It was all real. He was no longer preparing to join a caravan into the magical lands. The future was now. He was not five or nine years old anymore. He was not in his homeland anymore. He was fifteen, a year past the age of maturity, and he was the official healer's assistant for a caravan barreling its way to the Bridge. He was in a vile caravan and he often felt the gaze of his wretched master upon him. He turned and Erl was watching him.

Though not the winter season, the air felt as if winter approached. Caravans never traveled in winter, or in the peak of summer. Men and animals could freeze to death in the former, and both could collapse from heat exhaustion in the later. The time was spring, so why was the air so cold? He realized that he did not even have a good cloak to cover his body; a mistake he would never make again. He gripped the front collar of his tunic to also press his hand against his throat. One of the preeminent rules of being a healer or their assistant: you could never get sick.

Last Keep was a walled, castle city too but there was nothing majestic about it. It had a tower adorned with a large banner to signify it was a city under royal control, but they saw no noble knights or attendants at all. There was no welcoming committee to greet them and the population was far less than they expected. The residents of Last Keep seemed to care not about their presence, ignoring them completely walking to the city or from it. Traveler found the whole behavior strange but none of the men of Good's Caravan did.

He saw that one of the warriors noticed him looking around.

"Question, lad?" he asked.

The boy nodded. "What is the matter, sir? The people do not seem to care that we are here."

"Caravans rarely reach Last Keep—only once in a long time. Those that do usually have no money to spend. You gather men and supplies from Hopeshire, men and weapons from Ironwood, men and anything you missed from Goodmound's Castle, maybe have your last good sleep if you can afford an inn. Last Keep is simply to pass on through, stop if you must, buy meager items that you might have forgotten. The people of the other three cities live for the caravan trade. If the people of Last Keep had to, they would be starved and dead ages ago."

"Who do they do trade with then, sir?"

The warrior looked around. "Very good question, lad. I do not think any of us knows. They are never starving or in need. They are busy with the duties of life."

"They do not appear to be farmers, sir."

"Right you are, lad. A mystery then. Who are they trading with? Maybe there are other parties that pass through that bring a steadier, more reliable commerce to fill their pockets and the city's coffers."

"There is no value to the city for us, sir?"

The warrior shook his head. "None. Not even the robbers and marauders come this far. It is not worth the trouble. Last Keep is that last place you see before you leave the Lands of Man."

"Will we be here long, sir?"

"If we are, it will be to rest the horses. In this caravan, horses are more valuable than men."

The caravan did decide to stay in Last Keep for the night. The master-at-arms wanted to continue on but the caravan master wanted to rest within the walls of a city. The two were always contemptuous of each other in public, but this time they almost came to blows.

At night fell, the streets within Last Keep were empty of residents. Good's Caravan practically had the city for themselves. Most of the men took over a corner tavern and no one noticed, but Traveler saw the landlord had disappeared, leaving the men to pour their own alcohol and become an orgy of drunken brawling.

Traveler sat outside the tavern and after a while walked away to find a quiet spot to sit alone. No one was in the streets around him. All the establishments around were closed and locked, not even a hint of light or life within. He tried to fight the tears building in his eyes. It was a wretched caravan he was attached to. He wanted to leave them, but that meant going back to Goodmound's Castle, maybe back to Ironwood then Hopeshire and waiting. Waiting for days, months, or years for a good caravan that may never arrive.

He grabbed his head and shut his eyes. What to do? What to do? He opened his eyes and leaned back against the wall in the dark. The moon above came out from the night clouds. He would stay where he sat all night until the morning and wrestle with himself to decide.

Four men had died in the drunken brawling the night before. Traveler learned of it from a few of the caravan men laughing about it in the morning. He had barely slept a wink, but he had decided. Forward to Titan's Bridge, not back to Goodmound. He made it a simple choice of destinations and excluded everything else from his mind.

"Get up, boy!" The snarling face of Erl the Healer appeared.

Traveler glanced up at him.

"You have your duties to attend to. If not, you can remain behind here." The healer turned and walked away, around the corner.

Traveler slowly rose to his feet. He would begin his caravan duties—after he got something to eat from the tavern.

When Good's Caravan departed Last Keep there were no speeches. Many of the men regarded any more speeches from their hated caravan master as asking the

Fates to strike them all dead. Taner rode lead for the caravan horsemen. Ahead of them, marched their most fearsome warriors as front guard. Everyone else followed the riders. The rear guard was comprised an assortment of men considered their most depraved or useless.

As the hours passed, and they marched on, the land itself changed. Gone were the green fields, trees, and other plant life. The soil beneath them thinned and became replaced by dust, then dark gray rock. The caravan was also moving upward, as the land steadily inclined to higher elevations until finally leveling off to a flat plateau stretching beyond anything they could see.

Traveler already had a stride quicker than most men. He had moved to walk alongside the riders, near Taner's mount. Their master-at-arms noticed the boy then returned his eyes forward.

A man called out. Taner pressed his horse forward and it sprinted forward with several other riders following close. The boy saw Taner and the riders stop in front of warriors of the front guard. The men were talking but no one could hear the conversation. Taner turned and waved the caravan forward.

"We are at the official end of the Lands of Man," he said.

Traveler realized it was not he who the master-at-arms was speaking to but their caravan master.

"Have the men continue forward," the caravan master said.

"A caravan master who leads from behind." Taner looked down at the man with a snarl.

"What is there to show? There is a cliff and a bridge. We cross the bridge."

Taner led his riders away in a huff. The rider took point within the front guard. Suddenly, hands shot up. The caravan was halted again. Taner rode back to the caravan master with his men.

"Did you not tell us we should not start across the bridge unless it is at dawn?" Taner angrily asked him.

The man's eyes darted around. "Yes, you are correct."

Taner jumped down from his horse.

"If you strike me, I will not lead you to the magical lands."

Taner smacked the caravan master across the face, knocking him to the ground.

"You will lead us to the magical lands or I shall throw you off the cliff." The men glared at each other. Taner turned to his men and yelled, "Set up camp here for night. We set across Titan's Bridge at dawn."

Traveler rubbed his temple and held in his distress. The caravan master was going to get them killed. He was going to look back to see if he could still see Last Keep.

His view was obstructed by the rotund body of Erl the Healer.

"You have your duties, boy. Get to them then while I have my drink of ale and take a nap."

Traveler didn't know how close they were to Titan's Bridge. He had camped with a group of the warriors that he regarded with some respect—they were quiet, disciplined, and did not engage in endless drink or horseplay. Their skills as fighters were second to none which was why even Taner let them do as they pleased. As Traveler rested his head down on his blanket, his body close to the fire, he tried to recall all the stories he had heard about the Bridge over the years. Soon he would learn what was fact and what was fiction regarding its legend. Foremost among the stories was that it was a structure of such size that his eyes would not believe what it saw, a structure created by a legendary Titan of ancient Pan-Earth. As he let his imagination run, he fell asleep with a smile.

He always slept through the night; very little roused him even in a rowdy camp. Something woke him but when he opened his eyes, he saw nothing, though it was a well-lit night. By the time he realized that his head was covered and he was being dragged along the ground, it was too late.

The terror that overcame him was so crushing he was unable to move or scream. His body was falling into an emptiness that he was certain was his death.

Traveler's body lay on the side of the plateau bruised and broken. He had been staring up into space when it was dark and now up at the sky. The brutal pain had subsided, but he was scared to move because he certain that he had broken bones, maybe even a broken back. If so, even though he was not dead, he might as well be. His life was over. He knew who his murderer was but there nothing he would ever be able to do about it. He would never see the caravan, the magical lands, a gnome, elf, unicorn, griffin, fairy, nothing of the magical races or beasts, nor the Lands of Man ever again.

"What, look what I found?"

The sound startled the boy. How could someone be here? He was on the side of the mountain. When he saw the source of the question his mouth dropped open. Two elves stood on the side of the plateau watching him.

Traveler was so surprised by the strangers he hadn't noticed that he had sat up to get a better view. Maybe they were not elves but a different race of fae because their skin had a slight green hue, the tips of their pointed ears were at least six inches tall, and from their foreheads sprouted a long antenna above each eye. Beyond their physical features, they were dressed like human royals—expensive-looking tunics under leather jackets. They had long, well-groomed hair past their shoulders. Both elves carried a long light wooden walking stick.

"What might you be called?" the taller one asked.

"My name is Traveler," he answered.

"An ironic name for one in your predicament."

A realization of fear came over his face. He realized that he was sitting and looked down at his legs, wincing.

"Are they broken? Your legs," the shorter elf asked.

"I believe so, sir."

The shorter elf crouched down before the boy. He grabbed the boy's left leg then the right.

"There."

"There, sir?"

The shorter elf touched the boy's shoulder.

"And there."

"And there? What do you mean, sir?"

The elf stood. "You are healed, young one."

"What wounds did I have, sir?"

"The bones, muscles and tendons of your left leg were broken, torn, and twisted. Your right leg was broken in five places. Your ribs were cracked and bruised. But all healed," replied the shorter elf.

"What manner of profession do you do in your lands, young one?" the taller one asked.

"I am a healer—or I am training to be one."

The two elves giggled. "How does that work in your lands?" the tall elf asked. "A human healer. A race with no magic or advanced machinery."

"Yes, sir. I will never be able to be what you did for me now."

"Do not say that, young one," the shorter elf said. "Simply attain the magic or advanced machinery, then you will."

"Thank you, sir, for saving me." Traveler stood up slowly and quickly crouched back down. He stared at the elves. "You both are..."

The two elves giggled again. They were actually not standing on the side of the plateau. They had been floating all the time.

"What type of elves are you, sir?"

"We are fairy elves."

Traveler smiled. "Is that a separate race or a joined race, sir?"

"Our race are the descendants of a royal fairy progenitor and a royal elfin progenitor."

"It is my pleasure to meet noble members of the fairy elfin race. You are coming here from the magical lands."

"We are."

"Where do you travel to?"

"Last Keep."

Traveler gave him a puzzled look. "Last Keep, sir?"

The two elves giggled again. "You should be on your way, young one. You have been made whole and I am sure you do not wish to remain on the side of this plateau mountain, even if it is for stimulating conversation with fairy elves. Safe journey, young one."

The two fairy elves floated up into the air and disappeared. He could not see them anymore but felt as if they were still nearby.

Traveler turned his attention to the top of the plateau. He climbed to the top and stood as he stared off into the distance. It was well past dawn but Good's Caravan, the vile caravan, had only begun to depart.

Maybe the caravan had left at dawn. One comprised of thousands of men, disparate factions, under weak leadership could not depart without significant delays. Traveler was glad he blessed with a long stride because he knew it would not take long for him to reach the caravan's rearguard then find who he needed to in the main party.

Traveler had seen the lowly men of the caravan's rearguard before but today it was from a new vantage. As he quickly neared from a mile away, he could see their silhouettes glancing back at him. He saw them draw their weapons and some of them clustered together. However, when they were able to see him clearly, they relaxed, recognizing him. He ignored them as he marched past them and begun to scan the backs of the hundreds of men ahead of him.

One of the warriors looked at him and Traveler walked even with him.

"You decided to join us," the man said.

"Where is Erl, the healer?" the boy asked.

"With the riders at the front of the column."

Traveler walked ahead faster.

His eyes locked on Erl as quickly as his sorry frame came into view. The boy had his dagger in his right hand, held behind his back as he approached. Suddenly, the healer turned to look back as if someone whispered in his ear. The healer looked at him with shock then stopped his march. His face turned to a snarl. The man rushed forward at him.

"Where were you?" the healer yelled.

Traveler slashed him. Erl yelled out. The healer held his slashed right wrist with his left hand with all his might. All of Good's Caravan had stopped. Taner, the caravan master, and the riders encircled them.

"What is happening here?" the caravan master yelled at them.

"He bundled me up last night and tried to kill me by throwing me off the plateau," Traveler answered.

"That is a lie! Why would I try to kill my own assistant?" Erl snapped.

"Because you are a liar and a coward and no healer. I know more than you and everyone knows it."

"That is another lie." Erl looked at the caravan's leadership. "If I threw him off the plateau, how is he here before us? How could he survive such a thing?"

The men looked at Traveler for an answer. "I did not survive," the boy replied. "Or I would not have, but I was fortunate. Two fairy elves came upon me."

"Fairy elves?" Taner asked as he dismounted. "Where?"

"They are moving to Last Keep, sir, or that is what they said."

The news caused a stir among the men of the caravan.

"One of the men said he saw strange lights in the night," one of the riders said. "It must have been them."

"There have always been rumors of men seeing elves, dwarves, all manner of fae in the region near Last Keep," another said.

"Why would fae have anything to do with a nothing city such as Last Keep?" Taner asked.

"No one knows," the man answered.

"Yes, the lights last night must have been those fairy elves." Taner said. "What happened when they came upon you, lad?"

"They touched my wounds and healed me, sir," Traveler continued.

The men returned their attention to Erl.

"He is lying!" Erl yelled. "I did nothing. Where is the proof of it?"

Taner looked at the boy. "Is that it? You said your master tried to throw you off a mountain in the night and you merely cut his wrist. That is all your vengeance can manage."

"He is dead," Traveler said.

"Is he? He still stands and is still talking." Taner walked to his horse, mounted it and rode away.

When everyone's attention returned to Erl and Traveler, an arrow landed in the center of healer's chest. He immediately let the pressure go from his right wrist and began to bleed again. Another arrow ripped into his chest then two more. Erl dropped to his knees. The man's body shook and he doubled over and fell to the ground.

Taner rode back to them with a long bow in his hand. His quiver of arrows was on the side of his horse.

"Lad, if you learn no other lesson from me, learn that when a man is set on killing you, you better do much more than pass a blade along his wrist like a woman. You better kill him good and ensure that he is dead."

One of the nearby warriors swung and buried his battleax into the back of the late healer.

"He is dead, now," Taner said to Traveler. "Are you squeamish about killing because you are a healer?"

"I am not squeamish, sir, but I am a healer."

"You are a member of a caravan, far away from the niceties of law and order of a royal kingdom of any kind. You are a man first, a healer second. Are you not a man?"

"I am, sir."

"A man is one who can defend his own life. This is a caravan of men. Are you a man, lad?"

"A man, sir."

"If you think you have taken the role of healer so you can stay close to the warriors to protect you, I am going to instruct each and every one of them not to lift a blade to defend you. Understood?"

"Understood, sir?"

"Are you returning to Last Keep to be with your healing fairy elves?"

"No, I am continuing on to Titan's Bridge, sir."

Taner nodded. The caravan master moved closer to the boy.

"Young lad, you have moved up in position. You are the new healer of Good's Caravan."

Erl's body was not buried. Taner simply had a few of the men throw it off the plateau. Instead of preparing to leave, men broke out in celebration, which didn't take long to devolve into fighting. Traveler sat at a camp by himself listening to the brawling and a few screams. Before the caravan quieted down, three more men died in senseless fighting.

They left at dawn finally for Titan's Bridge—two days later. Normally there was some chatter among the men but not this time. Everyone had seen the first marker of Titan's Trail from many miles away—the rising mountains and the descending lands. When they arrived none of the myths and tales matched the true magnitude of seeing the Bridge for first time with one's own eyes. Off the edges dropped into a chasm so wide that it seemed an unfathomable depth. The sides of the chasm were barely visible in the far-off distance. Each side, on the other side of the chasm, was lined with unclimbable mountains and a sheer sheet of rock. The bottom was beyond contemplation.

There was Titan's Bridge. It was not a land bridge but a ridge, which made sense on sight, as no bridge could traverse the chasm without any underneath supports. However, the path surface was flat and smooth, as if polished, and over each side was the seemingly endless drop into the dark chasm. The Bridge was of the same dark-gray rock as the surrounding mountains, but it was only five miles wide. Such a distance would be considered a mammoth bridge anywhere else in the Lands of Man, but within the chasm, it looked like a mere string. It would take the whole day to cross, which was why they had to start across it soon after dawn. Though, they were already hours past dawn.

The signal was given for the caravan to halt its march forward. All the riders, Taner, the caravan master, the horsemen convened at the front to plan the formation of the men to cross. Restless men moved forward on their own to get a better view of the Bridge; others wanted to peek over the cliffs to see if there was any indication of its depths. Traveler looked on. Screams broke out!

The boy had just turned his head when the warrior standing right next to him was snatched away by a large shape. Traveler dropped back to the ground to see that the man had been grabbed by a slimy gray tentacle. His mouth and eyes widened as he saw the creature rising from the edge of the cliff, grabbing more men.

"It's a Carcolh!"

The boy had never heard the name before. Men attacked with swords, axes, and spears. A few arrows flew at it from within the caravan but they bounced off. The creature was both snail and snake. Its main body was a gigantic snail-like shell larger than a two-story hut and its slimy body was long like a snake. Its head looked like a giant snail but it had a teethed, circular mouth like a lamprey encircled by tentacles. Its long tail was also covered with tentacles. Chaos erupted as its many front and tail tentacles attacked—grabbing men, crushing them, feeding its mouth, swallowing screaming men whole, swatting men away.

"Lad!"

Traveler looked up from the ground. Taner had his arm extended down to grab him up to his mount. The boy slowly began to reach out to grab his arm but stopped. He looked at the terror of the battle with the creature.

He looked at Taner. "If I go with you, I will die."

Taner pulled his hand back with a smile. He saluted the boy and rode off hard. Taner and the riders left behind all the men of the caravan headed for the Bridge.

A man was screaming louder than all others. The caravan master fought futilely with all his might but finally the tentacle grasping him deposited him into the creature's mouth.

The vile caravan that took death so lightly in its travels would meet it here, finally. Most of the men had already fled, the ones remaining ran in every direction to escape.

Traveler was overwhelmed by anguish as he turned and ran as fast as he could in the direction of Last Keep. Good's Caravan was dead.

CHAPTER FIVE

Caravan of the Lost

Young Traveler was nearly fifteen years old.

He ran at a break-neck pace over the ridge, almost in a state of madness. A noise in the distance; he dropped his body flat against the ground.

Another caravan neared. From the standards held high—blue flags and white symbols—it was a large royal caravan stretching far into the distance. The boy watched them from his hidden spot. He thought for a minute—let them pass or warn them?

He leapt up from the ground. Moving so fast to them, he ran right into a fully armored single scout. Both males fell to the ground.

"You foolish boy!" the knight yelled and picked himself up. "If you had not surprised me I could have killed you!" However, Traveler was not paying attention to the man but behind him. "What are you looking at, boy?"

The boy sat up, watching behind him, ready to jump up and run again.

"What are you running from, boy?" the knight asked.

"The creature," Traveler answered, his voice wavered.

"Creature? What creature?" The knight drew his sword and watched where the boy was looking towards.

Soon a few other knights appeared and joined them.

"What's wrong?" one of the asked.

"The boy says he was chased by a creature," the scouting knight answered.

"Creature? What creature? Boy! Stand to your feet and answer us. If a creature comes, I for one would like to know what kind."

"I heard my caravan say the name but I never heard it before."

"What does it look like?" another knight asked impatiently.

"It's a giant man-eating snail with tentacles from its mouth and tail. I thought I was safe but the tentacles can reach out long distances. I swear I was nearly a mile away and it almost grabbed me!"

"That is not possible," the knight said as a new man in a hooded cloak joined them, as did knights on horseback.

"Speak someone. Who is this boy?"

"The boy says he was chased by a creature," the scouting knight said.

"Are you out here alone, boy?" a knight rider asked.

"No, I was with a caravan, sir, but the creature killed most of them."

"What creature?" the lead knight on horseback asked again.

"The boy is describing a Lou Carcolh—" the cloaked man began.

"That is the name they called it," Traveler called out.

"Lou Carcolh?" the lead knight on horseback said.

"The boy is mistaken," the man in the hooded cloak said. "What he describes is a slimy creature that exists only in the magical lands and there it inhabits dark, wet underground caverns."

"I know what attacked me only minutes ago and killed the men," Traveler said. "It came out from the side of the cliff as we about to descend to the path to Titan's Bridge."

The knights and cloaked man looked at each other.

"Maybe it found a dark cave on the side of the cliff to hide in," the lead knight said.

"But how did it get here?" the cloaked man asked.

"Fae of light are not the only fae that have been sighted in the parts around Last Keep," a knight said.

"You believe it was planted there by dark fae, sire?" the cloaked man asked.

"Why not? It is exactly the type of evil prank they would engage in. Hold onto the boy. Summon a troop of four dozen riders. I will lead it myself."

"Sire, your place is here. We will go."

"No, wizard," the lead knight said to the cloaked man. "I will lead the men and you will be at my side. If it is a creature from the magical lands, then we may need more than our royal swords to vanquish it."

"Yes, sire."

The lead knight moved his horse closer to the boy. "What is your name?"

"I am Traveler, sire."

"We will go find your creature and deal with it properly. Did it kill all the men of your caravan?"

"No, sire. The riders escaped."

"Then you will wish to rejoin them."

"No, sire. They were a murderous and ignoble lot. If the creature had not killed them, they probably would have done the same to each other in the next drunken brawl. I will not be rejoining them."

"I am sorry to hear that account of your caravan. Settle the boy in the camp and get some warm food in him. Men, let us find this creature of slime and tentacles."

The boy Traveler followed a knight into the royal camp. The stark contrast between the new caravan and his caravan of old was apparent in every activity and detail. Good's Caravan, with the exception of the horsemen, Taner and only a few of the warrior factions, was a wretched lot. The caravan before him was the professional operation he had never seen, but heard of and dreamed being a part of. Attentive, halberd-wielding armored sentries, two-per-unit, stood watch at regular intervals encircling the camp. Men within the camp were busy with duties: preparing meals, attending to horses, livestock in wagons, and guard dogs. Others polished armor and weapons, mended clothing, polished boots, others were carving wood into arrows.

"Have you never seen a royal caravan, lad?' the knight asked.

"I have, sir, but never one as well-run as this one."

"This is how our men conduct themselves."

Traveler saw in the distance men in fighting drills: fighting with staffs, wrestling each other, or practice fighting with swords.

"See there, lad, Mr. Melvin, the steward of the caravan."

The men he saw was every bit a royal in fancy clothing but also wore chainmail armor over his chest and had more than one dagger on his waist. He had graying hair and watched the boy with a stern face.

"You are the steward of the caravan, sir?" Traveler asked.

"I am, lad."

Traveler ran and hugged him.

"What!" The steward's emotionless demeanor was pierced as his face turned red. "Unhand me, boy!"

Knights around them burst out in laughter.

"There is no hugging in a royal caravan, lad!"

"What gives you cause to embrace our master steward so, lad?" the knight asked.

"Finally, I am in the presence of a noble caravan with noble men," Traveler said in a low tone and his eyes teared up.

"There is also no crying in a royal caravan, lad," Mr. Melvin said and tapped him on the shoulder.

"You did not have good fortune with the others before us?" the knight asked.

"No, I did not, sir," the boy answered.

"Well, do no judge us so hastily," Mr. Melvin said. "We only appear to be noble and well-trained. Determine it for yourself. Take our new young guest to some food and set him in the camp with some of the other lads."

"Yes, Mr. Melvin."

"What was your profession in your previous caravan, lad?" Mr. Melvin asked.

"I was a healer's assistant, sir."

The steward stopped. "Healer?"

"An assistant, sir."

"Are you any good?" Mr. Melvin asked.

"I have been training and practicing for some five years now, sir?"

"Trained where?"

"I began with the official leaders of a couple of royal courts, then moved out to apprentice with countryside healers, then a few traveling healers that provided care to the peoples of large regions."

Mr. Melvin nodded. "You are of interest to me now. Knight, put him with the lads near the healer's tent. He can assess him when he has a moment." To Traveler, "My only question to you, lad, is are you looking to join another caravan or were you on your way back to your homelands."

"Another caravan, sir."

"How far did you get on the Trail, lad?" the knight asked.

"Just before Titan's Bridge, sir."

"His caravan was attacked by a creature," the knight said to their steward.

"Creature, here? We have not even crossed into the magical lands and we are facing creatures?"

"The boy warned us of it."

"Good. A healer and a sense of duty to his fellow man. You will do well with us—if our healer accepts you."

"What is the name of this caravan, sir?"

"This is the royal caravan of Anfall Gates."

The healer of the Anfall Gates caravan was an old man whose busy white hair, mustache, and beard wound down to his knees. Traveler was certain the man was a wizard of some kind. For nearly a half hour the man had him sitting on a stool in the healing tent as the man wrote notes in a book. The healing tent was large, open and orderly. Along the wall were large baskets, each with a cloth with a single symbol. If it was a language, it was none that the boy had ever seen.

Traveler was a naturally calm boy but his impatience grew.

"Sir, why am I waiting here?"

"If I tell you, will you sit still?"

"I have been sitting still, sir."

The healer said nothing as he continued to scribble in his book at the table.

"Possibly, sir," Traveler answered the original question. "I do not like to be idle for no reason."

"If you were not sitting here, what would you be doing?"

"I would ask the men outside if I could be of any assistance."

"You would not simply lie around and eat as young men do."

"I did not come out here to do that, sir. I came to join an able caravan to the magical lands, not lay about. Sir, is there something I can be doing?"

The healer looked up from his table. "It is I who am waiting, lad, not you."

"What are you waiting for..."

The king knight entered with his several other knights. From their breathing and appearance of their attire, it was clear they had done battle.

"Your creature is dead, lad," the king said.

"Any of the men killed, sire?" the healer asked.

"No man will need your services, brother," the hooded wizard replied. Traveler now realized that the two men did resemble each other.

"Lad, your warning possibly saved many men in the days ahead," the king said to him.

"How did the creature get there, sire?"

"Who will ever know? It did find a very nice, tiny cave to hide in, resting between its man-eating feedings. But it will do so no more. We cut it to pieces and our wizard, here, engulfed each piece in fire. This very moment each piece still is in flight to the center of the world down Titan's Chasm."

The healer looked at the wizard. "My brother suspects a far more sinister explanation."

"The creature could have been a common snail and was transformed into the Lou Carcolh creature for sport."

"By whom, brother?"

"A wizard of course."

"We can speculate all day, but it is pointless. It is over. Healer, did you question the lad?" the king asked.

"He will do, sire. A healer's assistant is just that—an assistant. He looks able enough to do that. If he is frightened of blood and guts, we will soon find out."

"I am not frightened of blood and guts, sir. I have assisted in the sewing of bloody wounds of at least four men; one practically by myself, while the healer restrained the man."

"Good. It is settled then. Healer, you have a proper assistant after all, so you can stop complaining to me about not having one."

"Yes, sire." The healer sat up straight in his chair. "Boy, tell us the most impressive procedure you have done on your own to date."

"I restored a man's sight after he encountered a basilisk, sir."

The men looked at each other with smiles and sounds of astonishment.

"Well, brother," the wizard said. "I do not think you were expecting that answer."

"No, I wasn't."

"I do not think you can do that."

"Nor you, brother."

"Yes, sire. I have my assistant."

"Forward men! Across Titan's Bridge!" King Nathanial yelled as he gave the signal with his sword arm.

As the caravan descended down the path, each man noticed the large blackened spot on the barren rock to the edge of the cliff. It was where the caravan's knights and wizard did battle against the creature. Normally, the men marched silently but even such a disciplined party could not help but to gossip among the ones who were not present and brag by the ones who were.

"So, sir, are you a healer by magic?" Traveler asked.

"My brother is the wizard, lad. I am a man of science. My healing comes from knowledge and skill."

"I came across a duo of fairy elves—"

"Fairy elves? Where?"

"On the way to Last Keep."

The healer called one of the knights.

"Is something wrong, sir?"

"No, but I want the king to know what you saw."

The healer convened with the knight. After words were spoken, the knight ran forward to the front of the columns. The healer returned to his place in the caravan.

"What were you saying about these fairy elves?"

"They said that human healers can also use machines."

"Yes, that is true."

"There are healing machines, sir?"

"The Laurasian and Gonwandan empires have had such machines for ages. They are far ahead of all the other empires. Then there are machines from those in the magical lands. Then there is simple magic. The healing arts is wide and far in this world and all the realms beyond. You can spend a life of study and practice and master only a sliver of its totality."

"A healer I studied with in the countrysides outside one of the kingdoms, said that the best healers know a bit of everything but specialize in one of the arts so they can master it."

"That is a sound strategy, since you cannot master them all."

"Do you have a specialty, sir?"

"I do, but we can discuss that when we have a patient to attend to. Pay attention to your surroundings at all times, boy. You do not even realize your foot is about to touch the legendary Titan's Bridge for the first time."

Traveler jerked his head forward and his held his breath as his right foot fell onto it. Finally, he was on the true path to the magical lands.

A timeless bridge of such magnitude. Either side of the structure bordered by a dark chasm of such depth. The royal caravan of Anfalls Gate was an impressive sight to anyone who beheld them, but here, like all others, on Titan's Bridge they were no more than a speck.

None of the men spoke as they marched, Traveler followed the Healer Shane, surrounded by bearers. Knights before them and following had weapons in hand, though despite their weapons and armor, and their skill and courage, not one of them would welcome any sort of battle on the Bridge.

The healer glanced at Traveler. The boy looked at him and tried to maintain a brave face, though the healer well knew what the boy thinking. What if there were other evil creatures lurking over the edge ready to attack them? The healer showed the boy the dagger in his hand. Traveler smiled and reached for his own. He felt better with the weapon in hand.

Soon the next challenge for the caravan was the echo of thousands of men's feet and hundreds of horses' hooves on the stone. As the hours passed, the reverberating of the echo became so powerful and unnerving, men wanted to take off their boots and walk barefoot. The king and the senior leadership quickly dissuaded them. Men took to covering their ears.

"Men, on instruction of the king, we will not be stopping for the noon meal!" Melvin the steward announced walking through the columns.

However, as quickly as the announcement brought smiles to the men's faces, it was quickly replaced by apprehension and fear.

Men, on instruction of the king, we will not be stopping for the noon meal!

Men, on instruction of the king, we will not be stopping for the noon meal!

Melvin's words echoed and echoed all around them, seeming to shake the Bridge and the mountain ridges on either side. Men looked at each other with fear. It did not sound like an echo. It sounded as if the chasm was speaking—repeating his words—from its depths. Melvin, himself had to hide his fear, but he dared not speak another word. None of the men would say a single word as long as they were on the Bridge.

Traveler once caught himself looking behind again.

"What are you looking at, lad?" Shane asked in a whisper.

"Nothing, sir."

"Do you know, every time you do that you make every man behind us do the same, making them think something is stalking us on the bridge."

"Sorry, sir."

"Keep your eyes forward, your tongue still, and we will make it to the end of this Titan's Bridge soon. We are more than half way there. If you need something to look at, look at the sun in the sky. When it sets, we will be at the end."

Traveler looked up and overcast sky. The sun was not at its apex but slightly lower. That would be his focus.

Clang!

The boy was not the only one to jump in fear. Knights as large and as fearsome as he had ever seen were in near panic. Melvin raced through the columns.

"Everything is fine, men," he whispered. "One of the men merely dropped his sword."

At least the clumsy act lightened the mood of the men. Men grinned and whispered comments to each other in jest. The boy sighed and smiled himself. The caravan of Anfalls Gate was returning to normal.

Traveler kept his eye on the sun but it seemed that their march on the Bridge would never end. All his life he had heard the fabled stories of Titan's Bridge, however, there was nothing fabled about it to him. It was a scary place and he wanted to be done with it and never see it again.

Whether they had grown accustomed to it or acoustics of the rock had changed, the echoing of their march had subsided. The men felt free to talk amongst themselves to help pass the time. The sun was setting but still seemed to be no end in sight ahead.

The growing restlessness Traveler felt was also what he observed in the men around him. None were scared of the Bridge and its surroundings anymore. Boredom became annoyance.

"Look," a man said.

A smiling King Nathanial trotted in the opposite direction on his beautiful, grand, brown horse. He made eye contact with the men and nodded. Men returned the smiles and nodded back. They knew. The end of Titan's Bridge was in sight.

Not long after, there was another commotion ahead. Traveler got up on his tiptoes and jumped in place so he could see.

"Go on, lad," Shane the healer said to him.

"I am too old and dignified to engage in running anymore, but you certainly can."

Traveler smiled and dashed away. Men, at seeing the final edge of the Bridge, had taken to sprinting. Whether they ran or were content with walking or riding, every last man of Anfalls Gate made it to the end. They had traversed the first maker of the Titan's Trail to the legendary city of Atlantea, which sat at the end of the seventh marker of the Trail. The end of Titan's Bridge also marked the end of the Lands of Man—next would be the threshold Lands Between.

A euphoria took over the caravan's camp. Anfalls Gate's caravan celebrated more like Traveler's previous Good's Caravan with drink and music, but without the murderous brawls. Their king would allow the merriment to last for a full two days before they set out again.

The region that separated the Lands of Man and the magical lands of the fae was known by all humans as the Lands Between. The Mist Mires, aptly named, was the first of four regions that would have to be crossed before officially stepping in the magical lands.

The day of the march arrived and the caravan stood in its formation of three columns. King Nathaniel always led the column on horseback, with a vanguard of three dozen armed scouts on foot. However, this time they all waited. The thick mist ahead appeared as a gray, amorphous wall before them.

"I have never understood the science of mist," a nearby man said as he looked at Shane the healer. "If it is water, why does it hang in the air so, obstructing sight?"

"It is the science of nature, knight," Shane answered.

"What if there are creatures in the mist, healer?" another knight asked.

Traveler, standing beside the healer, swallowed. He kept his gaze downward.

"There are no creatures in the Mist Mires," Shane replied with annoyance.

"There were supposed to be no creatures at the starting point of Titan's Bridge but there was."

"Knights, my brother will use his magic to scout ahead for the caravan and search for any dangers ahead. I trust the only creatures he will find will be the ones in your own imaginations."

"If you say so, healer."

"There, my brother speaks." Shane pointed to the front of the columns.

"Men!" the cloaked wizard held up his arms, speaking in a booming voice. "We march forward through the Mist Mires. The realm is an enchantment spell, older than the Lands of Man itself. The spell makes human eyes see the darkest nightmares of their minds, causing terror and panic, causing those who wish to go forward to run back the way they came. I will cast my own spell. You are to walk forward when the king commands. You are not to stop. Do not concern yourself with the boggy ground beneath your feet, any puddles you almost lose your footing in, any sharp decline in the ground, move ever forward. You will also not need your eyes. My spell will cover and protect them from the spell of the Mist Mires."

Many voices were heard from men nearest the wizard but Traveler could not hear exactly what was said.

"Men have asked me: cover our eyes how? I will cover your eyes with magical blindfolds, men. It will appear around your eyes as soon as you cross the threshold of the Mires. Neither you nor the spell of the Mires will be able to remove it. Close your eyes and move ever forward." Blane the wizard moved to the side as the king, on horseback, moved to the same spot.

The king raised his sword arm. "Men, move forward!"

It was as the wizard said. As soon as one crossed into the mist, a blackness obliterated one's sight. Traveler touched his eyes and there was a cloth pressing against his head. He pulled his hands away from it and made sure to keep walking.

Either time passed by quickly or the distance to the other side was a short one. Traveler almost jumped when his eyesight returned. He looked around, then behind. He was on the other side of the gray mist wall of the Mist Mires.

"Men, the Mist Mires is behind us!" Blane the wizard's booming voice rang out.

The men cheered. Traveler smiled as he looked at Shane the healer, who managed a slight grin.

"Ahead men is the Howling Mountains!"

The men's cheering ceased.

The boy held his hood close around his head, his fist touching his throat. The valley of the Howling Mountains was colder than he had felt in many years. Not as cold as a winter in the Baltica Empire but here none of the men were properly dressed. The situation was made worse by biting cold winds that seemed to have minds of its own trying to blow the caravan off course and spook the horses. Then it began.

The howling sounds that echoed through the mountains on the either side of their trail were unnatural. Many of the caravan's men had traveled different lands, encountered similar lands with mountains and gusting winds. Winds were known to play tricks on human ears but this sounded different. The wind-swept sounds were eerie and unusually loud. Such sounds would better match the winds of a typhoon, not what blew through them at the moment.

The razor-sharp mountain range of either side also seemed like giant hands slowly closing around them.

"Do these Howling Mountains have ghosts?" a man asked.

"Absolutely not," Shane snapped. "Keep marching, man."

They all were thinking the same. The winds howled on and sometimes many of the men felt they were also...talking. A slow panic began to grow within the men.

Suddenly, their wizard bolted through the caravan on his own horse and a torch in his right hand.

"Move forward, men! We are moments from reaching the other side!"

It was as the wizard had said again. The caravan passed through and Mr. Melvin had the men set up camp. The patch of ground had its own eeriness—the Howling Mountains behind them and the Stone Forest ahead. Night fell, as if on cue, the moment the camp was began erecting its tents, building its campfires, and lighting torches.

Traveler sat at the campfire set for the healer by men of the caravan. The healer joined him, already eating something, though food was not served yet. Shane liked to carry pieces of bread in the pockets of his cloak.

"What do you think so far, lad?"

"We are making good progress, sir."

"We are."

"Though, sir, the Howling Mountains did not seem that formidable a barrier."

"Why do you say that, lad? Barrier?"

"The Lands Between are a magically created barrier to humans seeking to get to the Lands of Man."

"No, lad," another voice said.

Traveler turned and there was the caravan's wizard standing nearby.

"Brother, stop sneaking about the camp like a thief," Shane said.

"I am a wizard, brother. I have a wizard's reputation to maintain."

"Lad, ignore my brother's mysteriousness. It is all an act I can assure you."

"Traveler, the Lands Between were magically created to keep fae out of the Lands of Man, not the other way 'round."

"Really, sir?"

"Where do you think humankind would be if armies of fairies, elves, goblins, and creatures could freely move to and from our lands. There would be no Seven Empires and there would be no humans."

"I did not think of that, sir."

"I do not suppose you would."

"But the Howling Mountains seems less formidable than the others, sir."

"The more formidable barriers are ahead, but the key to both the Mist Mires and the Howling Mountains is who leads your party. I led the caravan. I knew the secrets of the Lands Between so the full magic of both regions could not affect the men. Had I not been with you all, and the one who led you through were unaware—lad, you all would not have passed beyond the Mist Mires. If you had, the region of the Howling Mountains would have magically been far vaster than you encountered—many times longer than the Titan's Bridge itself. Caravans have been lost in both and taken months to escape back to the Lands of Man. It is far worse for unaware fae or random evil creatures from the magical lands."

"Lad, my dear brother wants you to know we have his presence to thank for our fortunate progress through Titan's Trail so far."

"There is more to come, brother. A forest of stone then plains of illusion ahead. Then, lad, the caravan of Anfall Gates sets its feet upon the lands of the fairies and other fae."

Traveler smiled.

The caravan marched at dawn and once again men found themselves in a realm they had heard of in fables for years. However, the reality, even fore-known, did not prepare them. It was a forest of stone but much more—everything of the land was petrified. Men brushed past the petrified trees and brush; their feet crushed the petrified grass, turning it to gray dust.

Their wizard, Blaine, had spoken to the caravan the night before to prepare. "Do not think of gorgons or basilisks as you move through the Stone Forest. The realm was probably created long before the first gorgon ever crawled along this world."

Traveler was so thankful for the wizard's talk. If the men had not heard it, it would be all their minds would have fixated on as they marched. Here too there was an echoing effect from men's feet and horse's hooves on the petrified ground. The caravan marched but the stone trees went on beyond what their eyes could see. The atmosphere had reversed—shivering cold of the Howling Mountains to sweltering heat which made the march of those in armor dangerous. Traveler stayed close as Shane the healer walked through the columns visibly inspecting the knights who were breathing heavy, sweating more profusely, and were walking more slowly.

As the march continued, the entire caravan had slowed to a crawl. The sun above their heads was hotter than any of them had ever experienced. Even men not in armor felt they were about to pass out.

The first man stopped and fell to the ground with a cloud of dust.

"Follow me, lad," Blaine said as he rushed to the man.

More men stopped. Others sat on the ground or fell.

"No!" Blaine the wizard's voice boomed.

Everyone looked at him. The man was standing on top of his horse—almost floating.

"Men, it is another act of magic. Rise to your feet! The exhaustion you feel is an illusion. The growing heat of the sun above you is also an illusion. I am going to say something to you. You will not believe. You will think me mad, so I will lead the way. Line up behind me."

The wizard dropped down to the ground. He gestured for all the men on horses to dismount, even the king. The men who sat, dropped to their knees, or fell, rose to their feet. The men moved to line in in many rows behind the wizard and the caravan's leadership.

"Men! Run!"

Even the king was astonished. The wizard bolted ahead pulling the reins of his horse. He did not slow down but sped up and then he disappeared!

Everyone who could see, gasped.

"Where did he go?" a senior knight next to the king yelled. Other knights surrounded the king as if fearful of an attack.

"There is no need to ask that question." Shane the healer stood next to the king. "We simply do what he commanded." The healer looked at Traveler and said, "Shall we run into the next realm of this Lands Between together? It is probably the first and last time you will ever see me engage in this...running is it?"

Traveler laughed.

"Run!" The healer also bolted forward with the lad.

"Run, men!" King Nathanial commanded.

They all ran forward. They all disappeared from sight.

When Traveler passed through the magical barrier separating the Stone Forest, his ears were immediately overwhelmed by screaming. It was Shane's voice. The lad emerged into open plains of lush blues. The sky was quickly changing from day to night. But the shock before them was their healer Shane holding the corpse of his brother, Blaine. Traveler ran to the healer's side with a look of anguish. The wizard had been struck by multiple arrows. The lad looked up and in the distance, he saw several dark figures running away. He wanted to give chase, do something, but what?

The king and men came through the barrier. King Nathaniel knelt beside their healer.

"Who did this, Shane? Tell us who and we will avenge your brother."

Shane wept but forced the words from his mouth. "I think they were goblins. They are in black cloaks. I..."

The king touched his shoulder. "Say no more." The king stood and pointed to his knights. "Mount your horses. Mr. Melvin, I leave you in charge."

"Yes, sire."

The king mounted his own horse. "We will find these evil doers and avenge our fallen wizard. Ride!"

The king rode out with all the caravan's knight riders—four hundred strong. The sky had turned to night before their eyes.

"Men, set up war camp!" Melvin yelled.

Men quickly moved out as the steward patted their distraught healer on the shoulder.

Traveler's eyes were transfixed on the three arrows buried in their wizard's chest. The healer's eyes were closed in distress; the lad gripped one of the arrows but quickly pulled his hand back.

They left Shane alone to hold his dead brother. Within the hour, the sky turned back to day. Within an hour it was night again. Traveler watched them alone from his campfire within the war camp. All the men wielded their weapons, triple the men were on guard post encircling the camp.

As the sky of the magical realm continued changing between day and night every hour, a fear grew within the men. King Nathanial and the riders were not going to return.

"We must abandon the journey," Shane said to the gathered men.

A sullen Melvin stood across from him. The camp of thousands encircled both men—men closest sitting, behind them kneeling, the furthest on their feet. All eyes were focused on the steward.

"We can still make it, Mr. Shane."

"How? The two men who knew the way are gone—my brother and the king."

"But we can pass into the Mirage Plains ourselves."

Shane shook his head. "I heard my brother say many times that the barrier of the Mirage Plains is the most formidable of them all. If you do not know the way, you will cross over but where you will arrive...when you arrive is a far different matter. It will not be on the Trail. It may not even be in a part of the magical lands remotely near the Trail. It is a risk of madness. Neither one of us has ever been there. We know nothing of those. We know no one who could aid us. The two men who did are gone."

"I am willing to take that risk, Mr. Shane," one of the men defiantly yelled. Others cheered his words on.

"So am I, Mr. Shane," Mr. Melvin said.

"I am not," Shane said. "So, Mr. Melvin, you take the men who wish to go. I will take the rest back to the Lands of Man then home."

"Yes, Mr. Shane. I think it best this way. If we survive, we will do so for the honor of Anfall Gates."

"Yes, Mr. Melvin."

"Men!" Melvin yelled. "Those with me, prepare to march!"

"What about you, lad?" Shane asked Traveler.

"I return as well, sir. I am not so desperate to die. Your brother did say that to successfully journey through the Lands Between you must be led by one who knows the path. We do not have such a person anymore."

"No, we do not. And the king and his riders are among the best in the Seven Empires. Yet, they do not return."

"Sir, I am so sorry you lost your brother."

Shane's eyes stared downward. He was fighting the sadness again.

The caravan of Anfall Gates separated. Melvin led most of the men to a shimmering lightning-blue magic wall of the Mirage Plains. Shane and the remaining men, only a few hundred out of the thousands, including Traveler, waited and watched them depart.

Shane waved bye to them and in the distance could see Mr. Melvin, glancing back then return the gesture.

"We will wait until they cross into the magical barrier."

The sky had just turned to night again when the last of the men led by Melvin disappeared into the blue barrier. It was only for a moment, but the air was filled with the screams of many, many men.

PART THREE

FÄE-LAND MINOR

The Lands of Fairies, Sprites, and Giants

CHAPTER SIX

Caravan of Nymphs

Young Traveler was sixteen years old.

Shane and his men had remained in Hopeshire for about six months. It took that long for them to accept the fact that their king, their steward, and all the men with them were dead.

The boy was sad to travel all the way back to town but was glad to spend time with Shane and continue his training. Each day the healer would begin either with a new lesson or expand on the lesson before—diseases and symptoms; ointments, elixirs, pastes, and oral medicines; types of bandages, cutting techniques, building and maintaining a proper healing tent, proper way to dispose of corpses, graveyard creation. But the healer also taught Traveler about burial customs and rituals of not only men of the Seven Empires but what he knew of various fae races.

Sometimes at night, the lad could hear weeping. The men had been given use of the livery stable that the boy knew well. The healer and his few hundred men of Anfall Gates used it as their base doing odd jobs to earn money. Traveler knew that it would not last and it did not.

"I think I have taught you all that I know, lad," he said to Traveler one day.

"I doubt that, sir. You are an accomplished master of the healing arts."

"It is good of you to say, but my men and I long for home."

"I understand, sir. When will you leave?"

"At dawn tomorrow. It is a long journey back and we are eager to begin. We have remained as long as we could. Our king and his men are also lost. His wife, the queen, must be told."

"What will you do, sir? Will your kingdom try to reach the magical lands again?"

"I think not, lad. If the Trail has already taken from us all that we hold dear before we even reached the magical lands, then I fear what it will do to us once we arrive. No, lad. The journey of Titan's Trail will be left to others—like you."

"I am so grateful for your training, sir. I know I am a better healing assistant for it."

"I trust you are much more than an assistant by now, but yes, continue your training as an assistant. One day the healer you work under will simply say to you: you are the healer and I am the assistant."

"Yes, sir."

"It was good being your teacher, Traveler."

The men did leave at dawn. Traveler always got up before dawn so he was up and about to help. The men had given away most of their belongings already as they made their way from Last Keep to Goodmound's Castle. They would do the same from Ironwood to Hopeshire, each stop selling a bit more for money to live. They would march back to their kingdom and simply take on jobs to sustain themselves as they went. Traveler gave the healer a last handshake and he waved as the men of Anfall Gates marched on. The lad would never see them again.

Watchers saw their twelve-foot polearm weapons before the caravan marched into Hopeshire. Their scouts and vanguard included brutish knights were well over six feet tall clad in dark silver metal. Armored riders followed, one of them wore a crown on his head. The royal was surrounded by menacing men not in armor but in black attire with cloaks.

Traveler watched the caravan march in, at least one thousand men-strong and one woman. She was fat, ugly, with a perpetual frown on her face shuffling along pulling her own pull-cart. He had never seen a woman amongst a caravan. It was not the place for most men, let alone a woman. But there was something about her. He had no doubt that she could probably beat up most men to defend herself if she had to.

"What are you looking at?" He realized that she had yelled her question directly at him.

"I meant no offense, ma'am. I have never seen a woman on a caravan."

"I am not a woman, boy. I am the healer."

"Oh."

"Oh? What do you mean, 'oh'?"

"I am a healer's assistant looking to join a caravan, ma'am."

"Oh."

That was how Traveler met the woman, Burga.

She did not even wait for him to say more. Her hand pointed out the caravan's steward, a tall, thin man in black.

"Go see that man," she commanded. "When he accepts you, get your belongings."

She shuffled off, following the caravan down the Row. As he turned, he jumped. The steward stood next to him.

"Burga was sending you to me?"

"Yes, sir."

"Why?"

"I am a healer's assistant, sir."

"Good. We need one. Are you any good?"

"I have trained with several able healers."

"If one of them were killed or captured, could you stand in their place?"

"I...I could, sir, but I am—"

"That is all I need to know. Fetch your things. You are part of the caravan."

"What is the name of the caravan, sir?"

"Why?"

"It customary to know the name of one's caravan, sir."

"No, it's not."

The steward turned and walked away from him, moving alongside the caravan's moving column of men. He would later learn the steward's name—Deno.

The caravan with no name had not even made into Hopeshire proper to settle in, set up camp, and await men from the Seven Empires to queue up to be inspected by the steward and leadership. But already he was its newest member. He was cautiously optimistic but he had been so before. The furthest he had reached with any of them was the Mirage Plains within the Lands Between. Would this journey be different? He dashed to the stables to retrieve his hidden belongings.

Before dusk arrived, the caravan had doubled in size. Traveler sat amongst a few other lads near one end of the growing camp and took it upon himself to take charge and start a campfire. As he looked at the other boys, five in all, he could see himself in them when he was there age—uncertain and a bit scared.

"What tasks were you all hired for?" he asked them.

One was to be a bearer and the others were domestics to handle cooking and cleaning duties.

"I am a healer's assistant."

The boys smiled.

"Have you saved anyone yet?"

"Not on my own, but I have assisted in the saving of quite a few men. But I still have much to learn of the healing arts."

The oldest of the boys was twelve, the youngest was ten. Like most lads who joined these caravans, they were all orphans.

"Boy!" The woman Burga's voice was nothing short of unpleasant. Traveler grinned and grabbed his belongings and waved to the other boys. He had already decided to keep an eye on the boys as the caravan moved along the Trail.

"What did you say your name was?" Burga stood at the healing tent with her hands on her waist.

"Traveler."

"When you are old will you be Old Traveler?"

"Actually, yes, ma'am. And before that I will simply be Traveler."

"Traveler is a stupid name. Why could you not pick something better than that?"

"Journeyman. Trekker. They do not roll off the tongue so easily."

"How about the name your mother gave you?"

"What is the name of this caravan, ma'am?"

Burga pointed at him and gave a laugh. "Traveler it is."

"I wonder if I should want to be a member of a caravan that will not give its name."

"Says the boy who will not give his."

"I did, ma'am."

"Enough games. I need you to tidy up this tent. I want it all neat and orderly. Your job is to tend to the healing tent's supplies and the tent itself. Do your duties without fail, and I will be nice Burga. Fail in your duties, I will be evil Burga. You do not want to meet evil Burga."

"Yes, ma'am."

"Stop that! Do I look like a lady or princess? Burga is the name my mother gave me. Use it!"

"Yes, Burga."

"Better. Go do your duties."

"What will you do, Burga?"

"Eat and sleep."

She shuffled out of the tent.

Traveler stood at the entrance to the healing tent alone. He had completed his chores and watched new men as they settled into camp. The camp was outside of Ironwood and he imagined that they had doubled in size again.

"Are your duties done?" Burga returned from her rounds within the camp. Her face and demeanor was always unpleasant but he took no mind of it.

"Duties are done."

She brushed past him and looked at around in the tent. Baskets, pots, bags and supplied neatly lined the walls.

"You can almost eat off the ground."

"I keep a tidy tent."

"We shall see how tidy the first time we have to attend to a man who has had his arm severed and he is spraying blood everywhere or a man who sees fit to vomit all his meals from the prior three days straight."

"And I will make it tidy again."

"Why do you talk to children?" Burga asked as she sat on her favorite stool in the center of the tent.

"Children?"

"You know who I mean. I thought you were smart. You became a healer's assistant to befriend the warriors, so they would protect you on the caravan. But instead of talking to the warriors, you talk to children. Do you not wish to be a man?"

Traveler studied her. "Warriors accept idle talk from other warriors, not a boy. I will gain the respect of the warriors by deeds not idle talk. And I do not talk to children. I speak to those in the camp who are loners or have trouble fitting in such a large and chaotic camp."

"What job is that of yours? Let the steward do his job. Your job is healing assistant, not friend of all. I am surprised at you. One should not build friendships on such a journey. You may need to attend to one of those friends. You may need to bury one of your newfound friends."

"I know that, Burga."

"I hope that you do."

"And the young lads of this caravan are not children."

"Aren't they? They cannot defend themselves with a weapon."

"Why take them on, then?"

"Because the warriors are too lazy for the menial tasks. Let them do it."

"Why are you here, Burga? A woman on a caravan. I never heard of it."

"Haven't you? I was a great healing mistress of my lands. But scandal brought ruin to our royal house, so I had to seek refuge elsewhere. What better place than a caravan to the magical lands where I can find a new home."

"You plan to live in the magical lands?"

"Why not? Fae live in our lands. Some of us should do the same."

"There are fae in the Lands of Man? Where?"

"Wouldn't you like to know?"

"Maybe, Burga, you do not know as much as you pretend."

"Whatever I pretend to know, boy, is still far more than you actually know."

"Such as what?"

"No caravan of men can successfully cross the length of the magical lands. That is what legitimate caravans know."

"Know what?"

"Know what lurks in the magical lands."

A look of annoyance came over Traveler's face.

"Boy! You must learn to tell stories—great stories. Not for the sake of men but for the sake of fae-folk. In the magical lands a great storyteller can go far. Fae will do much for a great story. You better start practicing now."

Bruga stood from her chair and walked to him. She seems to be much taller now, though he was taller. She pointed right into his face. "In the Lands of Man, you must know good stories to take away the fear of a wounded or dying man. When they lie in your healing tent that good story could be the difference between them finding the will to live or not, or dying in agony or peace. Understand me, boy."

"Yes, Bruga. You have said something that finally makes good sense to me. I will learn."

"Good." She turned to return to her stool. "Go fetch me some food. I am hungry."

Traveler smirked. Bruga was like two people—one was a sage filled with gems of knowledge, the other was a rude, unkempt and uncouth layabout. However, Traveler was glad to have her as a teacher.

Peculiar to the caravan was that the leadership never mixed with the men. Their quarters were always separate from the general camp and well guarded. The caravan had many horses but they were all sold at Goodmound's Castle so that even their royal prince marched on foot. When he asked Bruga why they sold the horses, she grunted and ignored him.

When they reached the outskirts of Last Keep, they set up camp again. Night camp was often a nervous time for the men of the general camp. The royal camp kept the best warriors and the bulk of them. The general camp had men on sentry rotation duty which meant the quality of a given sentry was not guaranteed. Often sentries fell asleep and whole sections of the camp could be defenseless at night.

Burga and young Traveler sat at the campfire finishing their night meal.

"Tell me a story, Bruga."

"Why?"

"Tell me about the most amazing creature you ever saw, since you claim you have been in the magical lands before."

"Because I have."

"You also said you would live in the magical lands once you reached there."

"Boy, people need money to live in the magical lands too, especially if they are human and have no powers of magic. Telling stories only goes so far. Free food and drink for a night or two but not for a life."

Traveler focused on her as he ate his meal.

"Stop looking at me. A story? Most amazing creature? That would have to be the land kraken."

"Land kraken?"

"You do know what a kraken is, boy?"

"Yes, Burga, I know of the gigantic octopus creature that can destroy ships and whole seaside cities within reach from the ocean. How—why would such a creature be on land?"

"I said a land kraken, not a kraken on land. Krakens do not go on land. Land krakens live on land, burrow underneath, moving at great speed. They hate water. They live in the desert, in great sinkholes. They attack anything their tentacles can reach, on land or in the air."

"I have never heard of such a thing."

"Most of the races and beasts of the magical lands no human has heard or seen. You could live there a lifetime and see but a small fraction. There are parts of the magical lands unknown to other fae. So yes, there are land krakens. I will tell you where to find them though you will never get there unless you get an animal companion to fly you there."

"Yes, I would like an animal companion that can fly. Maybe a griffin or unicorn."

"Neither will allow any human like you to ride them."

"When we get there—the magical lands—what will we see first?"

"Once we cross into the magical lands from the Lands Between, we will be in Faë-Land Minor, the lands of fairies and sprites. The outskirts of those lands are also where the giants live."

"Giants."

"After that is Faë-Land Major, the lands of centaurs, fauns, satyrs, then elves, and also goblins."

"Have you seen all of these races, Bruga?"

"I have seen all of these races in the Lands of Man."

"Where?"

"I cannot tell you but I have. And do not ask me why I cannot tell you."

"What about dwarves?"

"They live in the Nether-Lands, far off Titan's Trail."

"Nether-Lands?"

"All fae that live underground are there. Underground realms as large and as vast as the lands above ground. But other things live there. Dark fae, what we call spider centaurs, undead creatures. Yes, boy, lycanthropes and ghouls and the like."

"You once told me Bruga that no caravan without a woman can get across the magical lands. What did you mean?"

"Do you know what sirens are, boy?"

"Singing mermaids that lure sailors to crash their ships onto the rocks of the coast."

"No, boy, they lure men in so they can devour them and they let their ships drift in to crash along the rocks. Well there are sirens that walk the earth. They are called nymphs and they can enchant a man to do anything. But human women are immune." She smiled.

"Then you should be the caravan master, Bruga."

"I am, boy. Once we reach the magical lands of the fairies and sprites, I will be the caravan's trailmaster and guide. I will be the caravan master and remain so until we reach the Giant Forest."

"You, Bruga?"

"Yes, I, boy. Without a good woman on this caravan, all you men would be lost."

"Bruga, you tell a good story. Believable? I think not."

The healer mistress cackled. "Not believable? Which part?"

"Which parts, you mean."

The unknown name caravan set up camp a mile ahead of the Titan's Bridge. It was all men could speak about as they waited. Those that had telescopes tried to get a look but they could not see because of the downward slope of the land ahead.

"You have crossed Titan's Bridge before?" one of the boys asked Traveler.

By now he was the official leader of the group of boys as he was the oldest. They all had their own separate duties but they ate their meals together and camped at night together.

"Hey!" one of the warriors stalked over to the second oldest boy who had some bread in his hand.

"Give me that bread! You are not a warrior, so why do you need so much food." The man was about to snatch the food from the frightened boy's hand.

"I would not do that if I were you," Traveler said standing to the side.

"Why is that, healing wench's assistant boy? Are you going to stop me?"

"No, I will simply poison your water."

The warrior stopped and stared at him.

"The poison will not kill you but it will reduce you to the state of a helpless pup. Imagine what will happen to you once we get to the magical lands. You may be snatched up a group of fairies and tossed off a cliff or thrown into a river to drown. Or I might just wait to get my revenge when you are wounded in battle. And yes, you will be wounded in battle. Maybe by elves or goblins, maybe a troll at night, or a man-eating ogre giant. I would be the one attending you then. Burga would not mind if I made sure you never woke up."

The warrior did not continue his advance on the other boy. He walked right up to a fearless Traveler and stared him in the eye.

"Maybe I will be punch you so hard right now that you will never get up off the ground ever again."

"Hey!" It was Burga. "Leave my assistant alone, you oaf. You do not want to make me into an enemy!" The healing mistress stood at the healing tent with her hands on her waist.

"Your healing wench saved your life, boy."

"No, she saved yours."

The warrior huffed and stormed off.

The boys were all smiles.

"Thank you."

"No need," Traveler said.

"Were you not scared?" the youngest boy asked.

"Actually, no. When I was a bit younger than you, it may have been the first time I came across a caravan, a man picked me up, and threw me against one wall after the next. My body was broken and bruised for almost a year. I do not think I was ever scared of anything after that. Though at the time, the shock and terror of the attack could have killed me alone. No, never afraid of another man after that. But...creatures."

"Creatures?" the boys asked.

"There are creatures on Titan's Bridge?" the youngest boy asked.

"Maybe I should not tell you the story I was about to. If I do, none of you will want to go. But I promise to tell you at night camp after we cross."

"It must be a scary story," another boy said. "I am not sure I do want to cross Titan's Bridge."

"It will be fine. This will be my fourth time."

The boys looked at each other in amazement.

"This is my fiftieth time!" Burga yelled, eavesdropping on the boys.

"No, Burga, it's your five hundredth time!" Traveler said back in jest. The boys laughed.

The royal scouts and the vanguard led by the prince left promptly at dawn. The rest of the caravan waited on the path down to the beginning of the massive. For everyone else except Burga and Traveler, the sight of the legendary structure supposedly carved into the world itself by an ancient Titan created a buzz of conversation among the men.

"You were telling the truth when you said you have been across the Bridge before," Burga said to him.

Traveler smiled. "And you have been across five hundred times."

She laughed.

"What is the difference between caravan master and trailmaster?" he asked her.

"A guide reads maps and leads. Nothing more. The trailmaster oversees the vanguard or front columns, also any advance scouts if there are any. As their name suggest, they make sure the trail is safe for the entire caravan. Then there is the caravan master. He, or me, does all that—guide, trailmaster, but also manages all the people and activities of the caravan whether on the move or encamped. In any real professional caravan across dangerous lands, it is the caravan master who commands, not even a king or queen is above them. The caravan master does whatever is required to keep the caravan safe and sees that every man, woman, and animal reaches the destination."

"Real caravans have caravan masters."

"Yes. If ever you hear them say they have a guide or trailmaster, run. That is fine for the Lands of Man, but not in the magical lands. You are asking to be taken to your death or worse."

"How would one know that a caravan master can do what he claims? Lead you to your destination."

"There are many ways. Boy, just watch what I do when we get there."

One of the scouts returned on horseback and gave the signal for the rest of the caravan to move forward. Traveler felt as if he was in a repeating dream. Every experience and feeling were the same as when he was with the Anfall Gates caravan. They too made it across as the sun was setting.

When released for the day by Burga, as the camp was set up, he joined his young camp mates. The boys were standing waiting for him. The campfire was already ablaze.

Traveler grinned. "Why do you want to hear my scary story?"

"You promised," the youngest boy said.

Traveler sighed and sat by the fire, then recounted the events of his last moments with the Good Caravan and meeting the Anfall Gates caravan for the first time.

When the story was done, the boys looked at each other in shock. The youngest stood to his feet and looked back at the Bridge.

"Hiding on the side of the Bridge. A snail creature with octopus hands."

"Tentacles," another boy corrected.

They looked at Traveler.

"I told you. I could not tell you until we crossed."

"Is it dead?"

"Yes."

"What is its name?"

"A Carcolh. Funny name but nothing funny about it."

"It killed your caravan?"

"It killed most of the men, yes."

"You are not sad?"

"No. I was with men who if a creature did not kill them, they would have likely killed each other for no reason at all."

"Maybe the Fates sent the creature as punishment."

"I do not believe that," Traveler said. "But if you want to say they deserved their fate, it would be hard for me voice any disagreement."

"What if there are more of them?" the youngest boy asked. He was on the verge of tears.

Traveler stood and put a reassuring hand on his shoulder. "There are no more here to harm any of us. Enough stories for tonight. We eat and then sleep. Caravans are always early to rise. Tomorrow, I will tell you new stories. About my travel through the Lands Between. I will tell you all the secrets so you will not be surprised by anything we encounter."

"Are there any creatures in the Lands Between?" the youngest boy nervously asked.

"None," Traveler answered.

As Traveler lay on the green grass looking up at the strange rainbow-tinted sky, most of their march through the Lands Between seemed like a distance memory. His hair was infested with mushrooms with weeds for stems. Grass enveloped his body and clothes. He could not move but not because he was restrained. He was simply too weak or...paralyzed by enchantment.

Burga's big head came into view with a crooked smile. "Are you dead yet?" She laughed. "You men are the weakest lot I have ever seen. We have been here weeks and you still have not grown accustomed to the magic of the realm."

"When...when will...we be normal?" he was barely able to utter his sentence.

"I believe the worst is over for you. I cannot say about the others." She tapped his body with her foot. "Get on with it. You have chores to do. With all you menfolk suffering from the enchantment, I have to do all the work. That will not do. You have to do all my work."

The healing mistress was queen of all now. Every man in the camp was in some state of incapacitation except her. Most of the men were in a deep state of sleep, unable to be awoken. Other were literally sleeping while standing up; others were sleep walking, wandering aimlessly from side to side or in circles. Most of the men were also covered with rainbow-colored flora—mushrooms, flowers, weeds, tiny trees—growing from their hair and clothes, between their feet and toes, on their noses, from their ears. Still others were covered with thick, dark cobwebs and others were encased in dirt that built up around their bodies.

A week more passed before the enchantment of the land was done with the human newcomers. But even still most of the men, and horses, were in state of lethargy.

"If I return to the Lands of Man and return again, would this happen to me?" Traveler asked sitting on the ground close to the campfire. His body seemed unable to keep in heat and he was always shivering.

Bruga had the unenviable task of preparing meals for the entire caravan, which she enjoyed for some reason. Boiling pots everywhere filled with broth and vegetables. "No, boy, once you go through it, you never have to again. The fate is for new arrivals."

"How long was I asleep?"

"I told you. Weeks. All of you."

"I do not believe that. Days maybe but not weeks."

She laughed. "Boy, in the magical lands you could sleep an entire year and it would seem like a day."

"That is a fairy tale."

"Yet we are in the land of fairies so I am not sure what point you are trying to make."

The healing mistress was gone on her new duties. Traveler felt drowsy and lay his head down on the ground.

"I hate this. I have no strength at all."

Normality would not return to the caravan for another few days. Slowly men found themselves with new vigor and daily activities of the camp returned to normal. All there was to do was sit around, gossip, smoke pipes, eat and sleep.

"These lands that we rest upon are called Beyond the Threshold," Bruga told Traveler as they sat at the night campfire for the last meal.

"Do we depart at dawn?"

"Unlikely. The prince is not sufficiently recovered and neither are the horses."

"I noticed that a lot of the men are overcome by a giddiness. Men who I have never seen so much as grin are given to laughing fits."

"We are in the magical lands. It arouses an intoxicating state of mind in humans. It will pass as you get accustomed to it."

"We are in Faë–Land? That is what the fae call it."

"No, that is what humans who have the good sense to respect the lands call it. Different fae races each have their own name for the lands in their own tongues. Only ignorant humans call these enchanted lands the 'magical lands.' But alas, that is what humans call it in the Seven Empires."

"I wonder when we will see our first griffin or unicorn. Or even flying horse."

Traveler grinned to himself. Bruga laughed. They looked around and most of the camp was fast asleep.

"Very good, boy, you must be of good stock. You are getting accustomed faster to this realm than most of the men."

When Bruga made her claim weeks ago, Traveler thought she was jesting. The healing mistress was fond of tall tales. But instead of marching to the healing tent, their new place was near the front of the columns right behind the royal vanguard.

"You stay back here," she told him. "I will accompany the prince."

"You really are the caravan master," the boy exclaimed.

She smiled as she left him standing where he was.

A caravan of nearly five thousand did not move quickly. The march was further slowed by men taking in the sights: a strange blue sky with long thin clouds appeared as inverted oceans, one man swore he saw a flying horse in the distance, and others said more than a few of the trees had eyes, which disappeared at second glance.

Traveler was no different; with a slight smile, he took note of anything and everything he saw. Then he heard gasps behind him from the men. They were marching along the bank of a large crystal blue river. When he turned, he too stopped.

"Look at those beauties," a man said. About a quarter mile away within the river itself, were several naked women wading through. Men were smiling; others laughing.

"I am looking for a new wife but if not one night will do!" one yelled.

Men laughed louder. The same man rushed forward and jumped into the shallow edge of the river and then waded forward, towards the women, as the river got deeper.

"Hello! Beautiful ladies!"

He was not alone long. Men dropped their weapons and followed after him.

"Stop!" Traveler knew it was Bruga's voice. "Stay on the land!"

Men ignored him. Traveler looked down the river again and was shocked to see that several women had increased to hundreds of naked women moving directly to the men—long, full blond, white, brown, silver, green, or reddish hair down to their ankles. The men could hear giggling and laughter from the approaching women.

"Get back on the land!" Bruga yelled.

"Shut up, hag!" one of the men said.

Traveler watched as the prince of the caravan rode forward to the river with a determined gaze fixed on the women. All the caravan's riders took their horses into the river.

Traveler looked as saw the camp boys looking at him, not knowing what to do. He gestured to them to walk to them. "Stay behind me," he told them.

"What is happening?" one of the boys asked.

"Nothing good," Traveler replied.

All the men, save the boys and Bruga, were in the river walking or running to the now-horde of unclothed women. Individual men embraced individual women with open arms. Traveler turned his attention to Bruga, who stood looking on, shaking. He had never seen their healing mistress afraid.

The youngest boy cried out. Traveler looked back to the river. All the men and women were gone! He stepped forward and could make out shaped under the water. In moments the women popped up laughing. None of the men reappeared.

Traveler turned to Bruga. "What are they?" he yelled.

"Nymphs."

Traveler looked back at the river with a stern look. "Get behind me!" The other boys were trembling in fear.

"Are we going to die?" the youngest buy asked.

"No," Traveler answered emphatically.

"My, how confident is the boy."

It was a strange sensation. One moment the women were in the middle of the river; the next they were all around the boys. Dozens danced in circles around the Traveler and the group of boys, singing in a melodic tone impossible to be created by human voices.

"What do you want?" Traveler asked with menace.

The nymphs stopped their playful dancing. One of the nymphs with fiery red hair, walked to Traveler and moved her face close to him. "Why are you in our lands?"

"Why did you kill all those men?" he asked.

"Because we can," she answered coldly.

"You would be with them, if you boys were actually real men," another nymph said.

"Leave them alone," Bruga said but not with her normal confidence.

"Do not interfere, human woman, or we will change you into a chicken and break your neck and toss you in the river," a nymph said.

"Maybe we can just eat you raw," another said and they all started laughing. Thousands of the nymphs encircled them.

"I do not know what you are but you are no nymphs," Traveler said.

The caravan of nymphs was silenced.

"Why do you say that?" their red-headed leader asked.

"Nymphs enchant. They do not drown and then giggle about the murder of men like children would giggle about pulling off the wings of a fly. No. I do not believe you are nymphs. Nymphs are noble fae. You are so far from noble with your fair skin and sparkling beauty; you are ugly and vile. When I see real nymphs, I am going to tell them what you did. I am going to tell them that there those impersonating nymphs, using their powers, to do vile things."

The nymphs looked at each other. There was a panic to their expressions. As quickly as they appeared on land, they were all back in the water. Their caravan moved away, sloshing through the middle of the river, then submerging, then gone. The bodies of the men began to surface but they were all pale from death. Soon the river was filled with drowned bodies, including the prince. They all felt sick as the beautiful clear river became littered with thousands of corpses floating away to oblivion.

Their journey was over. Their caravan was dead.

The shock of seeing so many deaths was too much for the other boys. Bruga was also not herself. She led them back through the magical barrier into the Lands Between. When they reached Titan's Bridge, she stopped.

"What's wrong?" Traveler asked.

"I cannot go back," Bruga answered back. "You know the way. Take the boys back so they can return to their homes and families."

"What about you, Bruga? You cannot go back there alone."

"I must. I have done so before. I cannot go back."

"Why?"

"I was the caravan mistress. I was responsible. The caravan master is always responsible if it is lost. They put their lives in my hands and I failed them."

"I was not your fault, Bruga," Traveler said.

She smiled with tears in her eyes. "Nice of you to say, boy, but it was. Take the boys home. You must leave now to reach the other side before nightfall. You do not want to be on the Bridge at night. Go on."

Traveler began to lead the boys across.

"Boys, you are in able hands with Traveler. Good luck with your lives."

"I am not going to see you again, am I?"

Bruga shook her head. "No. But do not fret. You will find far better and much better-looking healers than I to continue your training with. Good luck with your life, too."

She turned to walk back in the grayness of the Mist Mires. Traveler led the young survivors of the unknown caravan back across Titan's Bridge.

CHAPTER SEVEN

Caravan of Fairies

Young Traveler was still only sixteen years old.

He had seen many caravans at this time but never had he seen an army marching to the magical lands. Traveler was uncomfortable with the prospect where the fighting men outnumbered the domestics of the party by six-to-one. For the first time warriors who offered their services in exchange for a place on the caravan were turned away, bearers and cooks were turned away. He was the only person in Goodmound's Castle who was accepted, joining a staff of two lads and two assistant healers under the caravan's chief healer. He was a man with flowing silvery hair, beard and mustache and Traveler was eager to train under him.

The sheer mass of the army-caravan weighed on the boy's mind. They marched with a troop of flag bearers larger than most caravans he had seen—almost one hundred men. Hundreds of war horses, war wagons, catapults, giant crossbows, giant shields, wagons filled to the brim with arrows, endless thousands of men. He thought to himself if he were a fae in the magical lands and saw this army, the fae would undoubtedly believe humans were invading their realm. However, after the previous encounters, he wanted to get past the land of fairies and sprites and reach the lands of elves. The army-caravan of Spell Blade would get him there.

They marched like an unstoppable force across the Bridge, through the Lands Between. Beyond the Threshold, the men were incapacitated by the magic of lands. As Bruga had said, he was immune. But so were their full vanguard and royal leadership, led by King Owain.

At seeing he was the only person not in a state of sleep or madness, the king rode up to Traveler on his white warhorse.

"When were you last in the magical lands, lad?"

"Only a few months ago, sire," he answered.

"What happened?"

"All men were lost, sire."

"What manner of beasts or fae race?"

"Nymphs, sire. But they were evil to the core."

"Then they were nixes. Evil fae women of the water. They are also shape-shifters able to take the form of other living things, people or animals. It would cross their minds to appear as benevolent nymphs too. You were lucky. But you are of the age of maturity so why you were not affected?"

Traveler pulled a necklace of herbs from under his tunic, around his neck. "My healing mistress forced me to wear this, sire. I thought it was merely a superstitious charm but I now know that it has power."

"Yes, it does, lad. Your healing mistress undoubtedly saved your life. Good. Glad to have you among us. You will see those lands and much more. I made the mistake of venturing into the magical lands with mere caravans before. I have learned my lesson well. We are an army not to be trifled by fae or beast alike."

"Yes, sire."

The king rode back to his campsite as the boy looked on. Strangely, he felt more protected by his herb necklace than all the many thousands of men in the army-caravan. The words of the wizard Blaine echoed in his mind: "The Lands Between were created to keep fae out of the Lands of Man, not the reverse."

Even for the non-warriors, every man or boy was required to carry a bladed weapon and carry themselves as soldiers. Their healer marched in his column leading Traveler and the other healing assistant lads. They had set out at dawn and Traveler glanced back a few times. Every other caravan he had joined marched in three columns at the most; the Spell Caravan was ten across. The philosophy was the opposite of every caravan he had ever been a member which did everything to minimize the impact on the land. His new caravan-army seemed to want all to know they marched, blackening the path they cut through the flora with their thousands of footsteps, hooves, and wheels of their war wagons.

A few hours later the caravan began to slow and then stop altogether. Marching within a caravan of fifty-thousand men, where Traveler stood, the front of the caravan was at least five miles ahead. The vanguard was probably another mile or more further.

"Lads, draw weapons," their healer said to the lads.

Only Traveler could hold his small sword ably. The other lads looked awkward and unsure. But Traveler noticed that their learned healer did not inspire confidence with his own holding of his sword. Their healer was a gentle, bookish man.

"Lads, look at Mr. Traveler there. If we find ourselves in battle, we will all take refuge behind him," their healer said and Traveler grinned, as did the other lads.

"I am only a healer's assistant, sir."

"Of course, you are, lad."

A soldier quickly rode down the flank of the caravan. "We have encountered another caravan. A group of sprites." The soldier repeated the same two sentences as moved away to the very end of the caravan—a long ways away.

"Lads, let us move forward." The healer returned his sword to its scabbard. Traveler and the lads did the same.

Just beyond the front columns, was a caravan of several dozen halflings. Each of the sprites wore grayish robes but underneath were tunics and socks of outrageous colors. They looked human, but their eyes had a strangely glassy appearance. While speaking with the king and his royal staff, the sprite spoke in an overly animated fashion, loud, frequent laughter. Everyone in caravan was amused by them.

"You can accompany us, king," one of the sprites said. The healing crew now stood close to the king and the caravan's leadership.

"Very good, sir. We accept your kind offer."

"Never have we seen such an army of humans."

"We are of the kingdom of Spell Blade."

"Where do you travel to, king?"

"We travel to the fabled city of Atlantea."

The sprites gasped as they looked at each other.

"Never have we heard of human traveling so far into the magical lands," a sprite said holding his neck as if overcome with emotion.

"Yes, we do travel far," the king said. "But it is a journey worth the distance."

"How will you get across the Great Forest?"

"With my army, nothing will deter us."

The group of sprites burst out laughing.

One of the whispered as he stepped forward and said, "You have never been to the Great Forest."

"What should we know, sir?"

"It is also known as the Giant Forest."

"Giants live within it?" one of the king's men asked.

"Giant everything, but no matter. King, have you and your men had the pleasure of the food of fae?"

"No, sir, we have not."

The sprite wrung his hands. "King, you and your men are in for such a treat then. We have the most delightful spices, grains, cakes, and ambrosias in these lands. It will be our great pleasure to serve our new human compatriots a spritely feast."

"Thank you, sir," the king said.

As Traveler watched he felt a tickle in his right ear and brushed it.

Do not eat their food. We tell only you.

Traveler almost jumped and looked behind him. No one was directly behind. As he looked around, he saw nothing, but he felt a presence. It was not the first time he felt the presence of something—someone—nearby as he traveled in the magical lands. He felt so again; he would swear one or more persons stood near to him, but he saw nothing. His attention was returned to conversation between the sprites and the caravan's king.

News spread of the new sprites among the men. When dusk arrived, the entire caravan stood in line at the camp of the sprites. Dozens of sprites would enter a single tent of the serving line and come out with plates overflowing with food to serve—berries and grapes, other fruits, edible roots and stems. But above all were the sweet cakes.

The entire camp of men gouged themselves on the food as if it were the most succulent stag meat or plumpest fowl.

"Should we be eating this food, sir?" Traveler asked.

"Why would you ask that, lad? These are our guests. Eat up and do not be rude."

Traveler took not just one plate of food from the giggling sprites, but two.

"I am a growing boy," Traveler said to the sprite handing him the food.

Traveler walked back to the healing tent with his meal and set himself at the front of the tent. He noticed that the healer and the other healing lads took their time returning to the tent too.

"Where are your sweet cakes?" one of the boys asked him.

"That was the first thing I ate," Traveler answered.

The eating frenzy continued all night until men fell asleep where they stood. In the wee hours of the night every man in Spell Blade caravan lay in a deep sleep. Traveler, however, sat wide awake.

The camp of the sprites was silent. They had several tents but only one seemed to have any activity with light from a single torch inside. He noticed one of them peeking out from their tent and then tip-toeing out, followed by a second, then dozens.

Traveler stood from his post and walked to them. They didn't notice him until they were about to run into him, as if they could not see in the nighttime.

"What are you doing?" Traveler asked.

"Young boy, you should be asleep counting sheep. You did not eat your spritely food."

"What did you do to the men, thieves?"

"Thieves?" the sprites laughed in unison.

"We are not thieves, young boy. We are sprites."

"Why do you say that? 'We are sprites.' That means you are not sprites. What are you then?"

The sprites laughed. "We are sprites!"

"Guess what is in my hand?" Traveler asked them.

"What is in your hand, young boy?" they asked in unison.

Traveler threw a handful of sand at them—magic sand. But even he wasn't prepared for what happened next. The sprites screamed as they moved from him. Their faces violently shook and he saw their eyes—glass eyes—pop off their eye sockets. Smoke exploded from their bodies. Before him were several grayish humanoid creatures with bat-like wings, large pointy ears, and tiny horns poking through his skin above his eyebrows.

"Curse you, young boy!" they yelled.

With that, the creatures flew into the air and disappeared. Traveler looked and their sprite camp vanished.

Traveler was still awake when dawn arrived. He was in near-panic. Every last man was still fast asleep and there seemed to be nothing he could do to awake them; he had tried to awaken his healer master all throughout the night. He paced back and forth, tried to hold his fear in check but he was losing the battle as time went on.

His eyes widened as he looked out over the caravan. The men seemed to be sinking into the grass. He grabbed his head with his hands and closed his eyes. The situation overwhelmed him.

"What to do?" he asked himself.

He heard a scream and his eyes shot up to the sky. High up he saw a giant green bird wildly fighting something unseen, but the scream came from a man falling to the ground. Traveler ran to him. For a second, he stopped, when the man's body hit the ground, but then he continued to run to him.

When Traveler reached the unconscious man, his appearance was like he had never seen: white skin, green hair and a full beard of living grass and vines. The man also had horns and his feet were hoofed!

"Sir." Traveler reached down to touch the man.

"Do not touch him!" A high-pitched voice startled him. He jumped and looked behind. There was a tiny fairy no larger than a foot fluttering in the air with translucent wings. She had short dark hair, large bright eyes, and two antennae sprouting from the top of her head. The thigh-high casual dress looked to be made of leaves. "Move away from him!"

"Why? He is hurt."

"I warned you."

Traveler felt a presence and turned back to look at the green-haired man. The boy yelled out. The man was wide-awake and standing inches from his face with glowing green eyes and grinning with sickly green teeth. Traveler threw himself back.

"I warned you," the fairy repeated.

The green-haired male fae stared at the fairy. He lifted his hands and they grew in size and contorted. The fairy giggled and the male fae looked in the sky and saw an approaching swarm cloud. He growled like a bear then transformed into a green cougar and darted away, faster than seemed possible.

Traveler slowly stood to his feet. "What manner of creature was he?"

"Not a creature. An evil leshy," the fairy answered.

Traveler turned in panic to look at the men of the caravan. Only their faces very visible. The ground was indeed swallowing them up. He turned to the fairy.

"Please, help the men."

"Why?"

"Please. Can you not help them?"

"No!" The word came from not one voice but many.

Traveler turned and the swarm cloud encircled him—thousands and thousands of identical fairies fluttering in the air.

"Why won't you help the men? They were poisoned by fae."

"Humans. If you are so foolish to eat food from imps, you deserve your fate."

"Is that what the creatures were? We did not know this."

"Why do you come into our lands knowing so little?" asked several of the fairies at the same time. "You do not know of imps' evil ways. You do not know good leshies from evil ones. Go home, human."

"No," said a smaller fairy with a wide smile. "I have never seen a human before. I can keep him as my play animal."

Days passed as Traveler sat in a bird cage, his legs dangling over the side. The cage suspended from a lone tree branch by cobwebs. The fairy who wanted a "play human" tired of him after a day of shrinking to the size of a bee to buzz around and even sting him, then change her size to that of a giant to swat the cage around, knocking him across the woodlands. She showed him off to other fairies; he imagined he was looked over by hundreds of fellow child-like fairies.

As he sat alone in the cage on the tree, he reflected on another lost caravan. So many dead. Not even bodies to bury. His eyes only happened to look to the side and he saw them.

The male fae approaching him was another leshy with white skin but his hair was white too. He had the same full beard of vines and grass and vines. He wore a cloak that looked like it was made of brown tree bark but it moved like sheer fabric that reached the ground so he could not determine if the leshy had hoofed feet too. He approached with a tall brown walking stick and one other.

The leshy had an animal companion—a very large green dog but it did not appear vicious. Its long tail trailed on the ground behind it.

"You are the human boy," the leshy said. He stared at him with piercing green eyes. Traveler said nothing. He was hungry, dehydrated, and in no mood to talk. "Let us release you from your sanctuary."

"Sanctuary?" Traveler asked in a hoarse voice, though the derision was clear.

"Yes. The fairies had compassion on you."

"Compassion! They put me in a cage!"

"You must understand the nature of living things, human. Fairies are a long-lived race with tremendous energy for most of their days."

"Then they are like imps."

"Imps they are not."

"So I should excuse what the fairies did to me?"

"I did not say that. If you understand their nature then you will know how to interact with them, how to navigate around their behaviors. Their mischief is out of boredom and a genuine desire to play not for evil intent like imps or hobgoblins."

"They let all my men die!"

"Your men?"

The leshy had reached out his hand to touch the bars of the cage, which had no visible doors. The male fae pulled his arm back and watched the boy.

"It was the caravan I was a part of. I was a healer's assistant," Traveler said.

"Caravan? You mean the army."

"They were an army but they were a caravan."

"No, they were not a caravan. They were an army. They killed many sacred trees and animals. Their human king had been run off from these lands by fae before. He was told not to ever return. The fairies did him a kindness. Ironically, the imps they encountered did them a kindness, though that was not their intention. If your army had continued forward and came across other fairy clans, sprites, centaurs, or elves, you human boy, would have been cut to pieces and it would not have been a quick death. The death would have taken days."

The leshy tapped the cage and it disappeared. Traveler fell to ground. He just sat there, weak and exhausted.

"Do you wish to sit there or have some food and water?"

"What were the intentions of those imps?"

"Mischief. Steal all your belongings. Take your horses away. Maybe, even take all your clothes and leave you naked. It is always about mischief with imp-kind."

"I was told that fae food can be dangerous to humans."

"The wrong food can kill humans. But my kind knows the food your humankind can eat. It can have little or no magic in it. Come. We will get you food."

Traveler followed the leshy and his green dog on a path he hadn't noticed before in the grass. There was a clearing in the forest and the leshy grew in height and his arms elongated to pick fruits from its branches. He then reached down into the dirt itself at the trees bases and pulled up large vegetables. Both fruits and vegetables looked like those of the Lands of Man but they were twice the size and their outer skin was camouflaged to match the trees and their surroundings.

The boy looked at the food that the leshy handed him.

"Do I need to wash them? Or..."

"Wash them? Why? The dirt is good for you. If you plan to remain or return to our lands you better become accustomed to them. Eat."

Traveler sat down on the grassy field. "How can I tell a good leshy from an evil one?"

"Benevolent ones have white hair and evil ones have green hair."

The boy was about to take a bite of the pear-like fruit.

"But all leshy are shape-shifters so they can make their hair appear any color they wish," the leshy continued. "You can tell from their eyes."

Traveler bit into the fruit. He was so hungry that he devoured the sweet fruits and vegetables that had a meaty texture. The green dog moved to him and the boy let him sniff his hair.

"My companion has never met a human before."

"I have never met a green dog before."

"He is not a dog. He is a cù-sìth. Humans have called them 'fairy dogs.' I would suggest that you find yourself an animal companion too if you plan to remain or return to our lands."

"Yes, a good dog would suit me. I have always been partial to wolf-dogs."

"I do not mean an animal companion from your lands. I mean from ours. One from yours would hardly be of any benefit to you here."

Traveler looked up at the leshy. "I want to go home."

The leshy stared at him then nodded. "Then you shall."

The male fae chirped like a bird and soon more than a few birds appeared and landed on his outstretched arm. Humanoid and bird conversed in birdsong, his green dog watching. The bird flew off into the sky.

"She will find one of his animal friends to return you to your homeland. As any fae of light, I would wish your memories not to be of death and distress in our realm. I told her to find a specific friend. Have you ever ridden a flying unicorn?"

CHAPTER EIGHT

Caravan of Night Horrors

Young Traveler was still only sixteen years old.

He had spent so many years on the Row from Hopeshire to Goodmound's Castle that he recognized people—residents of the various towns and cities, thieves and scouts for the marauders. The realization depressed him. He also saw other men waiting on the Row for the next "best" caravan. Upon eye contact, they would nod to him or mumble a "hello." Other smiled to themselves.

"Yes, I still live," Traveler said under his breath as he quickly walked to his job working at one of the taverns in Ironwood.

The Windsong Caravan was another not seen before. They were of a nomadic kingdom that roamed a territory in the Baltic Empire. Though it was not winter, they arrived wearing their animal pelts over their armor. They were a horse people and Traveler had never seen so many horses—exquisite and powerful animals everyone. Every man rode a horse; there were no wagons among their three-thousand-strong caravan.

There was no respite for workers at his tavern.

"You go out there. You don't come back," the owner said when Traveler said he wanted to speak to the caravan for only a few moments.

Traveler walked up to the man and shook his hand. "Thank you for taking me on, sir. I hope my work was satisfactory."

"It was, but I knew I wouldn't keep you here."

Traveler left the tavern, slowly closing the door behind him. The streets buzzed with the news of the new caravan seeking men. When the boy reached the inspecting lines, he accepted the fact that it was going to be a long day and possibly night. Thousands of men and boys were already ahead of him.

"You there, boy!" a horseman called out to him directly.

Traveler, surprised, looked at the men standing in line with him.

"Yes, you! Yes, I know what you look like!"

"Yes, sir," Traveler said as he stepped out of the line and approached him. The horse was larger than he had ever seen in the Lands of Man.

"What services do you offer?" the man asked.

"I am a healing assistant, sir."

"Good. Follow me."

That was it. He was accepted into the caravan and assigned to one of the camp stewards and also got his own horse. Later, he learned that the caravan's leadership had run into a group of men in Baltica who spoke very highly of him—Shane from the old Anfall Gates lost caravan.

The Windsong Caravan departed in two days for Titan's Bridge.

It was the third caravan he had joined to traveled across the Bridge and through the Lands Between without incident. What he prayed for was to be able to march from the lands of fairies and sprites to the lands of elves. However, the fortune that the caravan possessed was replaced by disaster the second they moved from the lands Beyond the Threshold.

Only Traveler was unaffected and he alone had the task of watching over three thousand men and horses. As men regained their normal senses after a few days, they joined in the patrol and sentry duties. But Traveler was still in reality the man-in-charge. They were all so groggy and slow-witted. Most of the horses that awoke were in a constant state of unease.

A roar pierced the air! Traveler yelled out and grabbed his ears as did the men who were on patrol with him. When they looked towards it, their mouths hung open in shock. A giant golden griffin flew away into the clear sky with two of the horses in its claws. Never had they seen the fantastic beast before—the body, tail, and hind legs of a lion and the head and foreleg talons of a giant eagle. In the Lands of Man, griffins had always been a symbol of good fortune but they all recognized that it possibly foretold the opposite for them in the magical lands.

In horse cultures, horses were more valued that the men. Traveler watched as a near mutiny erupted between clans within the caravan at the loss of two of the horses. Without their horses, the men would be reduced in rank and not much better than a domestic.

"We have no choice!" the bear of a man, the king yelled. He was the largest and fiercest warrior of all the men in the caravan. "We move on."

The two men without horses stormed off to their new position in the formation—at the rear.

"Sirs," Traveler said to the men as they neared. "I can give up my horse."

"No, you cannot," the healer scolded, riding beside him.

"But they are warriors."

"A noble offer, young one, but our fate is sealed and we accept it," said one of them before both men continued to the rear of the caravan.

"In these lands, kindness may get you killed, boy," the healer scolded.

Traveler said nothing.

The Windsong Caravan moved faster than any other he had been a part of. Galloping fast for a few miles and then casually strolling, then walking the horses. They moved through the magical lands with a steady determination. No idle gossip among the men. Conversation was always only about protecting the horses, rather than the men.

"Hold him!" the healer yelled.

Traveler struggled to hold the man down on the now blood-soaked ground of the healing tent. Mr. Caladrian had his own battle—fighting to close a deep gash down the man's side. The man was flailing and screaming.

"Leave him!" the healer yelled to Traveler as he stood to his feet. "If he will not remain still, there is nothing we can do."

"No!" one of the healing lads yelled standing in the corner of tent. Both boys had thrown up from the sight of spraying blood.

Traveler smashed the man's face with one of the test's storage chests knocking him unconscious.

"Sir, you can sew the man's wound shut now."

The healer smiled. "Lad, I now know the difference between a noble healer who practices under the auspices of a king and a countryside one who must make do with what's at hand. Yes, let's save this man." Caladrian looked at the other two boys. "Get my needle and sewing twine from the chest. You have already vomited out all your guts so there can't be anything left in your feeble bellies."

Another deafening eagle shriek rang through the air.

"Forget the creatures! Move!" the healer yelled.

The lads quickly found the items and put them in the healer's hand. Traveler assisted by holding firm the flaps of skin for the healer. The horrible wound was made within the blink of eye by one of dozens of the fantastic beasts. Outside the tent, they heard the fierce battle continue, eagle shrieks, men's scream, flapping of wings.

"Mr. Traveler, survey outside. I can manage now. Don't get yourself killed!"

Traveler got up and slowly stood to one side of the tent's entrance. Then he stepped outside to fully view the carnage the camp's battlefield. Many men lay dead, but not all the horses were lost. In the distance, he could see the hippogriffs flying away—magical animals with the hind half of a horse and the front half, including head and forelegs, of a giant eagle. The beasts came for the horses. They succeeded in killing three but they were not allowed to take their kill away for a meal. The king formed most of the men in tight circles around the horses to fend off the hippogriff attack.

"Attend to the wounded, boy!" the king yelled.

"Yes, sire!" Traveler yelled back and ran back into the healing tent.

It would be a long day and long night for the healing crew. They saved fifteen, but the caravan lost fifty-four men.

Traveler had offered his horse to a warrior before. The next day warriors took his, the healers and the other healing lads away. The wounded men could not be left to rest. Instead riders rode double; Caladrian the healer did all he could to bind wounds as securely as possible. At least the land was flat and level he said to reassure them.

There was a feeling of doom among the men as they marched. The boy could see it in their faces—a growing number wanted to turn back, though they would never say so aloud.

The sky above darkened as dusk approached and that was when they felt a faint rumble beneath their feet. Men on foot looked at each other.

The healer got down on all fours and pressed an ear to the ground. Traveler and the other healer lads waited with him. The man got back to his feet.

"Many riders. I count at least a few hundred," the healer said.

"Over five hundred," one of the warriors on foot corrected.

"Men!" It was the cry of the king. None of the men waited to react. They drew their weapons.

"Look!" a man yelled.

In the darkening sky was a swarm. Traveler stared at it. Not a fairy swarm but whatever the insects were, their size was equal to that of normal birds. The figures of the approaching riders could be seen on the horizon riding fast, along with sounds of cackling.

The healer grabbed Traveler. "If I do not survive, you are to take charge of the boys."

"But, sir—"

"No 'but,' do. That is my standing command should it be my last."

"Yes, sir."

"Boys, stay with Mr. Traveler. He is the oldest and he knows the way back to the Lands of Man should it come to that. Do you understand?"

The boys nodded, tears in their eyes.

"We are forming up," the healer said.

The men formed up into three circle formation around the horses. As the cackling riders drew closer and the insect swarm gathered above their heads, Traveler was overcome by a sickening feeling.

"Sir," he looked at the healer with a pained face. "It is not us. It is the horses. They are after the horses."

"We are a horse people, Mr. Traveler. We will defend them to the death even if it costs our own lives."

"Men! Brace for battle!" the king yelled. He raised his sword in the air.

No one could see what one of the dark riders threw, but the black shape ripped through the king's chest and he collapsed to the ground dead.

The riders were witches and their steeds were not horses, but animated bones of a myriad different animals draped with cloth. They plowed through the formation; men impaled on the bones of their dark magic steeds.

The hags had pure white wrinkled skin, with high foreheads and flowing white hair. Their eyes were black and their teeth were more like that of a shark.

Their swarm descended on the men in a thick cloud. Dragonflies larger than a foot covered the bodies of the horses. The poor horses cried out and bolted from the circle column created to protect them as the dragonflies burrowed into their skin.

The hag riders cackled as they trampled, impaled and threw black balls of magic—each attack killing more men.

Traveler looked to either side and Mr. Caladrian the healer and all three of the healing lads were dead. He turned from caravan and ran. All the horses, not too far away, had collapsed to the ground, writhing in horrific pain as the demonic dragonflies feasted on them. The hag riders reveled in killing Windsong's men.

Traveler never looked back. No doubt, both witch and insect beasts, saw him but a single human boy was inconsequential to them when thousands of men and horses were trapped in their grasps.

PART FOUR

FÄE-LAND MAJOR

The Lands of Elves, Hoofed Fae, and Goblins

CHAPTER NINE

Caravan Academy, or the Secret
City of Last Keep

Young Traveler was nearly seventeen years old.

He hated Last Keep. There was nothing there for him—neither work nor prospects—but when he emerged again from the Lands Between and took the day to cross Titan's Bridge alone—again—he literally had no more energy other than to collapse. When he finally made it to the city, after not eating for days, he simply sat on the side of the road, mentally and emotionally crushed, his eyes red with tears. He had always found the people a strange lot, none paid any attention to him and moved about on their way. At one point he closed his eyes and simply wished he could be carried off into a distant land or...die.

"You there, human. Why are you sitting on the ground, crying?" a man in very loose-fitted clothes said. He had a flowing dark cloak, wore a pointed cap, and held a tall walking staff.

"I am not crying," Traveler snapped

"Little human boys often cry, so you would not be the first."

"I am not a little boy. Let me alone. I do not want to speak to you nor anyone else. Let me alone!"

"You cry because you cannot join a human caravan. Though on such a journey you would surely be killed at some point. You humans are a curious race—so illogical and simple-minded. Well, I will do as you ask and let you alone."

The man continued on, tapping the ground with his walking staff as he strode forth. He noticed the boy following him.

"You are not human?" Traveler asked.

"Why do you ask that? Do I not look human?"

"What kind of fae are you?"

"Who says I am fae?"

Traveler studied him. "You said."

"Certainly not."

Traveler noticed the man's over-sized feet.

"You are a fae with big feet. What kind of silly fae is that?"

"I am a sprite more powerful than any human you have ever known."

"I doubt that. Maybe you are not a fae at all, simply a human with big feet trying to trick passersby."

The man laughed. "Well, at least you retain a healthy skepticism. Maybe there is hope for you. Where was your last caravan headed?"

"The kingdom called Atlantea."

"I was born in Faë-Land and I do not know the way to Atlantea, so how would some random human know? You follow human men into a land they have never been to get to a fabled kingdom most fae cannot find. That, boy, is idiocy. Besides, humans can never get their alone."

"How do you not know the way?"

"Why would I know the way? Our magical lands are many, many times more vast than your Seven Empires and all its seas and oceans combined. I have no desire to travel to Atlantea. The question is: how would you know for certain that the men you join know the way? Well?"

Traveler stood thinking. "I do not know. How?"

"Who guides a group of men or full caravan on a journey?"

The boy straightened himself. "The caravan master."

"Yes. A guide leads you there. A trail master manages the journey along the path. However, it is the caravan master who is both and more; he commands all. To get to

Atlantea any real caravan master would be an elf or a sprite, rarely a dwarf because the Trail is far beyond their lands."

"Never humans?"

"Goodness, boy. You do not even know the path, by reputation or legend, yet you risk your life to go to the place. That is jumping from a cliff before checking to see if there is a body of water to catch you. Titan's Bridge is merely the first marker of seven on the year or two-year long journey to Atlantea."

"I thought you knew nothing of Atlantea?"

"I know of its reputation."

"Well, it will remain a tale for me."

"Why?"

"I will not be going."

"Why? Have you given up so easily?"

"All I wanted to do is see the races of fae, a gnome, a wizard, a unicorn or other fantastic animal, maybe stay a short time to earn money to return with."

"Are you an oracle too?"

"Why?"

"How many times have you tried?"

"Enough, and I was almost killed each time!"

"Boy, you would never have made it no matter what caravan you ventured with. You were not listening to me. A caravan of humans alone will never make it across the magical lands. Never go on any caravan unless the circumstances are right, whether you have to wait a week, a month, a year or three."

"Then, I might as well not go."

"Well, if you feel that way, then I shall be off."

"If I could only see some fae here, I would feel better. Preferably without big feet because that is unimpressive."

The man laughed again. "Is that all?" He watched him, then sighed heavily. "I will be asking for much trouble to rain down upon me, but you are only a boy. I will take you to the place within the Lands of Man where fae live.

"Here? Where?"

"Last Keep."

"Last Keep?" Traveler frowned. "This is Last Keep. There are no fae here."

"This city is certainly not the real Last Keep. That is the human one. The real one is a secret city, invisible, filled with fae, and since I'm fae, I can enter." He smiled "And bring a guest."

Traveler smiled.

"But listen well, boy. You will have an opportunity that most humans in your entire Seven Empires will never have. If I were you, I would not leave Last Keep until I learned every possible thing humanly possible to learn. Every day, I would seek out a new fae to learn from. I would sleep the very barest amount of hours and eat standing up, because I would always be on the move. If you are destined to make the death-journey to Atlantea, this may be where your journey really begins. Sometimes that's how it works in the land of magic. You move in the opposite way of the one you wish. Because there is knowledge and people you must encounter first. Then, and only then, will the Fates allow you to move forward on your path."

The man with the over-sized feet said his name was Alwing.

Traveler grew suspicious when the man told him that they would leave at nightfall for the real Last Keep.

"Why would we need to leave at night?" the boy asked him.

"Because that is when one goes to enter a secret fae city. Do not look at me like that. I am not a child-snatcher or some fiend. They exist, of course, but I am not one of them. The nightly visit is for your benefit, not mine. You humans have such poor eyesight as with all your senses. I can see the entrance but you need the aid of the moonlight."

"Why can we not go during the day?"

"Because we cannot. Should we forget the whole matter?"

"Only if there is not a real secret city of Last Keep."

The man chuckled and for a moment the boy saw he had a third eye between the two.

"You do know I can see your third eye."

"I have been around you too long, human. My spell is fading."

Traveler noticed that it was a full moon as the men walked out of Last Keep.

"I hope you are not a lycanthrope."

"Human, you have a very strange sense of humor. One day you will say that to a real one and then where would you be?"

"Those creatures haunt the magical lands?"

"Certainly not. One is sighted and all of Faë-Land hunts them until they are found and destroyed. The creatures remain in the Dark Lands or find their way to yours. But often we send hunting parties after them. We would not want them to turn your entire race to their kind. Why I am speaking about this! Lycanthropes, indeed. The ones you humans are fascinated with are so rare as to be extinct. Were-ravens, rats, bears, boars, and cats are more plentiful. But enough of this Dark Land talk. We go to a fae city and you will see none of that there, or your vampires or ghosts or any other fiend."

Alwing led the way and in not too much time, Traveler saw the walled city sitting upon a mountain plateau. With walls well over twenty feet he was astonished. He had traveled by day many times but had never seen the city or plateau ever before.

"I told you, human. The city is invisible to humans. Unless one who can see it shows you."

They reached its massive door, also more than twenty feet tall. Alwing knocked and then it opened. The boy was blinded from the daylight within.

Traveler stood with his mouth hung open. After a gush of air that whipped around him and seemingly lifted him from the ground to pull him in, he stood within a wonderful castle city.

It might have been night outside its walls, but inside there was a bright blue sky with a white sun beaming down on them. The walls of white marble towered tens of feet above them. The streets were made of what he thought was fine black dirt but it was a fine black sand. All the buildings along the streets were a combination of buildings of human-style construction but also tree or cave-like ones or, in one case, a giant shoe.

He suddenly glanced back to see how he had passed through. A closing hole a few feet away. It disappeared and all that remained were open castle gates and green pastures in the distance.

"Do you plan to stand there all day?" Alwing asked.

The boy turned around. "I do not understand. The city is not invisible it is..."

"It is in a pocket-realm," the man said. "A realm invisible to all outside of it. Its entrance only known to fae."

The man clapped his hands. His pointed cap grew to cover his head. White hair grew to adorn his face with a full beard, mustache and bushy eyebrows. His nose and ears doubled in size. The ghostly third-eye he saw was actually a golden symbol on his cap on a tip that touched the bridge of his nose.

The boy stared at him. "What...what kind of fae are you? Not a gnome or dwarf or..."

"Are gnomes, dwarves, and elves the only fae you humans know? There are so many other races of fae, you could say each name at birth and still be reciting our names until you die as an old man."

"What fae race are you, sir?"

"Call me a glenn. We are a simple fae people who frequent the green fields of fae."

"Are you a wizard?"

"No, but we can do magic like many fae."

"Why is this real city of Last Keep hidden?"

"This real city of Last Keep has been here before you humans had your Seven Empires. Many thousands of years before that. This city is a sanctuary for us fae traveling in the Lands of Man. We can rest and engage in commerce free from meddlesome humans or any other living things."

"Other things?"

The glenn smiled. "Humans and fae are not the only races that live on this world."

Traveler shook his head. "I do not want to know."

"You are wise to say that. You know of the dark ones already but you do not know of the travelers who call other worlds home."

"Other worlds?!"

"Come on, lad. I am hungry, as I am sure you are. I will get you settled in some lodging. I have to depart tomorrow."

"You are not staying, sir?"

"No, I travel further, but you can remain. You want to meet fae. Well, here are all the fae you need, without the danger of venturing into Faë-Land with human caravans destined to be slaughtered or enslaved along the way."

"A human caravan cannot make it across the magic lands."

"A human caravan cannot make it across the magical lands *without fae*. Otherwise, it is impossible."

"You plan to leave me here alone?"

"There is no danger here. I will leave you with gnomes. You humans like gnomes and gnomes can tolerate your kind. They can mind you."

Traveler smiled. "Gnomes. I like gnomes."

"You never met any gnomes."

"But I know I like them."

Alwing had left the real city of Last Keep a week ago. Every day was a joyous shock. A city filled with gnomes, dwarves, elves, fairies, humanoid animal people, such as rabbit men, bird men, and cat men, and humanoids with animal features such as wings, boar tusks, and beaks. His first few days was simple sitting at a tavern and smiling with a big grin as he watched from sun up to sundown.

Traveler had settled into a nice daily routine under the apprenticeship of a clan of gnomes. Alwing left him under their care as guardians. The boy turned the arrangement into more; a chance to learn and train under multiple vocations.

"We do not understand," a gnome asked him.

For the day, the gnomes traveled in one of the many gardens in the city. The gardens were their own pocket-realms—vast open green fields or dense woodlands or thick forests. The gnomes were showing him how to live off the land—what roots, seeds, vines, and plants could be eaten by fae or human. Further which ones had medicinal purposes.

"Why did I continue?" the boy asked.

"Yes. Why do you keep at this quest to the magical lands? The mark of a fool or a child is not accepting what is foolish or impossible."

"I agree, perhaps. But those who accomplish great things are always called fools and children. The problem is there is no way to really tell the difference between the accomplished person and the fool, until the end when you are looking back, which is easier to do than looking forward. I saw every journey as my time to become more experienced in my own determination to master the quest."

"A quest master, or end up dead."

"Oh, I wanted to ask. Sometimes when I was in Faë-Land I had the feeling of someone close but there was no one to be seen."

"Someone was there. They were invisible."

The boy snapped his fingers. "That was it. I knew I wasn't imagining it."

"You were not. Likely a fairy or sprite of some kind, maybe a bird or small animal of fae."

"I was in no danger?"

"You likely could have been in danger. Not only benevolent beings can become invisible. Many fae can, like elves or gnomes."

"You can become invisible?"

"To the eyes of humans, yes. But so can evil beings and dark creatures."

The boy looked at him with concern. "How does one protect oneself then, or see the invisible?"

"That is another lesson. No. Two lessons. You have not even learned this one yet. Today the lesson is food gathering. Tomorrow the lesson will be another art that humans are terrible at—fire-lighting. Basic skills, young human, is what will save your life on your quest. Tackling invisibility will be another day."

"Yes, Mr. Greenboots."

The fae halfling sprites were always in high spirits--amiable, love of dancing, singing and music. The clan he was in the care of had long white beards on their mature faces and wore green conical hats and green clothes.

Traveler lodged in a tiny hut with over two dozen of the gnomes. They had bunk beds and he had his own in the corner. After a long day, the gnomes had a rowdy last meal of the night with lots of ale, then as quickly they fell fast asleep as soon as their head hit the pillows of their beds. Often, he would lay quietly and watch out the single window to watch passersby on the night street. Gnomes were day fae, and he learned that when the sun set, so did they. However, there were many night fae and those like humans who could be active as they wished.

He was tempted to sneak out but his guardians told him not to. As a human, he was a guest of the secret city. If he ran afoul of any of its rules, he would find himself standing in the middle of the human Last Keep with the magic snap of a fae finger. Traveler was going to stay in the fae Last Keep city as long as he could. There was so much to learn.

There were gnomes, with many, many different varieties and clans—green gnomes, blue gnomes, red gnomes, yellow gnomes, tree gnomes, cave gnomes, sand gnomes, water gnomes, night gnomes, cloud gnomes, mist gnomes, tall gnomes. There were gnomoids—like gnomes but some had horns like a goat, or tails, or cloven feet, or clad in the shell of a turtle or snail.

Traveler learned of brownies, pucks, pech, nisse, kobolds, dwarves, more leshy and many other types of sprites. Because he truly was a healer-in-training and sincerely studied in medicines of all kinds to heal the sick or wounded, his gnome guardians freely shared the information. They also allowed the young boy to venture onto the streets to strike up conversations with fae of the city. Not only did he have the pleasure to meet so many fae from all corners of Faë–Land, but all their wonderful animals: fae dogs, fae birds, fae cats, giant animals all kinds, beasts he never saw before, or read in stories, like carnivorous ostrich or stags, hippogriffs, zebragriffs, liongriffs, tigergriffs, elefantagriffs, axexs, and fire birds. There were splendid griffins, and their cousins the owl griffins. There were a few unicorns, and a flying white horse. He saw his first keythong, a beautiful beast, a griffin without wings. The boy was in a wonderful world.

One day he saw a fairy and immediately left the streets. His gnome guardians watched him return to their hut.

"Human, that is not very wise," one said as two of the gnomes entered the hut. The boy sat on his bed watching the window.

"Do not let your one unfortunate encounter with fairies taint your view of every fairy you ever see. Come with us."

The boy rose and followed the two gnomes from the hut. They led him down the busy street, which was lined with lodging for visitors on either side.

They arrived at a tavern that the boy had not been to yet. At the first table they reached upon entering sat a tall female with almost translucent skin. If she were a fairy, it was the tallest one he ever saw. Her bent knees reached up to her very large eyes. She had many insect-like wings and two head antennae.

"Lustra," one gnome said. "This is our human ward you have heard of. He trains in the ways of fae. He trains in his vocation as a healer for both human and fae."

The fairy smiled and nodded.

"But he is fearful of fairy-kind. We need to rid him of it if he is to one day be a healer to fairies if needed. He may be on Titan's Trail and it may occur. You, Lustra, are the greatest fairy child-minder we know. If the human can learn to mind a fairy child, he can deal with any fairy of the magic lands."

"Lustra is mother to three thousand of her own fairies," the other gnome leaned over to whisper to the boy.

He cocked his head back with a perplexed face and grin. "Three thousand?"

"How old is the oldest, Lustra?" a gnome asked her.

"She is nearly five hundred, thank you."

"That's older than my birth city," the boy said with a laugh. "Three thousand?"

Traveler learned of all fae foods, ambrosias, cornucopias, herbs and spices. He learned to cook fae cuisines from fauns, fire-lighting from brownies, and tending to animals, whether livestock, burden, or guardian from nisse.

"How have your lessons with Lustra progressed?" a gnome asked the boy as they strolled through one of the city's open markets.

"It all makes perfect sense, Mr. Tidyfields," the boy said. "It is as the leshy told me. They are not malevolent; they are like bored children, and need direction. I thought of a dog I once had as a child. It was a terror of the streets but all I had to do was play with him for a little while and he would not misbehave anymore. Direction."

"Yes, indeed. They are overflowing with exuberant energy. If you learn how to mind fairy children, you won't need to be a healer of humans, fae will hire you for that skill alone."

"What are we here to buy, Mr. Tidyfields?"

"You know of pocket-realms so you will learn another secret of fae."

"Circles?"

"Not yet, but soon. No, something else. A magic pocket or pouch. Sometimes it is called your bag of tricks. With it you do not need a beast of burden or pull-cart or wagon. You simple carry it all with you in your own pocket."

"Like a small-realm?"

"That is another term for it."

"But is it safe?"

"Safe? Interesting question when dealing with things of magic. Safe from most fae? Yes. Safe from imps, pixies, and hobgoblins? No. But that reminds me. You should learn about pixy dust too."

"Then how do you protect your pockets from imps, pixies, hobgoblins?"

"Magic, either a spell or a guardian. But there is what we want."

The gnome pointed to a merchant with a cart of hand-sized pouches of different colors and textures.

Traveler studied the list.

"One needs all this on a caravan?" the boy asked sitting under a tree in a garden near the city's street of book vaults, libraries, and schools.

His gnome guardians had left Last Keep City on their own quest into the Lands of Man. His new guardian was dwarf named Blok. Never very talkative but the boy was learning much from him in regards to what made a proper caravan into the magic lands.

"Baker and barber?" the boy asked. "No baking and the men can cut and groom each other's hair."

"A caravan does not need to be a royal one to have such niceties."

"Blacksmith, yes."

"They are different than a weaponsmith which is far more important on the Trail. The best would be for the weaponsmith to be a forge too, and with his own magic smithy."

The boy took notes, and continued to scan his list. "Carpenter? Cooper?"

"Men, fae or human, need a proper shoe."

"You crossed out harness makers and saddlers."

"Never travel with horses into the magic lands."

"What of unicorns or pegasi?"

"Unicorns and flying horses are of magic. They are not horses. Heed my warning."

"I do not need to, Mr. Blok. I saw with my own eyes what horror can befall such a caravan, especially a caravan of a horse nation."

"Yes, you do know. A mistake made by many a human caravan."

"Do you miss your people, Mr. Blok? I am told your lands are further away than all other fae."

"I do miss them. Once my mission is complete, I will return as quickly as my legs can carry me."

"I never knew there were so many fae in the Lands of Man."

"And there are many humans in ours."

"Maybe I will have a chance to visit your lands too, Mr. Blok."

"It is a barren land. No green or fauna. But no less beautiful to our eyes. The many minerals and gemstones of the earth are as rainbows to us. My people are at home in the vast underground lands. We are also the protectors of the magic lands from those forces from the Dark Lands."

"Creatures?"

"Creatures, demons, and their servants. The handsome elves and vivacious fairies fill your books of fables about our lands, but we dwarves are the true champions of the realm."

"I believe you, Mr. Blok. I will visit your lands."

"And if you do, I am sure we can fit your thin human form with a magnificent suit of armor to fend off any beast or creature, good or evil."

"But could my thin human form bear such weight, even when I am fully an adult?"

"Probably not. But dwarves are the best forges. We can fashion other metals more to your suiting."

Blok the dwarf would be Traveler's guardian for only a few days but in that time the boy learned all he could about the metals dwarven-kind mined, forged, and fashioned for warriors all over the world. Blok, in particular not only knew of dwarven metal, but elfin, goblin, and all fae races—both good and evil. He also knew of the rarer and sometimes more powerful elemental metals, which Blok knew of but had never touched.

There were other humans in Last Keep City. Traveler learned of berserkers, those human warriors that could tap an internal rage of magic to battle stronger and longer than any normal human. Few berserkers knew of the real Last Keep, but those that lived in Faë-Land all did. But it was a member of another group that became his new guardian.

"Is there a reason why I am being kept from the non-sprite sections of the city?" Traveler asked the wizard as he worked at a table making charms with herbs, roots, and vines.

"Are you ready to meet the elfin races, Master Traveler?"

The boy grinned. "I am not a master. You are the master, Mr. Nigelle."

"Well, are you?"

"Why would I not be?"

"Because elves are very much like humans. We live similar to each other—kingdoms and villages. Similar class structures; we both have royalty—kings and queens, princes, princesses, dukes, and duchesses, lords, generals and knights. Same notions of religion, the time-before and the after-life. Same notions of battle and honor."

"Then I should enjoy conversing with them, Mr. Nigelle."

The wizard stepped closer to him. The man always wore a dark navy robe. He looked like a wizard would look. Long white hair, combed back past his shoulders. His face was clean-shaven otherwise. He tapped the table with his multi-ringed hand.

"You do not need to tell me. I know the difference between elves and goblins," Traveler said.

"I was not going to tell you to never call an elf a goblin or vice versa. What I was going to tell you is to be careful of elves. They are not all the same. Always remember that. Never, ever fully trust them until you know that you can. In that regard they are like humans too. Some can be trusted, others cannot. Some are even less trustworthy than goblins and you never trust goblins."

"Is there a story behind your warnings, Mr. Nigelle?"

"Yes, but that is for another time. Are you not training to be a healer? How are your charms coming along?"

The boy held up the necklace. The wizard touched them and nodded.

"Magic without being a magic-caster. Without a charm you are helpless against nymphs and many other enchanting fae."

"Can nymphs enchant women, Mr. Nigelle?"

"No. Woman and males before puberty are immune from their enchantment."

"What enchants women and not men?"

"The questions continue, do they, Master Traveler? Actually, all proper caravans will have women, in case of nymphs, fairies, and sirens. Our human kingdoms frown on the presence of woman, but the wise ones traveling into the magic lands or fae kingdoms always do because of those real dangers posed by enchantment."

"But what beings enchant women and not men? I need to know, Mr. Nigelle, if I am to be a proper healer in Faë-Land, for men and women."

"Okay, Master Traveler, you have made a reasoned request. But I know how your human mind works. I will answer but no more questions. Strigoi, demons such as incubus, and there are rare male sirens."

"Strigoi? Is that not a vampire?"

"There it is. What is with you young people and the fascination with vampires, zombies, and werewolves? How quickly you tired of elves. Charms, Master Traveler, charms are what we are learning today."

Mr. Nigelle's fae friend was a four-armed cyclopoid. A cyclops but not a giant. Each of his four arms could move independently as if they had minds of their own.

Otherwise, he looked human in every other way. Nigelle was a wizard who could do healing spells. Gorb was an actual fae healer practicing the arts for many decades, even working as a member of fabled flying caravans that Traveler began to hear much about. The boy knew of land caravans but never knew of the great flying ones.

"In humans, Master Traveler, bright red is what?"

"Artery blood; carries blood away from the heart to the body."

"Dark red."

"Vein blood, which vampires don't like, carry blood low in oxygen from the body back to the heart for replenished with more oxygen."

"Ignoring your poor humor, how many different colors of blood do fae-kind have?"

"Every color there is in the Lands of Man and even more colors in Faë-Land, but I do not need to know all that. Bright is artery, dark or dull is not."

"Good. What can you tell me about setting up a healing tent for a caravan?"

"Will that be my decision as healer? It will be up to the caravan master or steward."

"It will be up to the healer who takes charge. Even with magic, healing is not for the faint-hearted, young human. Blood, guts, vomit, excrement and urine, not to mention bodies that have to be burned and buried, if not guarded to protect against animals or creatures."

Traveler nodded. "I will learn it all, Mr. Gorb. And Mr. Gorb, what kind of fae are you? With four arms you must be able to attend to how many patients at once?"

"My fae people are born to be healers, young human. I would take full advantage at working under my tutelage, and Mr. Nigelle's. You will undoubtedly come across other human wizards, but likely will never see my kind again."

"Why Mr. Gorb? Your people will not be seen by humans again?"

"You will learn, young human. Most fae races are never seen by humans or fae. My people are also oracles and we chose to depart from the lands of human and fae for some time."

"I am saddened to hear that, Mr. Gorb. There would have been many who would have enjoyed you as their teacher of the healing arts."

"Good of you to say, young human. Then it is up to you to learn all you can so you can teach them for me."

As if Nigel the wizard and Gorb the one-eyed fae healer wasn't enough, a third healer joined the team of healing arts tutors. Traveler was lucky to be in the city to attend a meeting of fae healers from every part of Faë-

Land and, as he learned, other magic lands of other realms.

The woman was not big, rotund, and gruff like Bruga but the slim, tan, and short woman reminded the boy of her nonetheless. She commanded attention and knew the art of medicinal potions.

"Vapors!" she yelled at him.

She was not the friendliest or patient of teachers but he was determined to master the art of mixing medicines, herbs, potions, by boiling them—vapors.

"You can cure many more men than only one with the art of vapors. Erect a tent, big pot, filled with plenty water on a big fire. Mix your medicines and boil it. Saturate the air thick with its power. Magic medicine can be used for men or animals. All they have to do is breathe. No paste or ointments or liquids to drink or needles to stick. Breathe."

"What is this healing art called?" the boy asked.

"*Arbularyo*, *kulam* and *pagkukulam*. Magic of the earth, herbs, and candles," she replied. "You learn this art and you will be better than most healers in Pan-Earth, fae or human. So few know of it but it is so powerful. So many uses."

Traveler nodded. He had found his particular specialty to master in the vast healing arts.

"Will you travel again?" she asked him.

"I am not sure."

"So you will stay here all your life?"

"Why not? I am doing noble work."

"One does not remain an apprentice all one's life. You learn, grow, and move on. Fae don't need a human healer but humans could have great use for a human healer trained by fae."

"True."

"More than true. But I know your heart. You will go. As soon as the right party enters this city and tempts you away. Why do you want to go to the magical lands?"

"The same reason as most men—see fantastic lands, people, beasts."

"No, you are not being truthful. You have tried many times before you came here. Your quest to go to the magical lands is an obsession, it borders on madness for a human."

"We call it unwavering determination."

"No, it is madness. Men braver and more learned than you would have squelched their desire to ever venture into the magical lands every again, but you continue. Why? The truth this time."

"My father was a great adventurer. He went to far off lands, every corner of the empires, distant realms, distant worlds. All in his mind. He wrote stories of all those adventures. He told them to me as a child. He would have done them all but he met my mother. They had me. He had responsibilities. Rose in rank and status. But his heart longed for those adventures and he collected stories too. Books, accounts. He knew as much about these distant lands as our own kingdom. There was a war and he was struck by a random arrow in battle. He lived for a week afterward but there was nothing the healers could do. It was his intention to go on those adventures when he reached his elder years. He lived those years, longed for it every day. Then to have that taken from him. It was too much for him to bear. He should have lived for months; he lived only a couple of weeks more. My mother died when he died. Not physically but she did. She was gone too. I was an orphan from that point on. She died in her sleep a couple of years later and I became a ward of the relatives I had never known.

"The one city in the magical lands my father was most fascinated with was Atlantea. So that's why I go. I want to walk into that kingdom, find a patch of ground, and bury the last thing he ever gave me—a ring he swore was given to him by a fae as a boy. I would be able to say that I made the trip for him."

Nigelle stood in the tent listening, quietly. The wizard was physically moved by the account.

"Then why do have men believe you became a healer simply to be popular with the knights and warriors?" the wizard asked. "You were always going to be a healer."

"A means to an end."

"Also good," the woman healer said. "Learn to tell good stories. Very important. Stories are like money in the land of fae."

"I did not anticipate your response. You are already the only human residing in Last Keep. You can just as well be a human residing in Atlantea," Nigelle said.

"Have you ever been there, Mr. Nigelle?

"Never. Most fae have never been there. Atlanteans are not really fae at all."

"Not fae? What are they then?"

"Think of Atlantea as similar to the true Last Keep. Its residents live in Faë–Land but they are from another realm. They also do not like fae. Humans they do not mind but not fae."

"Why?"

"Wars. But we humans never made war on them."

"Because you are too inferior to do so," the fae healer woman said.

Nigelle smiled and threw his arm around her.

"Leave me alone," she said as he tried to kiss her on the cheek.

"She loves humans."

The boy laughed.

"I would not be that harsh," Nigelle said. "But many fae do have that regard towards humans, in a benevolent way I would say. Are you surprised?"

"I am. I think of fairies and sprites and elves. Races that have existed before the Lands of Man ever were."

"But the Titans and dragons were before us all, and the Atlanteans were here then. They were civilized and advanced in magic and machines when we were roaming savages upon the world."

"Yes, they would like you," Nigelle said.

A smile grew on the boy's face. "But can I get there?" the boy asked.

"With a fortune or the right skills, you can," the wizard said. "But that you know. And you are still alive so I would count that as great fortune. Did you not tell me that you flew on a winged unicorn?"

Traveler chuckled. "Yes, I did, but I was so scared."

"Scared in the good sense."

"Have other humans like me been so lucky to have found the real Last Keep on their own?"

"Oh, yes. Through the centuries, yes. The one advantage they had that you did not was the ability to speak a fae tongue. That will have to become part of your lessons from a future tutor."

"Learn to speak fae?"

"A human does not speak fae. Humans have a hundred languages. Fae have hundreds of thousands. Pick one and that is the one you will learn."

"Which one do you recommend, Mr. Nigelle?"

"Elvish, of course. Either an elfin caravan or one led by an elfin caravan master is the way you will likely get to Atlantea."

The boy smiled. "Elvish. Why in the future? You can start teaching me tonight?"

"Me? Master Traveler, I'm not an elf. I don't speak elvish, human."

The boy laughed.

Actually, the human wizard spoke many spritely languages, a bit of centaur, and dwarvish. Traveler learned that languages were a kind of magic themselves and by speaking one fae language one could understand fae speaking another, as long as the fae language one spoke was true. He immersed himself in his language studies on his own as much as he did with his study of fae healing arts.

One day, Nigel, Gorb and the female fae healer, Wu, gathered their people to depart with their own caravan.

"I hope you realize the tremendous good fortune you have stumbled upon as a human. You have learned much in your time here. More than any human could have learned in a lifetime on the Trail in one caravan or another."

"I will have much to offer the proper caravan as a healer, Mr. Nigelle."

"Healer? Why not a steward, trailmaster, or even a caravan master?"

"As a mortal with no magical powers or object or weapon, any vocation as a caravan master would be extremely short-lived. Caravan masters have to be able to battle creatures and win. I am content with the role as healer, and I aim to be the best one there is."

"You are already on your way to be that. However, if you were to obtain that magic weapon or perhaps a magic companion, I would not be so quick to dismiss a higher role. You have all the traits to be a great one."

Traveler bid them all goodbye and all three of them each gave the boy a gift for his "magic bag of tricks."

CHAPTER TEN

Caravan of Drows

Young Traveler was nearly eighteen years old.

For the first time, Traveler had his own lodging in the secret fae city of Last Keep. He managed his own days with his studies of the healing arts primarily and learning elvish, fae customs, and of caravan management. For money, he worked part of his time in the city's main apothecary. As a human boy, he became quite the attraction for fae visitors, many of whom, had never seen a human in person.

He had purposely avoided the elfin parts of the city because he too felt that the moment he entered, he would come across an elfin caravan that would take him from the city. There was still much to learn.

When it was day on the outside it was nighttime inside Last Keep, or so he was told. In the more than a year he lived within the city; he had never once ventured out. He had lived in the human Last Keep; there was nothing there for anyone to want. But he did learn that its residents secretly traded with their fae sister city.

One night, he walked home to his hut left to him by the gnomes. The sprites had paid for the lodgings for as long as he stayed in the city. It was one of the few nights that there was not a soul on the street but him. Most of the visitors and residents of the city were day fae. From the taverns that were open he could hear rollicking brownies.

"Hello, young lad," a voice said from behind him.

Traveler turned to see a man slowly ambling toward him as if drunk, there was a bottle in his hand.

"I heard from others that you are keen to see beasts. I may be able to help you."

"Thank you, sir, but maybe another day."

"Day? Why the day? The night is the best time for beasts."

The man dropped his bottle to the ground and it shattered. Traveler instinctively ran.

The boy burst through the door of his hut and slammed it shut. He stepped back as he realized that doors in the fae city had no locks. The door was kicked open. The man stepped in with a low laugh. Traveler was at the other end of the one room hut with his back against the wall.

"Don't you want to see beasts?" he said.

The man's head, neck and shoulder began to shake violently. The man grew in size as his upper torso began to transform. Thick hair sprouted from the man's skin. His nose elongated. Wolf ears sprouted from top of his head, on the sides. Traveler watched the man change into a werewolf but it was impossible. No lycanthrope could enter Last Keep City, any more than a gorgon or manticore. The man was something else.

"You are not afraid," the man said with his wolf's mouth.

Traveler suddenly disappeared into invisibility.

The lycanthrope's head looked all around in shock. "Where did you go, little human? Why do you hide from Goar? I am not here to hurt you. I am here to eat you."

Traveler watched the beast man from his pocket-realm. From his view it was private reading room filled with reading books and parchment for notes. It was his traveling study room but tonight it was his sanctuary. The wide entrance was invisible to the man but Traveler watched him grow much taller, so much so that he had to hunch his back over.

"Goar can smell you."

"What are you?" a new voice asked from the street.

Traveler could not see who asked the question. The gigantic lycanthrope's body blocked the front entrance of the hut.

"Goar will show you."

The lycanthrope lunged but promptly yelled. Traveler heard sounds but was not sure of what. The beast man collapsed to the ground. The lycanthrope transformed to a giant of a man, ugly, bald and with vicious teeth.

At the entrance were several elves. But elves with dark-blue skin in the night.

Goar was a grendel. A shape-shifting giant fond of the taste of humans.

Traveler's savior were not blue-skinned elves. They were drows. It was a lesson he learned with the punch to the jaw from one of them when he thanked the "elves."

"Call me an elf again, human, you will join your would-be killer on the floor of your hut! We are drows."

Traveler made a note that it was time to learn of all the different elves that existed, and those mistaken for elves by humans.

The boy had never seen them before but Last Keep City did have its own magistrate. News spread fast of the carnivorous shape-shifting giant that had gotten into their walls. Traveler was questioned many times by the fae magistrate, as were the drows. Another reason the drows had for not liking him; they were being inconvenienced for coming to his aid.

He was late to work at the fae apothecary but his boss—a leshy fond of green fae cats that infested the store—knew without him having to say why he was late.

As the close of business neared, four men entered in hooded cloaks. Traveler was dusting shelves at the time. The store was a maze of shelves with bowls, flasks, cups, small boxes, powders, and pouches of products. The boy returned to the main counter. His boss almost never attended to patrons when the boy was on duty working.

Traveler recognized one of the drows as they stopped at the counter. The one who punched him.

"We are told you are a healer."

"I am."

"In search of a caravan to join?"

"Why would drows need a human as a healer? There are drow healers."

"But unfortunately, ours got himself killed in battle. We do not wish to return home to find another. We do wish to move forward with our quest on the Trail."

"A human healer. You would trust a human healer to attend to drows?"

"Impatient men do foolish things. Will you go?"

"What will you pay me?"

The drow smiled. His white teeth sparkled in the dim light.

Drows didn't hate humans, but they didn't like them either. Traveler knew there was a real reason as to why they were willing to hire him as their healer. However, he'd have to figure that out for himself on the Trail. Traveler bid his boss goodbye but the fae had always known it was a matter of time and gave the boy a supply of herbal medicines for his healing bag along with his final wages.

As they left the apothecary, the one who hired him told the boy to wait at his hut. He would summon him when the caravan was about to set out.

"Am I part of the caravan or not?" Traveler asked. "If so, I want to see your full caravan supplies, weapons, defense and meet all your leaders."

The four drows looked at each other. The one who hired him laughed.

"The human is not so foolish after all."

Their party was nearly five hundred. Smaller than most caravans and they were not dressed as warriors. They reminded him of assassins, or robbers. Dressed for stealth and speed. They did not have swords but long dual daggers on their waist belts. They had many dire-cats, saber-toothed wolf-sized felines with jet black fur. They had many wagons tied to giant tail-less lizards.

"No archers?" Traveler asked.

One of the drows pointed and he saw more drows come out of invisibility, many dozens of archers and led by drows with swords.

"Our caravan master," one drow said.

The tall drow looked him up and down but said nothing and made no attempt to shake the boy's hand. Traveler simply greeted him a nod.

"I am the steward," the drow said. "Those are the only titles of importance for you."

"Where do you want me in the camp, sir?"

The drows were surprised by the boy's good manners and respect. The caravan master grinned. "When you return with your things, healer, I will show you."

When Traveler returned, he was ready for work. He reported to the steward, a drow named Dr'alak, with his own healing bag of supplies. He joined the laborers making the final check of supplies. Of interest to the young healer were those supplies he could use for his healing duties: a billy, the small cooking pot with a handle on top, he could use for boiling water, bedding supplies, bandages. He took note of their tents: lean-tos, a three-sided shelter with one open side; large tents, he could use for a healing tent; and tunnel tents, low profile tent that were long and rounded. He also made check of the caravan's kindling. Most fae knew fire-lighting as if second nature but he wanted to make sure there was plenty for him.

"Are my provisions satisfactory?" Dr'alak asked. Like most fae, they appeared out of nowhere when one wasn't looking.

Traveler turned to him. "Yes, sir. I was checking the supplies of tents you have. Whether we need a large one for more patients or smaller ones, if in battle. You have all that I need. If it should come to it, may I be assigned a person to help with my duties, moving patients or bodies, getting supplies, the like?"

"Yes, of course. I will see to it."

"Also, I know of drows but not much more. If you can teach me of drow ways and especially the protocols of your caravan, I'll be sure to conduct myself accordingly."

"Yes, I will. You can join the men for meals. You should get accustomed to eating drow food."

"Yes, sir."

Traveler joined the drows for their meal but either they did not speak at all in his presence, or whispered in their own language, which even knowing some elfin words was unintelligible to him. He knew it would take some time for the men to warm to him. But any good healer doesn't wait.

"Excuse, sir," he said to the closest drow to him. All of the men were scattered along the woodland earth of their pocket-realm sanctuary. "What will be our greatest threat on the Trail? I want to ensure I can prepare against any attack on the men."

"Goblins," another drow said. "Prepare for goblins and all their dark allies."

Hobgoblins, spriggans, bugganes, boggarts, bugbears, dire-wolves, rat-bats, and Redcaps. Traveler had to learn all about the dark sprites and creatures. For a moment it was overwhelming that goblins traveled with such creatures as normal. All they had were dire-cats and tail-less lizards. But the healer kept his comments to himself.

On the second day, the drow caravan marched out the secret city of Last Keep under the cover of the night. As Traveler stepped across the threshold of the pocket-realm city, he breathed in the air of the Lands of Man for the first time in over a year. It felt invigorating. The breeze. The moonlit sky above. The caravan of drows would be his first caravan as a new man with all the knowledge and skills he accumulated from so many teachers. He glanced back at the secret city with a smile. His temporary home had given him so much and he would return to it one day, if even for a visit.

The drows did not need to tell him where they were going or when they would stop. He knew; the foot of the Titan's Bridge. They camped in their pocket-realm and would wait until dawn, like he had done with so many other caravans.

Some of the drows viewed him with indifference, others ignored him altogether, but some watched him suspiciously or with disdain. He still did not know why they would hire a single human for their drow caravan.

"What is your name, human?" a drow walked up to him from behind.

Traveler looked up from his seated position in front of fire by himself. "Traveler is my name, sir."

The drow knelt to join him by the fire. "I am Dr'raen. Do not mind the men. Drows are very suspicious by nature. Most have never seen a human, only read about them."

"I have never met drows before, only read about them."

"I heard about you from the others. I heard you were able to bear up even under a swift drow punch."

Traveler smiled. "What is your occupation in the caravan, sir?"

"I am a cleric."

"Both of us interested in the well-being of men," Traveler said.

"That is true. Mind, body, and soul. I have spoken to our caravan master. You will camp with me and my men."

"Thank you, sir."

"You are brave, human, to so freely join a people you know little about on such a dangerous journey."

"No different than other caravans I have been a part of."

The drow caravan made it across Titan's Bridge faster than any previous one. Traveler was certain they used some type of spell that made every step they marched the same as two. As a result, they had made it to just out of the Howling Mountains when night fell. However, rather than stop, they continued forward using magic to illuminate their way with magic torches. They had crossed the Mirage Plains and set up camp. All were exhausted and for those not on night guard, sleep came fast.

Traveler, so eager to get back out on the caravan trail, ignored the most basic of his rules: if your instincts says a caravan is not right, then avoid it like the plague, there will always be another caravan to join right behind it.

The caravan moved through Faë–Land Minor, the land of fairies and sprites, with equal quick speed. For the first time he beheld the fae city of Fae–Wick. A castle city unlike anything he could have imagined. The main castle floated in mid-air and was made of shimmering ivory rock. The centered main entrance was shaped like an open mouth on a crowned humanoid head. On either side were slits where sparkling white water spilled outward and down about one hundred feet into a moat of mist. A winding, unattached white drawbridge path floated before the entrance. The sky above Fae-Wick was filled with beasts—griffins, flying horses, flying unicorns, giant birds, and other winged fae creatures.

But they neither stopped nor entered. The caravan marched past. No caravan moved as quickly as they did. Traveler knew they were retracing a path to get to a specific destination on the Trail, not to move along it. But what destination?

They entered the valley of the fae city of Arion's Spear. Another fae city Traveler had never seen before or could have imagined. A mammoth white rock statue of a horse on its hind legs, reaching for the heavens; a golden spear wound around its body and pointed upward. The caravan, every drow with their hood firmly covering their heads, avoided all others on the valley path, both travelers and camps. Traveler saw sprites, elves, fauns, his first centaur and other fae everywhere. Again, the caravan bypassed the city. Always setting up the camp far away from city and any other camps.

One morning, Dr'raen the cleric told him that they had crossed into Faë-Land Minor, the land of elves, hoofed fae, such as fauns, satyrs, and centaurs, and...goblins. A day later, Traveler learned what the truth of the caravan was.

They neared another, larger, drow caravan. The caravan master greeted the new caravan leader, who Traveler knew was royalty of some kind from his attire. Large ornate blue feathered shoulder pads, a unique ragged sword strapped to his back, and a pack of dire-cats around him tended to by the tallest drow he'd ever seen. The drows spoke in whispers and watched him from afar. The boy realized that it was not one caravan but two. The one that fetched him was a scouting caravan.

Traveler looked at Dr'raen. The drow cleric looked away. The boy could feel his anger growing.

The drow caravan master waved to him to approach.

"This human is our leader, Dr'oyn," the drow caravan master said.

"What is the name of your caravan, sir?" Traveler asked.

"We have no name as such," the drow leader answered. "We are a caravan of royal thieves."

"I did not know there was such as royalty for thieves," Traveler said.

"There is and that leads us to your task as healer."

"A wounded drow, sir?"

"A wounded something. You are to attend to the creature."

"Creature, sir?"

"Cleric, take the human to his new patient. See to it that he restores it enough so we can continue our interrogations."

Dr'raen nodded.

The drow cleric lead Traveler into the new camp. Unlike the smaller one, the drows were dressed in full armor. There were many tents but one had a large contingent of guards. The drow cleric stepped into it as Traveler followed. The boy had to let his eyes adjust to the dim light. Only one torch hung from a corner of the tent. In the other was a large cage. Someone was inside, propped up on an elbow, on the ground.

"Mr. Dr'raen, we humans do not have the gifted sight as drows do. I need better illumination."

"Yes, of course."

The drow cleric left the tent.

"A human," the cage prisoner said in a gruff, condescending voice.

Traveler stepped closer. "Who are you?"

He heard low laughter. "Either these drows will kill you, or I will when I escape."

"Why would you say that to a healer here to help you?"

"Help me? You mean keep me alive so they can continue to torture me, the drow thieves. That's why you are here. Get a human here so their own drow healers need not sully their hands on the flesh of a goblin."

"Goblin?"

Dr'raen returned with a few other drows with long torches. The tent was properly lit and Traveler returned his eyes to the cage. A goblin. A large bulky and tall green-skinned humanoid with a big flat nose, pointed teeth, and large pointed ears.

"Human." Another drow had entered the tent, a drow bodyguard on either side. "I am the caravan's chief healer. You are to tend to the creature's wounds. Then we will question the thief further. You will stay close so that if there are more wounds to attend to, you will see to it."

"You hired me onto your caravan for this?"

"You accepted the assignment. You were paid. Why complain? We will leave you to the creature. However, be careful. We drows can defend ourselves. You humans are a fragile lot. We'll chain him appropriately but he can still kill."

All the goblin did was laugh at him. The drows chained the goblin so completely he was like a mummy wrapped in chains on his back. Traveler had to fight the chains to examine the severe chest wounds.

"What did they do here?" Traveler asked.

"Are you not disgusted touching the skin of a goblin?"

"I asked you a question."

"You are quite angered by your benefactors, human. They tricked you. What did you expect from a clan of thieves?"

"They said you are the thief."

"I am, but I did not torture anyone to steal what we did."

"What did you steal?"

"A teleportation spell. We stole it, my goblin party and I, from an elfin caravan. We had an army of Redcaps occupy them as we snuck into their camp. Our hobgoblins dealt with their guard animals. Then these drow thieves stole the spell from us. We tracked and attacked them. I found it, ran, and hid it. They killed my men but they can't kill me because they do not know where I hid it. That is why you are here, human. Their drow healers would never touch a goblin. Their warriors will continue to impale me with their swords and you will heal the wounds so they can do so again. However, I will never talk. I will gladly die. Drows and elves are the same vile dung to all goblinkind. When they are done with me, they will kill you. That is what drows do. Why do think fae don't trust them and they hide their faces with their hoods all the time."

"What is your name?" Traveler asked.

The goblin laughed. "Why? Will you cast a spell on me?"

"Goblin, do you want me to attend to your wounds or not? I do not care either way because at this moment, drows and goblins are the same race to this human."

The goblin laughed. "Yes, you would feel that way. I would too, in your shoes. Why do we not make a bargain? You help me escape and I will rescue you when they try to kill you."

"Goblin, I am a human, but I am not a stupid and gullible one. You just told me that I am nothing more than a lowly human. So, I am not much better in your eyes than a drow or elf, you simply are not consumed by hate for humankind. You'd kill them out of racial hatred. You'd kill me because I am a nothing to you. Why am I bothering with this quest of mine through Faë–Land? The great fae. What a laugh. No different than humans. I will go back to my tent and you can all just kill each other, I will take your possessions and wait for a noble caravan to join. Free of drow or goblins."

Traveler stood from the bound goblin and left the tent.

Traveler tossed the bag of coins he had been given to the caravan master's side. The drow sat at a campfire with their leader, the chief healer, and a few warriors.

"I will wait outside my tent. Since I won't aid you in your scheme, you can kill the goblin now, be done with him and move on. I'll wait here for another party or caravan. I can live off the land like any other fae."

"But can you defend yourself like any fae, human," the leader said coldly.

"Why do you care, drow?" Traveler said. "Not your concern and not your life."

Traveler walked away from them and grabbed the one thing he did have, a satchel, from the smaller caravan. He marched to a secluded spot away from both camps and sat on the ground. Drows of both caravans stood there watching him.

The caravans erupted into a shouting match more intense than he'd seen in past caravans. The most dangerous of caravans were ones of disparate factions that either hated or had no respect for the other. Such caravans were dead long before they had to do battle with their first creature or enemy along the Trail. The drow caravan was divided against itself. On one side was the king, caravan master and chief healer; on the other were the majority of the drows including Dr'raen. Traveler did not need to speak drow to know that capturing and torturing a goblin, an enemy race to drow for ages, was still an act of much dishonor for the drow caravan. The boy was watching a mutiny of the men against their leadership.

As Traveler sat quietly and watched, he felt a presence. He did not bother turning; he would not see anyone. However, his eyes began to make out a shadow on the ground. Traveler turned to see a tall elf in golden armor with long flowing white hair, pointed ear poking through. The elf stared at him with ice-blue eyes.

"They tricked me, so I'm not part of their caravan anymore," Traveler said calmly and returned his attention to the yelling drows who had not yet noticed the elf.

On the ground he saw many more shadows of elfin knights appear. But it was far worse, arrows flew from the opposite side of the woodlands and battle cries. Scores of large, brutish, green-skinned, goblin riders burst through the wooded forest, heavily armed with spiked maces, battle-axes, and spiked war hammers. Goblin archers on foot followed them. Goblin warriors, on the back of giant black dire-wolves, attacked the drows. They too, did not see the growing army of elves.

At that point, Traveler thought the wisest action was to slip away and hide in his small-realm. He watched as not one but three armies battled. Each side was battling two other armies. No general alive would do such a thing. Traveler sat at the threshold of the realm entrance and watched the slaughter. Soon the battlefield was littered with elfin, drow, and goblin bodies. There was a madness to it all. He had always heard of the nobility of elves but their actions were no better than human marauders—blind fury and killing, every elf for himself. No formation, defense or strategy other than to kill anyone not an elf. Soon it was over.

Some sanity seemed to return to the remaining elves and drows. The enemies agreed to do one thing together—kill all the goblin warriors and their beasts. They did. Then the elves tended to their dead, and the drows did the same.

Traveler stepped out of his small-realm when he saw the wounded drow, Dr'raen. The stumbling drow cleric had a staff in his hand and he walked to the remaining elves and threw it to their feet.

"There. You can take it with you," the drow said with a sneer.

The staff was broken in two. An elf picked it up from the ground and saw that the magic staff could not be made whole.

"It would appear that neither one of us will be able to teleport across these lands and the Great Forest. We will have to march through like all others."

"See to it that we never meet again, drow," the elf said.

The remaining dozen or so elves pulled all the bodies of their fallen elfin comrades together. It would be slow work to gather all the bodies together, and retrieve all weapons. Half the number of drows remained. The sneak attack by the goblins had done its damage to the drow caravan.

Traveler neared a dejected Dr'raen, holding the gash in his stomach.

"Assign me one drow and we will attend to the goblin bodies. Burn and bury them. You attend to your men."

"Yes, of course," Dr'raen said.

The work of both parties went on until nightfall. Traveler decided to return to Last Keep City. The remaining drows decided to accompany him.

CHAPTER ELEVEN

Caravan of Pale, Blue, and Green Elves

Young Traveler was still nearly eighteen years old.

Traveler had a new guardian—the drow, Dr'raen. They returned to Last Keep City and the boy was amazed that now he carried the magic of the city forever. Unlike most humans, he could see the secret city by eye even in the day. He laughed as walked straight to its entrance, knocked on the massive front door, and was let in by a humanoid gerbil in a hooded cloak. The drows followed him in.

Dr'raen was a cleric of some note in the drow kingdoms. Neither he nor the other drows would tell him the full story behind what he had seen—a near-mutiny within a drow kingdom's caravan, brother drow against drow, capturing and torturing goblins rather than killing them in battle. He might never know. Instead, Traveler used their time together to learn all about drows, their customs, languages, and lands.

The other drows left the city days later and only the cleric remained. Traveler surmised that Dr'raen was waiting for a new drow caravan to fetch him.

"Are you in trouble?" Traveler asked the drow cleric at their lunch meal in a fae tavern.

"Hardly."

"You do not have to say, if you do not want. Only I was told that drows do not make war on one another, and neither do elves."

The drow cleric almost choked, bursting out laughing while drinking his ale.

"Elves do not make war on one another? That is certainly not true, human. Never believe all the fables you are told about them."

"Then, what is the truth? I would not know. I am a human."

"True."

"For a healer, you seem much more interested in other duties," Dr'raen told him. Both Traveler and the drow cleric were spending many hours in the fae city's deepest and most ancient book vaults of their libraries. Traveler didn't know what information Dr'raen was searching for, but he continued studies of the healing arts while he asked about other topics.

"If portal magic can make caravan travel across the Trail obsolete, why not master it?"

"Master Traveler, do you really believe if were so easy that any of the fae kingdoms would do so? The Great Forest is made of magic, older than either fae or human. No magic portal could traverse its domain so easily. The quest to and from Atlantea is not a onetime life event. Caravans seek to travel to its fabled walls often."

"So it is possible if for a onetime event. Open a portal doorway and step through from here to the gates of Atlantea."

"It is possible, young human, but not by any being either you nor I would ever want to meet."

"Are you suggesting demons?"

"I am suggesting beings from other realms on other worlds."

"Other worlds?"

"Do you not know there are other worlds? There are networks of pocket-realms and realms everywhere on Pan-Earth, and the same exist on other worlds."

"Have you been to these other worlds, Mr. Dr'raen?"

The drow cleric smiles. "I have not, but there are some drows who have." His smile faded.

"Did I inadvertently touch upon another sensitive matter for drows?"

"It is not your fault. You are a curious human. Both a blessing and a curse for your kind."

"Why do drows hate elves, Mr. Dr'raen?"

"That is a question, Master Traveler, that cannot be answered in one afternoon in the bowels of Last Keep's great libraries."

Traveler learned that Last Keep City's greatest value to fae in the Lands of Man was as a depository of ancient knowledge. In the magic lands he learned that the greatest libraries were in the scholarly centaur city of Chiron, a cloud city of the giant oracle cyclops, and the celestial elves. The latter two being the most inaccessible to most fae.

Days later they heard of an approaching elfin caravan to Last Keep City's gates. The drow cleric gave the boy a glance.

"Maybe this is the caravan you seek," the drow said.

"If they try to hire me, without so much as a proper question, I will certainly know it is not."

The drow laughed.

"Mr. Dr'raen. Royal thieves? Was that the truth? You are too noble for that."

He smiled. "Good of you to say but 'thief' is probably not the correct word in your tongue. My people are very emotional despite our often-calm exterior. We hold grudges and vengeful. A difficult mix for a people who are also honorable."

"You steal from those that deserve it."

"Our clan steals from those whose who stole from drow-kind. There is honor in that for us. To right wrongs against our people by our enemies. I am sure it does not make sense to you. But it does for us."

"It makes sense to me, though I disagree with it. But it is not my place to say either way. I take it that is also the source of enmity between drow and elf."

The drow hesitated.

"Do not ever repeat what I am about to say to any drow or elf ever."

"I promise."

"There was a time, eons ago, there were no drows, only elves. We were all the same people. But some clans were mesmerized by the power of magic. But only day magic was permitted by all fae. However, there were those enchanted by the power of dark magic. They rationalized it to themselves by saying they would use dark magic for good. But that is always the fallacy. Use dark magic to fight creatures of darkness and demons and the like. It only led to war—vicious and long. When it was done, there were two races—drows and elves. Drows lost themselves. The war turned from elves and became a civil war of drows between those wanting to abandon the use of all dark magic and those who wished to continue on. The war was so immense that is almost destroyed all drow, elves, and other fae.

"The drow civil war ended. We abandoned, and rightly so, the use of dark magic for any reason whatsoever. However, it left our race stained forever. The stain of that use of dark magic by our ancestors. Fae see it as a mark of shame. We see as our proud birthright. We were so staunchly against evil that we made war against our own kind in a war that almost destroyed us all. We see that as an honorable history."

"Did all drows agree with the outcome of the civil war?"

"No. One race did not, and tried to continue. We drows view them as enemies to this day. Night drows. Their skin is dark purple from continued use in the dark arts, though they claim it is for good. It is also why we drows became much more interested in religion than even elves. We have a strong cleric class. We recognize how even the most noble drow among us is vulnerable to the basest temptations that reside in the soul of us all.

"But I did not tell you that history, young human, only for you to know about drow history and the temptation of dark magic. There were plenty of other elves too. Night elves. Celestial elves, and star elves."

"Why did their ancestors not become drows?"

"Good question. Maybe one day they will transform into night drows."

"Night elves," Traveler said to himself. "Nocturnal elves."

Dr'raen nodded. "That is it exactly. Drows are often called night elves by humans."

"And get punched in the mouth."

The drow cleric grinned. "That too."

"What is the scariest creature you ever encountered in the magic lands?" Traveler asked the drow cleric.

"How is this conversation even remotely productive?"

"I was told that the most destructive on land is a land kraken."

"Land kraken?" Dr'raen scoffed. "They are so rare and when you encounter the larger, more frightening sea cousins you will not think a land kraken is so scary."

"You encountered a real sea kraken?"

"And roc—"

"The giant bird the size of a mountain that can blot out the sun."

The drow laughed. "And manticore."

"Manticore!"

Other fae turned to look at the two men standing with their backs against the wall of the main receiving street of the city. Everyone had gathered to see the arriving elfin caravan. Such arrivals were common and did not usually attract the attention of visitors and residents but these elves were renowned.

"Sprite storm," Dr'raen said.

"What is that?"

"When sprites run at high speed in a circle, they can create a cyclone to suck a human like you off the ground. No, the scariest thing I ever encountered was a fairy storm."

"Fairies? I used to like them, then not, now I like them again because I know their nature. But how are they scary?"

"Millions of them in an attacking swarm? That, young human, is a gruesome death I would not wish upon even an elf. Blot out the sun? They can blot out the sky with their numbers. Pull your skin apart, fly down your throat, nose, ears—"

The same fae turned and gave them scolding stares. Traveler and Dr'raen looked at each other trying not to laugh.

The first elves he saw were tall and had pale skin. Whether dark hair, blond or white they all looked very similar with their matching armor and attire. They were the same race of elves he saw battle the drows and goblins before—high elves.

The next party of elves clad in elfin armor wore bright blue attire. Their skin was not as pale but their eyes were bluer than the boy had ever seen. Dr'raen told him they were water elves. The last were woodland elves. Their attire seemed to be made from green leaves of trees.

All their armor was impressive and they made their way down the packed streets.

"What makes these elves so special, Mr. Dr'raen?"

"Elfin basilisk hunters by vocation and one of the high elves is a gorgon hunter."

The drow saw the amazement in the boy's face. "I could talk to them," Traveler said.

"There is no medicinal cure for the magic death-gaze of either. You see them and you die as a block of stone. There is not even magic to reverse the evil deed."

"Then how do they kill them?"

"That is the secret of a hunter. There are the same hunters among drows, though very rare as we are less likely to come across the creatures. Such hunters are revered by all fae. You should join them. After they settle into their lodging, they will likely occupy the nearest tavern for some time, long into the night, with stories."

"Thanks Mr. Dr'raen. I will do that."

The drow cleric watched the boy head off after the elves, following the fae crowd.

The elves did take over a tavern, as they mesmerized all inside and those listening outside with their exploits.

"These gorgons have their own worshippers as black and blind as the creatures. They see with magic like eyeless hags and are equally cannibalistic. We had to deal with both the creature and a dozen worshippers."

The high elf reveled at the attention. With his stories he was higher than a king holding court to adorning followers.

Traveler sat in a corner of tavern listening to all their stories far past midnight. By the time even the elves were ready for bed, the crowd had grown from day fae to include night fae such as brownies, night fairies, and frowning full-bearded halfling men with pointy hats called haltija, a clan of them called a väki.

The elves were indeed traveling back to Faë-Land and the next morning they began hiring promptly at dawn, even though they all had but an hour night's sleep. Until their arrival, Traveler had been the only human he knew of in the secret city but other humans arrived—berserkers, and members of the elfin caravan. He did not know if they hired because he was a human or a healer, but he was hired.

As the caravan's head healer's assistant, he accompanied a thin woodland elf to the livery stables to inspect the caravan's pack animals—giant boars.

"You, human."

One of the high elves stood at the stable's entrance. Traveler and the woodland elfin healer turned to him.

"Is it true you lodge with a drow?" the high elf asked. The woodland elf glanced at the boy.

"Why? It has nothing to do with this. I was on another caravan and he was a member," Traveler said.

"You are banned from being part of this caravan for associating with drows."

"Banned?"

"That is the rule."

"Why?! That's not fair."

"No, it's not, but I'm doing it anyway. Go home, human."

The high elf left the stables.

"I am sorry, human. You would have been a fine addition but I am only the healer, not the steward. He is."

Traveler stormed out of the stables.

When he returned to his room at a fae inn, he marched in, still angry, and threw himself onto his cot. He and the drow shared the room with a bird man, who was always sick in bed and a squirrel man who read all day. Dr'raen already knew what had happened.

"Don't fret, young human. They won't make it if they don't take you."

"They banned me because they said I lodged with a drow. What a stupid caravan."

"They will reconsider."

"How do you know? No. It's over. I will have to wait for another."

"I will be leaving in the morning."

Traveler sat up. "Leaving?"

"Yes. It is time. My last lesson to you is when you talk to a drow, regardless of the clan, talk with them as if annoyed. To do otherwise is seen as an insult. You are on the path to understanding all of drow-kind."

"Thank you, Mr. Dr'raen."

"Visit me in Faë-Land when you have a chance. You are resourceful. The village of Blue Mist. Spend some time among drow and continue your training."

"I would like that."

"A drow would never join a caravan run by an elf and an elf would never join one run by a drow."

"What about a human?"

"Human, dwarf, centaur, any but an enemy."

"You will be missed, sir."

"Be wary of star elves. Until we meet in Blue Mist then."

"Yes, sir." The boy shook the drow cleric's hand.

The elfin caravan of Lake Pegasi marched from Last Keep City in two days and Traveler was its chief healer's assistant.

The caravan was a thousand-man party of woodland, water, and high elves. The human berserkers did not join them, as they were hired by another caravan bound for one of the kingdoms in the Seven Empires, as soldiers in some war.

Traveler did return to the fae city of Arion's Spear—the kingdom with a mammoth white rock statue of a horse on its hind legs, reaching for the heavens; a golden spear wound around its body and pointed upward. As before, the valley was filled with elves, sprites, and other fae all the way to the large castle entrance. For some reason, fae eyes were on him as the only human.

"Why are they looking at me, sir?" he asked the woodland elf healer.

"Humans do not make this far in Faë-Land Minor. They are merely surprised."

They entered the bustling fae city and Traveler was immediately overcome by the crowds of fae—average human-sized ones, giants, some flying, humanoid, animal-like, humanoid animals, fairies. The flood of languages—humanoid, chirps, grunts, purrs, barks, singing. The blast of different smells in his nose, from aromatic to pungent and foul. So many people and animals. Traveler felt as if he were suffocating. A hand on his shoulder. The woodland elf pulled him off the street into a cul de sac in front of a shop.

"We can wait here," the woodland elf said. "I will watch the group and we can join them when they reach their destination."

"Why are we here, sir?"

"For our caravan master."

"I thought it was the high elf leader."

"He is but the steward."

"I did not thank you for helping change his mind about me."

"It was no burden. I needed a healer assistant and you have a good reputation in Last Keep."

"I do?"

"You do. Your knowledge and skill in the healing arts was attested to by many fae."

Traveler had seen centaurs before in Last Keep and on caravan, but never had he seen a winged centaur! The fae was wonderful in his eyes with a perfect physique, carefully groomed hair, golden band on his head, and angelic wings. The boy was drawn to him and ran to get closer. He had so many questions. Suddenly, there was blackness.

Traveler lay on the ground gasping for breath. He felt something wet on his arm and realized that the flying centaur had woken him by urinating on him. The boy jumped up, disgusted and stumbled down, holding his chest. The winged centaur had kicked him.

"Pegataur!" another centaur yelled at him with the elves of his caravan standing around him.

"What is wrong? It is only a human," Pegataur said.

"The boy is a member of our caravan."

"A slave?"

"A healing assistant."

"Look how weak their frames are. I could have kicked in his entire body and killed him."

"Why would you do that?" the woodland elf healer asked.

"Because I can."

"You should be elsewhere, centaur," the woodland elf said with contempt.

"What if I chose not to?"

In the blink of an eye both woodland elf and flying centaur were aiming arrows from their bows at each other. Traveler had never seen movement so fast and did not know where their weapons magically appeared from.

"The age-old question," Pegataur said with a grin. "Who is faster?"

"Who is better?" the woodland elf said.

"Pegataur withdraw!" the centaur caravan master yelled. "You kill one of them and I will kill you."

"We will kill you!" the high elf steward said. He too aimed an arrow from a long bow at the flying centaur.

All the other elves joined him. Pegataur lowered his bow and the woodland elf did the same.

"You elves are partial to your pets. I will leave yours alone. I would recommend you give it a bath."

Traveler rubbed his chest, glaring at Pegataur. The flying centaur jumped into the air, his giant wings flapping but creating no wind. He grinned at the boy a last time.

"See to it I never see you again, human."

The flying centaur flew away from them all like a projectile.

Traveler would not meet the flying centaur again for many years, but he would often hear of the vile Pegataur from other caravans, especially other centaurs who despised him and his evil deeds. Traveler made the note to himself that a fae so beautiful in outer appearance was actually so dark in their heart. He took it to be a lesson that might save his life in the future: Do not be fooled by outer beauty, or outer ugliness.

"Ignore him, human," the centaur said to him as he trotted closer. His skin had a golden tan clad with muted golden armor on his torso. His hair and beard were black and flowing. "He hates humans, he hates fae who work with humans, he hates fae who work with other fae, outside of centaur-kind. Many call him Pegataur the Vile. The name is well deserved."

By the time the Caravan of Lake Pegasi reached Faë-Land Major, they were five-thousand strong, all elves save their accomplished centaur caravan master, Therolus, and Traveler. They were a caravan of archers, knights, shield men, and trident bearers, but thought it odd that there were no wizards. He thought of it because Mr. Shane of the Caravan of Anfall Gates told him no caravan could make to the end of the Trail without at least one wizard.

Traveler was happy to be a member of the elfin caravan. He learned so much about his elfin comrades and elfin-kind in general. He even got to practice a bit of elvish with his woodland elfin healer. At the moment, he marched at the elf's side. Already they could see the beginnings of the Great Forest in the far distance. It would be the furthest he'd ever been on Titan's Trail.

They heard the first elfin scream.

Elves fell to the ground. The shadowy attacker moved quicker in the tall grass than even they could react.

"Run!" the woodland elf healer yelled at him.

"But—"

"Run! We will fight the creature! You get to the Forest!"

Traveler did so as the elfin healer drew his dagger. All he heard were screams and commotion as he ran as fast as he could. He glanced back only once to see their grand centaur caravan master ripped in half from the waist, separating his human half from the lower horse body. The elfin caravan was in a frenzy of terror.

Two hours of running. The screams long gone. But something was chasing him!

The boy ran faster still but his stamina was quickly waning. He had first seen the bright green-leaved trees towering more than one hundred feet in the air more than a week ago when his caravan first came out of the valley from Faë-Land Major. His clothes in tatters, feet bare and raw, sweat and tears in his eyes.

In his mind, he had convinced himself if only he could get to the threshold of the Great Forest, he might have a chance. A chance for life. He ignored the pain, the fatigue, fear that the creature may be right at his back to throw himself with one final burst of energy into the Forest. He fought his own body which wanted to lie prone on the ground and pass out to crawl through the four-foot blades of grass. He saw it. He crawled and pulled himself across the greenish dirt to a single giant daisy at the foot of a giant tree with a trunk tens of feet wide. The daisy itself was at least nine feet high.

The boy reached it and threw his back against its stem—firm but he could almost make it sway back if he had the strength. A dew droplet landed on his forehead, falling from one of the giant daisy's petals. But there was no time to study the giant flora of the Great Forest, or wonder if any giant insects might be nearby that might take offense to him taking temporary residence under the canopy of its petals. Traveler stared at the giant blades of grass he had crawled through.

His eyes could make out a form slowly pushing through. First a vague shadow, then what appeared to be a man's face became more visible. The creature had a man's face but its eyes were black as night. Its smile revealed not one but three rows of yellowed, ragged teeth. One of its clawed hands came through the giant grass to set on the ground.

There was no energy in the boy. But there was no fear either. He was too tired to be afraid. Traveler was content to simply await his inevitable end. He had cheated fate so many times before. Caravans lost, but he was always one of the survivors. Not this time. He would join his caravan in the after-life.

The creature's eyes widened as it noticed something behind him. Traveler was too weak to turn to look. A light of such intensity flashed. The boy yelled as he closed his own eyes tightly with all his might but the light still was blinding. He heard the creature yell too, but knew the yell was of its death.

PART FIVE

THE GIANT FOREST

The Great Uncharted Magical Lands

CHAPTER TWELVE

Caravan of Sky Elves

Traveler had curled up his body to shield himself from the intense light. Then it was gone.

"The creature is dead, human," a voice said.

His eyes opened but he was still blinded. As the seconds passed, his sight returned and there stood an elf of a race he had never seen before. He stood tall at over six feet, slim frame, his dress had a geometric construction and was a silver white. The elf's white hair reached his waist, his skin pale, and so were his eyes then they turned a gray white.

Traveler looked up, noticing. More elves floated down from the sky. Most were men but others were female. Their attire was different—grays and blues, flowing over their bodies. Their skin was equally pale and their hair was black, browns, or blond. The boy stood to his feet at the giant tree they gathered.

"You must be the most fortunate human alive," one of the other elves said. "The chances of our caravan being above and observing. Deciding to intervene on your behalf, when we had no reason to. You are a lucky human, indeed. Crawling manticores are deadly fast and thoroughly efficient in their killing. Your elfin caravan was no better than a human one in their defenses."

Traveler turned to look in the direction of his old caravan.

"They are all dead," one of the female elves said.

Traveler's face held a deep sadness.

"Should we leave him?" another elf asked the white elf.

"Why would we save him, then leave him here in the Great Forest to die?" the white elf said. He shook his head. "Human, I am Sol-ren the star elf. My comrades are cloud elves of the kingdom of Nimbus Blades. You will accompany our flying caravan of my kingdom of Phoenix Titan. What was your title in the elfin caravan?"

"I was a healer's assistant, sir."

The star elf looked at the others. "There. A healer's assistant. He can attend to our own humans. And he is well-mannered. I say he will do nicely in a royal flying caravan. It is settled. We return above." The star elf stepped forward to stare at the spot where the land manticore was vaporized. "Nothing will grow there for ages after we are both dust, human."

He stood straight and pointed to the cloud elves. "Hold him properly. I doubt the human has flown before into the clouds."

The cloud elf lifted Traveler as they flew straight up, through the sky, into thick clouds, and emerged. Never had he seen anything like it. A giant castle floating high above the clouds anchored to clouds themselves. Scores of camps, elves, and beasts walked on the clouds as if they were as solid as the earth.

"You will not be able to walk on the clouds as we do, human. Your place will be in the castle," the cloud elf said.

He was set down on the open courtyard of the rear of the castle. Several human men ran to the cloud elf.

"Attend to the human," the cloud elf said to them. "Who remains as the chief healer to the humans?"

The men looked at each other nervously.

"Never mind. Settle him in."

The cloud elf unhanded Traveler and rose in the air. The boy noticed that the elf stood on his own small cloud, flying above them all and away. Traveler turned to his human minders. The men stood there as if wondering what to do.

"Do you wish for me to settle into where I will camp?"

"Yes, yes, yes, sir," the men said and led the Traveler through the busy court.

There were many humans hard at work scrubbing, washing, or stocking wagons with magical wings. There were flying chariots, giant catapults, cannons, and crossbows. There were giant metal golems standing lifeless in formation. There were humans polishing golden spears, javelins, daggers, swords; all strewn on the marble grounds. Most of the men at work had noticed him, but kept working, glancing up occasionally, and quickly as he was led through.

The men led him to empty quarters and left him at a cot in a row of cots. They nodded, smiled, and promptly left. There was not a person to be seen. All the men were outside working. He sat down for a moment. The loss of his centaur-led elfin caravan had hit him. Another dead caravan.

After a time, he found himself looking out the windows of the quarters, no glass, curtains, or shutters, just holes in the stone of the structure. Human men feverishly working.

"What are you thinking?"

Traveler imagined fae enjoyed appearing from nowhere to startle a human, but he was immune to the prank. He turned to see an elderly cloud elf.

"Nothing at all, sir. Other than the loss of my old caravan and all its members."

"Elves?"

"Woodland, water, and high elves. A centaur as caravan master."

"My apologies. Travel along the Trail is a deadly business. No less so for fae than humans. Those who travel by land are, in my mind, foolish. I do not mean to be disrespectful to their memory."

"They had no wizards amongst them."

"None?"

"No."

"Then you share my assessment."

"They allowed me to escape."

"Yes. A noble act in the end." The cloud elf looked out the window himself. "I observed a note of disapproval in your face as I watched you from the court. The humans are not slaves if that was where your thoughts were going. They can leave and return to your Lands of Man whenever they wish."

"They seem especially servile."

The cloud elf looked Traveler in the eye.

"They are not you." The elf stepped away from the window. "Follow me. I will give you a tour of the castle. The humans no longer have their own healer, so that role will be assigned to you. Unfortunately, he died in an accident. I have only known you, human, for mere moments but doubt you will be as clumsy as he to step off our cloud foundation to your death.”

The floating castle served many purposes for the many flying caravans that traveled in the skies from Faë-Land to Atlantea—staging area, supply market, and rest area. As flying caravans and their lords came and went, Qiro, the elderly cloud elf that met young Traveler, was the permanent steward of the castle and master of all within its walls. He was diplomat, general, merchant, wizard, and sage. Often, he would make his rounds and greet visitors with the human at his side.

“I am Qiro, the master of this castle under the Kingdom of Nimbus Blades.”

Traveler stood behind the elf, quietly, and like him, held his hands clasped behind his back. Elves were fae that loathed the handshakes and hugging greetings fond of by humans, dwarves, and sprites. Greetings were no more than nods.

For the first time Traveler met plant people. The party of humanoid plants arrived from the Chasm of Flowers. Among them were spidery, dog-sized plants that he learned were their “animal companions.”

“We are honored to be among the cloud elves above our lands.” The plant man was not speaking. A magical band around his neck read his thoughts and spoke to the elf aloud.

"My aid will show you to your quarters," Qiro said.

Traveler was the castle's chief, and only, healer to all its human servants. But the human men always worked and were healthy, whether because of drink, magic or both. Qiro elevated his status to be the cloud elf's right hand in attending to non-royal visiting parties or those with nobility recognized by the elves.

Traveler was fortunate to have his own aid. A fae he had taken under his wing. Froth was an urisk. In appearance like a satyr or smaller stature, with a human torso and shaggy goat legs. An elfin party had snatched the urisk from the wild for a pet but grew tired of the lonesome fae quickly. Urisks were extremely introverted but also able fae guardians of the woodlands and especially of animals.

"Will your companions remain with you, sir?" Traveler asked the twelve plant people. Qiro had already left them for his other duties.

"Yes, we are never apart."

Traveler led them down the vast hallway with his own urisk aid following along.

"Mr. Froth, check with the kitchen to make sure their meals are being attended to."

"Yes, Master Traveler." The urisk ran off ahead of them and down another hallway.

"Humans among cloud elves," a plant man said.

"Yes, I have been here almost six months."

"Have you ever visited our lands?"

"No, sir. The Chasm of Flowers, is it?"

"Do you eat meat or vegetables?"

Traveler turned to look at the plant men. They had no eyes, or face as such. The boy looked at where eyes would be with a grin.

"You are trying to trick me, sir. I am a meat eater, of course. Does this mean I would be allowed to visit your Chasm of Flowers?"

The bodies of the plant men shook and swayed. Traveler confirmed with Qiro later in the day—the plant people were indeed laughing.

Traveler's spirits were high after spending most of the day with the plant people, conversing and learning about their lands, people, and the many creatures of their subterranean realm.

"Mr. Froth, the stories I will have to tell from being here," the boy said as he sat on his cot relaxing for the night.

"Yes, Master Traveler," the urisk said. "Fae are very fond of good stories."

"Yes, Master Traveler. No, Master Traveler."

The smile disappeared from the urisk's face as he crawled under the covers into the cot next to Traveler.

Traveler's status had been elevated but he remained in the human quarters. Well over sixty men and Traveler's urisk in the giant room. Traveler sat up on his cot, his feet resting on the marble floor. The man speaking gave Traveler a dirty look, as did several men who stood with him. All other men sat or lay quietly on their own cots watching.

"We have been here for many years and we were never been asked to be an aid to any of the cloud elves, or get our own fae slave," the man yelled.

"Mr. Froth is my aid, not my slave. You know that because you were there when I rescued him from the elves mistreating him."

The man gave him a dismissive wave.

"I do not need to stay here with you," Traveler said. "I had nothing to do with Mr. Qiro choosing me for the role he has put me in. All I did was be rescued by them after my caravan was slaughtered. Mr. Froth, the men here do not wish our company. We will go elsewhere."

"Yes, Master Traveler."

The urisk followed as Traveler grabbed his one satchel and walked out of the human quarters. The castle had quarters for fae servants such as grunts and a race of fae similar to brownies called domovoi, with thick mustaches and beards touching the ground but Traveler decided to simply find a corner in the courtyard outside the quarters and step into his small-realm.

Qiro always walked fast and he walked fast when giving instructions.

"Tomorrow, a caravan flies in from one of the northern kingdoms. A very delicate meeting. The kingdoms of moon and night elves, but the kingdoms' names must never be spoken. You will oversee service of both the fae and human servants," he said.

"Yes, Mr. Qiro," Traveler said as he scribbled notes in his book, effortlessly following the elf.

The boy stopped and looked out the window.

"Mr. Traveler?" Qiro said and joined him.

A trio of star elves kicking a black ball between them in play. The boy's face had a look of shock.

"That is an animal they are kicking."

"Mr. Traveler, you are to ignore them."

Traveler dropped his book and stormed out of the main hall.

"Mr. Traveler!"

The boy ignored his cloud elf master. He stepped onto the grassy royal courtyard and marched in the direction of the star elves. They had seen them and waited, watching him with squinted eyes and pursued lips. When

Traveler reached the ball on the ground, he picked it up. One eye, then a second opened. Traveler was holding a black fox. As he tucked the animal in his arms, he glared at the star elves.

"How would you like it if someone kicked you around, helpless?" Traveler snapped at them.

"How would you like it I kicked you out of the castle, literally?" one star elf said starting towards the boy, but he was restrained by another.

"Mr. Traveler." The star elves looked past the boy. Behind him stood Mr. Qiro. "Please follow me to continue your duties."

The black fox in his arms buried its head into Traveler's chest. Its eyes were teared up.

"That is not a fox, human," a star elf said. "You have in your arms a little goblin who will devour you in the night."

Traveler stopped to say something else to the star elves.

"Mr. Traveler!" Qiro called, already back in the castle hall.

"Humans have a fondness for furry little things," a star elf said to his comrades. "Even ones that will kill them. Take the goblin with you, human."

Traveler angrily went back inside. He saw the cloud elf elder and ran after him. They went into one of the rooms, stepped in, and Qiro slammed the door.

"Mr. Traveler, your behavior and judgment has been exemplary, until now."

"Mr. Qiro, is this creature a goblin or not? I do not believe the star elf lies because I have seen a goblin."

"You have?"

"Yes, Mr. Qiro. I saw elves and goblins battle, kill each other. I know of no goblins that appear as foxes. And I know of no elf who would kick one around, playing like a little human child. Goblins kill elves, and elves kill goblins. Or am I incorrect, sir?"

"You are correct, Mr. Traveler."

"Then what is it I am holding?"

"A race of shape-shifting fae called by many names. Phooka, pooka, púca. It does not matter. They may not be goblins but they have the disposition of hobgoblins and mischievous destructive nature of any imp, pixy, or gremlin."

"Is it dangerous?"

"Mr. Traveler, you seem to have a talent for collecting fae no one wants. Keep your creature but I never want to see it. I doubt it will harm you after you risked your life on its behalf. And remember, human, that is exactly what you did. You are a human boy, not even a full adult in your species. You confronted not one, but three star elves. Three star elf warrior knights. I would not be so bold."

"You are a cloud elfin wizard, Mr. Qiro. They would have been no match for you. I saw the fear in their eyes."

"Mr. Traveler, people who are afraid of you can kill you nonetheless. Never do that again. Anger does not suit a human on a floating city of elves and fae."

"Yes, Mr. Qiro. I am sorry."

"When you can defeat an elf in battle then you can be so bold. When you defend against a magic spell attack, you can be so bold. Until then your human intellect is your best defense. That is why I picked you for my role as aid."

"Yes, Mr. Qiro."

"Go put your creature away and let us return to our duties."

"Yes, Mr. Qiro."

Traveler enjoyed walking with Qiro on his rounds. It was his chance to speak with the cloud elf steward without interruption. He knew his new master enjoyed the conversation equally.

"What really is Atlantea?" Traveler asked. "Why do so many covet it? Is it simply treasure? I cannot believe that. Maybe for humans, maybe dwarves, but not elves or other fae."

"You are so correct, Mr. Traveler. The fabled kingdom of Atlantea is much more than a realm of treasure. It is a realm to other realms. Its people are from the time of the Titans and beyond. In fact, they are not from Pan-Earth at all."

"Master Qiro!" an elf appeared in a panic. "Lord Sol-ren's flying caravan is landing."

Sol-ren was far more than a star elf; he was a star elf over-lord. Traveler did not know the full meaning of his noble title, likely in command of a vast army, the elf returned to the castle with a full contingent of star elf riders. The star elf leader had a strange dog-like creature with the paws of a panther and a golden necklace around its neck.

A full banquet for the star elf and his men was in session. As both feast and a meeting, elves of all kind reported the news to Sol-ren directly of other flying caravans throughout the skies, battles, dangers, and gossip. Traveler pretended to manage the servants of fae and humans without concern of matters of state, but he secretly listened to every word being spoken. All was in elvish but Qiro told him months ago that every elf on the floating castle knew that he understood elvish fine.

Qiro always stood behind the star elf lord to directly attend to any requests and to watch over the banquet hall.

"Master Qiro!" Sol-ren yelled with a goblet in hand.

"Yes, m'lord."

"Where is this human of yours? You, human, attend me."

Traveler for a split second wondered if he should pretend he hadn't heard or not. He turned and ran to the main banquet table. Sol-ren sat in the center. On either side were this warrior knights.

"I heard about what you did, human," he said. "A human unafraid of us mere star elves."

The other elves of the court laughed.

"What makes you so brave, human?" Sol-ren asked.

"And for a blackish goblin," one of his knights added.

"Not bravery, sir, lord, I mean."

"The title of lord is for elves alone. Sir is fine, human."

"Yes, sir."

"Master Qiro tells me that you truly are a healer. You call yourself a healer's assistant but he says your skills and knowledge for a human is far beyond most human healers. Master Qiro, I borrow your aid."

"Yes, m'lord," Qiro said.

"You, human, will travel with my warrior knights into the Great Forest. You cannot hide amongst the clouds forever. You will accompany a meager caravan for no less than treasure. Perhaps use your healing skills at the side of one of our elfin master healers as an additional treasure to you. Master Qiro, get the human ready to fly."

"Yes, m'lord."

The party of elves descended to the edge of the Great Forest. Dozens of elves riding griffins. Traveler sat on the back of one giant griffin, the only human in the party. In fact, there was no other fae besides cloud elves.

They landed in an elfin camp of giggling star elves. The boy surveyed the scene as the fantastic beasts landed softly on the earth. There was the structured elfin camp but the remnants of another camp scattered everywhere at the base of the gigantic trees. He realized that the star elves were laughing at the carnage of human bodies.

A few cloud elves accompanied the boy as he walked through the bodies. He had never seen what he did with his own eyes before. All the dead were human. Some had grown to the size of giants, or parts of their body had. One man's head exploded from its gigantic size. Another man's belly had burst apart. Other were suffocated by their own gigantic hands, necks, one man's tongue had ripped open his head from the inside. There were men who had shrunk and something had crushed their bodies into the grass—stepped on them.

"So many humans still to this day do not know they cannot eat certain fae food," one smiling star elf said who followed after them.

Traveler said nothing as he continued to walk through the remnants of the human camp.

"There were a few humans alive but they since died," the star elf said still pointing.

Traveler led them to where he pointed. He knelt beside three bodies. The men were dead. In their case parts of their body had shrunk. One man was all but a head, his body below the neck shrunk to nothingness; the other two were piles of flesh, their insides had shrunk.

The boy stood. "What was it you thought I could do here?" Traveler asked.

"We do not know," the star elf replied. "They are your kind."

"Do you have a shovel?" Traveler asked.

"That we have," a cloud elf said and summoned a piece of a cloud from above. The cloud became the form of a shovel and he handed it to the boy. It was as solid as iron.

For the hours that passed, Traveler alone dug graves and buried the bodies of the human men. The star elves engaged in silly horseplay to pass the time. The cloud elves simply watched his every move.

More elves had flown down from the floating city. A group of woodland elves, but they were the unfriendliest Traveler had ever encountered. They moved through the area, sometimes glancing suspiciously at him, and kneeling on the ground to touch the earth. Traveler watched the woodland elfin scouts as they walked through the destroyed camp. One began to say something but a cloud elf quieted him with a gesture: the human can understand elvish. He could no longer hear their words; obviously due to some concealing spell.

Night approached as Traveler buried the last corpse. He stood up and straightened his back. Backbreaking work gravedigging was. By now many more elves had joined the camp. A new party of night elves arrived—dressed in purple. He had hoped to see his first celestial elves but the only other race of elves that joined them were forest elves. They all searched for something.

"A survivor!" a voice rang out.

Traveler ran in its direction. He noticed balls of light above him and looked up. The star elves were magically lighting his path. A man lay on the dirt ground but he was already encircled by elves, including Sol-ren. Traveler knelt down beside the man.

"Are you wounded?" Traveler asked.

The man looked at him, then up at the elves. He closed his eyes. "My chest."

Traveler had not seen it at first. He had to lift his tunic to see that the man's chest looked to be made of glass. He could see his organs and blood moving.

"What did this?" Traveler asked.

"It was the sprites that attacked them," Sol-ren replied for the man.

The man nervously looked up at the elves then at Traveler. "Yes. They attacked us."

Traveler lurched back as the man's shadow moved on its own and a form grew from it. The night elves were shadow elves! One rose pulling a necklace from the man's pants.

"Strange place to hide a necklace," the shadow elf said. At the end of the necklace was a trinket in the form of a box. "What is this?"

The shadow elf ripped it off the necklace, threw it, and a doorway appeared before them.

"Bring him!" Sol-ren yelled.

A star elf kicked the magic doorway open. The elves carried the man and pushed Traveler into the pocket-realm. A floating castle of many, many stories. Each floor spinning one way, the floor above or below another. The entire structure spinning from top to bottom to back up.

The elves stormed the castle, both star and cloud.

"Beware of booby traps!" Sol-ren yelled. "We must find it!"

The night and woodland elves watched Traveler and the man.

"There is a stray sword on the ground there," a night elf said.

One of the woodland elves reached down for it and was immediately impaled through the head.

"A mimic!" the elves yelled.

They drew their swords as the creature leapt at them, transforming into a blob-like form and its sword appendage fatally slashed another elf. Its form was amorphous except for the multiple sword appendages that attacked the elves like tentacles from an octopus.

Star elves appeared out of invisibility. The man threw dirt at them and the elves screamed.

"Save me!" the wounded human yelled at Traveler.

"No one can save you!" a cloud elf yelled raising his sword to strike as he stepped into the realm. Both Traveler and the man disappeared.

The dirt thrown at the star elves were magic metal mites. They screamed as they quickly stripped off their armor and dropped their swords. The metal of both rusted away and turned to dust.

Beside the one sword mimic, there were more. A chest mimic that had already eaten one elf, a table mimic that used its legs as both spears and tentacles, and a flying shield mimic. Soon all the different elfin races ran into the pocket-realm for battle.

"We do not have much time," the man said.

"What is happening here? Why did they kill your men?"

"It is our fault. We tried to double-cross them so they killed them. Forced them to eat the deadly fae food. Star elves are very good at torture."

"Double-cross?"

"I am an alchemist and they needed me to break into a vault they stole."

"We need to get you from here."

"You do not understand. The star elves stole a vault from celestial elves."

"What is in the vault?"

"A piece of a Titan sword."

"I do not know the significance of what you say. I do not know why the elves brought me here."

"They needed a witness, but I ruined that plan." the man said, laughing. "You were to be the trustworthy human to tell the celestial elves what you saw."

"Witness? Bringing me here made me a witness. Leaving me at the city would not have."

"What are you?"

"What?"

"You are not a human. Your inner organs are not right. What creature are you?"

The man's hands grabbed Traveler throat to strangle him. The hold was like a vice. Traveler watched as the man's face start to change. The man's face was turning into an exact imitation of his own.

"Not a nice doppelgänger," a voice said from Traveler back.

A black fox jumped over the boy and attacked the man-creature. The man screamed as the black fox, now a goat-headed gorilla, pounded the creature's head to a pulp. Traveler saw one and grabbed the pouch from the man-creature's body. The phooka returned to his form of a black fox as they watched. The man was now in the form of grayish humanoid whose body resembled the texture of clay. More pouches appeared on the ground around him, many more. Traveler swept them up in his own invisible magic bag.

"Are not doppelgängers cousins of trolls?"

"Yes, they are Master Traveler," the black fox said with human eyes.

"I thought elves and trolls are enemies."

"They are, but these are not good elves."

Traveler stepped through the portal onto the floating city. The doorway closed behind with a hint of smoke in the air. He immediately walked to the work yard of the human servants.

The men saw him approach from the castle halls. Since he no longer stayed in the human quarters, they only saw him at Qiro's side during rounds and specific duties with the boy overseeing their work.

"I have one question," he said to the men. "Are you able to leave this floating cloud city whenever you wish?"

There was silence and Traveler could see the tears growing in the eyes of some of the men.

"Please explain," Traveler asked.

"We have been here too long," one man said. The one who challenged Traveler that day and caused the boy to abandon lodging with the men. "If we set foot in the Lands of Men, we will grow and die within days of arrival. This is a realm of magic and we are humans not of magic. Time effects fae and human differently. One must understand that. We did but too late. We are prisoners of this castle."

"The elves did not tell you."

"No."

Traveler tossed a pouch to the man. "Then if you are to be a prisoner in the magic lands, make it elsewhere as a prisoner to no one."

Traveler started away but stopped once more.

"Tell me one other thing. The shape-shifter creatures they keep," Traveler began.

"The golden collars around their necks are to control them against their will," another man said. "The creatures are not from this world."

"The celestial and star elves invaded the creatures' world and imprisoned their entire race. Shape-shifters whose power is not of magic," another man said.

"Thank you, men. Safe journey in your new life."

"You as well, Master Traveler."

Traveler returned to the interior of the castle hall.

An enraged Sol-ren ran through a portal into the castle's royal keep. An army of elves followed.

"Qiro!"

The castle's steward came running up the stairs.

"Where is that human?"

"M'Lord, was he not with you?"

"If he were with me, why would I be here asking for him?"

The elder almost swallowed his own tongue.

Sol-ren looked at the other elves. "Can he escape from the castle?"

"No, m'lord."

"How could he escape?"

"There is no way, m'lord. Unless he can fly one of our chariots or wagons."

"Can he?"

"No, m'lord. A human cannot command any of our flying animals."

Sol-ren had already seen the elder cloud elf's face.

"The urisk can!" Sol-ren yelled and ran, followed by every elf in the room.

Urisk held the reins of the white pegasi with all his strength. Traveler sat in the chariot watching the rear. The black fox sat on his lap. The floating city was almost out of view.

"Master Traveler, we can make it all the way to Atlantea," he heard Mr. Froth say.

Boom!

Traveler saw the flash. He grabbed the fox and threw himself at the urisk. All three plunged off the side of the chariot. The chariot exploded, shredding both of the beautiful flying horses into body parts, bones, and blood. Elves never missed when they fired an arrow. There was no reason to believe their aim with a cannon was any less deadly. But never did he think the elves would kill such noble beasts to stop them.

Traveler rode the black gazelle across the barrier and both collapsed. Traveler lay on the grass barely able to breathe. The pooka lay beside him in the form of a rabbit headed pig, smiling with a human mouth.

"Will Mr. Froth live?"

"If I cannot heal him, I will find those who can," Traveler said.

The pooka was no longer beside him. Traveler sat up and saw a black mouse hiding behind him. Traveler looked forward through the barrier toward the great oceans. The bridge to Atlantea to one side. He sat on the beach stretching to the magic waters. A figure came out of invisibility.

Sol-ren crouched down and peered across the invisible barrier. The only indication of its existence was a faint yellow glow hanging above the sand. The star elf tried to punch through it but it repelled him. Traveler heard the bones of the elf's hand shatter. The star elf looked at his hand and smiled.

"Human, you better never leave Atlantea for all your short years of life. I will wait all those years outside Atlantea's kingdom. I will have others wait all those years. Your foot crosses that barrier and we will fly you into the skies to be devoured by the creatures of the clouds. We will cast you into the voids of the heavens as if never to have existed. I will remember you, human."

Traveler pulled the weapon out from his magic pouch—a sheathed sword with glistening glass-like metal. Sol-ren stared at it with shock.

"I will hold onto to this then."

Sol-ren spat at the barrier in front of Traveler. "I will kill you, human."

"Then you will never enter Atlantea, star elf, or your clan!"

Traveler was startled too. He stood and stared at the being behind him, as did Sol-ren. Traveler, for the first time, gazed at an Atlantean.

CHAPTER THIRTEEN

Caravan of Pookas

Young Traveler was nearly nineteen years old.

Traveler climbed up the hill of rocks. His three grinning pooka companions watched from afar.

"Why am I here and you there?" Traveler said from on top of the rocks.

"You will see."

A monstrous arm came out of one of the crevasses and grabbed Traveler. In shock, he instinctively drew his dagger to slash at the creature. At first, he thought it was some type of snake but after he stabbed it, it did look like a giant's arm with pulsating thick veins. It tried to pull him into the crevasse, he stabbed and pushed his body away from it. Long black tentacles grabbed the boy and pulled him away from the arm monster, which yanked itself back into its underground hole.

The three pookas could not stop cackling and rolling on the ground in the form of large black ground hogs with tentacles for arms. Traveler stood there watching them but without anger. This was their nature and there was no changing it. They weren't evil but their spirit was no different than an imp or pixy.

Much later, on another caravan, he would learn the arm monster was called an Il-Belliegha.

Traveler spent many months with the pookas. One led him to two others, the three led him to more. With the shape-shifting sprites he explored the main paths of the Great Forest. The common paths they could travel on their own; the more dangerous ones they traveled with other caravans of the Great Forest, nomadic fae who had done so for ages. Traveler took no risks; he was learning the ways of the Forest and the people who called it their home for eons.

"A caravan master who can travel by land from point to point is more valuable than any other," a pooka told him. "Don't be fooled by flying ones."

"I won't be fooled by the flying ones ever again. Or star elves," Traveler said.

Mr. Froth, the urisk, did not survive his wounds from the elfin cannon blast. But the meek sprite had thanked the human for his loyal and sincere friendship.

"Be careful, Master Traveler. There are bad star elves and good star elves. Bad elves and good ones. Bad goblins and good ones."

"Good goblins?"

"Bad pooka and good ones. Can you tell which one are we, Master Traveler?" The pooka began to cackle.

"I am not sure yet," he said with a smile.

Traveler remembered the day when, for the first time, he walked clad in full fae armor. He had held swords and shields, but never both in full armor. He did not ask the pookas where they "found" it, but he was more than a healer. He was an honorary caravan master even if he was not fully ready for the responsibility yet. That's what he was for the pookas and himself.

The pookas took him many places in the Great Forest like the lands called Vivaria, where giant fae lizards roamed; mountains of perytons, flying beasts with the antlered head and legs of deer and wings and body of a bird; and even to Titan's Fall, the fifth marker on Titan's Trail to Atlantea. But then Traveler had already been to Atlantea and lived there.

Traveler learned that pooka had their own villages, hidden in pocket-realms. His three traveling mates took him to their home lands. Hundreds of pooka occupying a village of tree huts, where the creatures caused mischief all day—throwing things at each other, chasing each other, dancing, singing. Traveler was told that they could drive humans or fae insane with their antics but he didn't mind. It was their nature. They came to realize he was immune to their chaos.

"Good night, Master Traveler!" they would all say. When Traveler lay his head to sleep in a cot he made for himself out of giant grass of the Forest, they went to sleep too—smiling with their human mouths.

In the night, they could all see the stars and they could see streams of light. For Traveler, all he thought of were the elves that traveled in the voids of the heavens.

One morning, the human found a nice branch on a morning walk with his pooka comrades. From it, he carved and fashioned a fine walking stick. He had learned to be quite the performer and they had grown fond of his many stories.

Traveler gathered them all together.

"One day we will have a great mission!" the boy declared, holding his staff up high above his head, pointing to the sky.

Every pooka in the village was enraptured by his words.

"You will be a clan of new pookas. Your names from today and forever will be... darklings!"

"Yes! Yes! Yes!"

The pookas danced and applauded for hours. They never tired of their new name given to them by Traveler. He and the darklings went on many other caravans through the Great Forest.

PART SIX

THE OCEANS OF FÄE-LAND OMNIS

The Empires of Merfolk, Water Fae, and Sirens

CHAPTER FOURTEEN

Caravan of Kobolds

Young Traveler was twenty years old.

The ship bobbed up and down in the ocean, gently for once. In a storm, the vessel could sink dozens of feet and rise hundreds of feet. This was the sailing life in the Oceans Omnis, the lands of merfolk, water fae, sirens, and sea serpents.

Traveler examined and cleaned the cupboards of his healing storage cabin, filled with medicines, herbs, and supplies. The knock on the door was slight as it opened. The ship's captain and a sailor entered. Both fae were Klabautermann, the sea-faring race of kobolds. Hunched, large bodies, ugly faces in human terms, dark leathery skin in their grungy sailor clothing.

"Mr. Traveler," the captain said.

"Yes, captain," Traveler said.

"You behave as a brownie or nisse, constantly tidying what does not need to be. This is a sailing ship, not a royal cottage. One day of rough seas and all your work will be on the floor."

"No, captain, they will not. I have also tied each to their shelf. No fae will die under my watch because I am unable to find the remedy I need."

"If you say, Mr. Traveler. We will take on our new passengers soon."

"To Atlantea."

"Yes. Goblins. Many of them. We wanted to ask again about your decision to stay aboard."

"You do not mind them."

"Goblins, elves, humans. You are all the same to us."

"Are there any fae-folk kobolds are partial to?"

"Dwarves."

"Yes."

"Goblins may not hate humans as they do elves, but they do not like your kind."

"I will stay aboard and perform my duties, captain."

"You would provide healing services to a goblin."

"A patient is a patient."

"I know of no human who would say such a thing."

"You take them aboard and I am a member of your crew."

"I take them on because they are paying handsomely for the privilege, like all others. Coin is coin to me."

"Yes, captain."

"I do not want any trouble, human. You may be a healer but I know you are scheming something. Kobolds can smell it."

"There will be no trouble at all, captain. I will behave as I always do and I have never given you cause to think otherwise, despite what you may or may not be smelling."

The kobolds grinned.

"Yes, Mr. Traveler. See to it that you remain in my good graces."

"I shall, captain."

The goblin caravan arrived to board the next day. The kobold ship was docked at a coastal kingdom not far from Titan's Fall. The fifth marker on Titan's Trail was a gigantic waterfall peak that fell a hundred feet from the shore to the ocean. From far distances it was said to look like an arm from open hand to elbow.

A thousand goblins marched onto the Iron Siren with their dire-wolfs. Hundreds of hobgoblins and Redcaps stayed behind on the shore under the command of a squad of goblins. Once aboard, the ship raised gangplanks and soon moved out to open waters. Goblins, hobgoblins, and Redcaps disappeared into invisibility as they headed back to the Forest.

The ship crew were all kobolds. All had been with Captain Tunik for many years and were a tight crew. Traveler, as a human, would ordinarily never have been allowed aboard but their long-time kobold healer grew too old for the seas and returned to their lands, but not without testing the young man for several trips.

The old healer had to admit to their captain, "The human knows more of healing arts than I do," he said.

The ship was nowhere as huge as others, but had sailed longer than most. Despite its name it was not made of iron but a wood as strong as any elfin or dwarven metal. The top deck with the captain's cabin, bridge and navigation room, deck mate's quarter; galley, and ship's stores and cargo hold were manned and guarded by the kobold crew at all times. Traveler had his own cabin next to the galley, adjacent to the infirmary.

The accommodations would be tight for the goblins and their creatures in the lower decks in between, but they would not mind. All the goblins cared about was getting to Atlantea as quickly as possible. But even sailing with the best winds with no attacks from mermaids or sea creatures still meant sailing for at least four months.

Traveler had expected it, even though he had not gone any further than his cabin or the galley once the goblins boarded.

"A human."

A half-dozen goblins entered the infirmary, dressed as if going into battle. Traveler sat at a single table facing the door, a book in his hand. He looked up at them for a moment, then returned to his reading.

"Are you seasick?" he asked. "If you are, you can go up to the main deck and hold onto the side to vomit out anything."

"The human is not afraid of goblins," one goblin said to the others.

"Because there is nothing to be afraid of."

His table was smashed to pieces by the blow of the first goblin's forearm. Traveler's eyes moved up from his book to the goblins' faces.

"I will have to let the captain know that you destroyed his favorite table. He will expect you to pay for it or he will throw you overboard."

A goblin threw coins at the human's chest. Traveler picked one of them up from his lap and squeezed it. "Is goblin money worth anything these days?"

The lead goblin laughed. "The human is fine by me. I don't smell any elf on him."

The goblins turned and they filed out of the room.

Goblins at first did not trust there being a human aboard the ship. But he completely ignored them as he went about his daily duties. The captain always ate in the galley with his senior kobolds and the goblin leaders began to join him. Soon other goblins began eat their meals in the large room and to converse. Traveler continued not to mind them.

"Why are you here?" a goblin asked him.

"I am part of the crew, obviously."

"A human in these lands. On a fae ship. In these waters. Do your humans not think you mad?"

"I really do not care. I am here to learn healing arts not possible in my lands. When I return, I will be able to open up a healing academy and become very rich doing so from all that I learn."

"Assuming you live," another goblin said. "These waters have many creatures and sirens that would find a human a tasty meal."

Traveler said nothing as he swallowed the last of his beverage in his mug. "Enjoy your meal, goblins." He stood and left the table.

After that the goblins started not minding Traveler's presence at all. He blended into the background like the kobolds.

"Why do goblins hate humans?" Traveler asked the goblin. Several of them were sitting at his table as they all ate their meal.

"Hate?" The goblin grunted. "You humans are a constant reminder of that future lost. Goblins could have ruled all of Pan-Earth! But the elves."

"You are mad at elves because they did not allow you to slaughter humankind?"

"Yes!"

"You are a wretched race."

The goblin stood up and pulled a dagger from his waist.

Traveler was unafraid. "Put that away. I am not here to battle with you. Wait. Tell about your goblin metal. If I am to be a well-rounded healer, I must know of all fae metals."

The goblin looked at his dagger. "Such as?

"What kind of weapon can cut an elfin or goblin blade?"

"None."

"Stop lying. Celestial elves and maybe star elves have them."

"Night elves too."

"Lying beast."

"If you know, human, why ask?"

"What is this metal they have? Where is that metal found?"

"Why? Even if you had such a blade an elf would run to you, take it from you, and plunge it into your belly, human."

"Yes, that thing they do. I call it 'blink' motion. I know there is a fae term for it. Blink once and they move from point to point, and have done what they have done."

"Goblins can do it too."

"No, you cannot. Where is this magic metal found? That these sky elves have."

"Where you puny humans could never get to it. On another world."

"Other world?"

"Metal from the Titans."

Traveler laughed. "So goblins cannot get at it either."

"The metal is here too, fallen to the earth. The metal from the Titans is guarded by the dwarves. Another in Borea guarded by the Ice People."

"There are no people on Borea."

"Like the Great Forest, there have been fae living there longer than humans."

"Did they side with the elves against your goblin plot?"

The goblin did not answer.

"Then I like these Boreans too," Traveler said with a smile. "I was once told that humans could train to use swords of this metal to defeat elves."

Goblins laughed, except one. The goblin stood and walked to their table.

"No goblin would teach any human such fighting skills."

"Even to fight elves."

"Fight or kill?"

"Fight to kill."

"No goblin would."

"Who then?"

"Are you a healer or swordsman?"

"I have never wielded a sword. I am merely a curious human collecting stories."

"No goblin would but maybe one could pay a half-goblin to. They have far less honor than goblins."

"Half-goblins. I did not know there were such. Where do they hide?"

"Goblins do not hide. Full or half. Damdread is one place."

All the while, Captain Tunik watched Traveler's conversation and smiled.

Traveler used a heated clamping tool to remove the giant leech from the back of the kobold lying on his back on the infirmary's healing table.

"I told you not to be on the main deck without proper clothes," Traveler scolded.

"Just be done with it, human. If not a leech, then a jellyfish. You work the decks; the ocean will throw a creature at you."

Traveler finally pulled the animal from the kobold's skin.

"There. Finally."

They had heard commotion above for minutes. Another kobold burst through the door.

"The captain wants us on deck," he said to the kobold on the table.

Both kobolds raced from the room. Traveler put all his things away and ran after them. He did not like being on the deck but did so when needed. The ocean did not just throw creatures at men from its depths. Creatures from its depths also reached out for men on the deck.

As soon as Traveler reached the main deck, his face was stung by the splashing water across his face. The waters were getting choppier. The captain and his top men stared out over one side. Human eyes were not fae eyes. He saw the shapes but needed his telescope to see better. One destroyed ship floated in the distance, then they saw a second.

Goblins also appeared on the deck and ran to the side for a view.

"What destroyed those ships?" the goblin yelled.

"We saw ships manned by mer-captains but we are not sure it was them," the captain answered.

"Mer-captains?"

"Ship manned by mermen."

"They are that deadly?" the goblin leader asked.

"They can be." The captain yelled at the kobold crew to ready for battle.

"Captain, we are only weeks away from Atlantea."

"I know exactly how far we are, goblin. I am the one taking you there. Get below with your men. My crew will handle any attack on the Iron Siren. We have been doing so for many years."

"Remember, we paid you and there will much more when we arrive."

"Goblin, dead men cannot buy a thing. Get below!"

"Mer-ship!" a kobold yelled.

The ship looked more like a giant cocooned pod than a ship, breaking through the ocean's surface and flying over the kobold ship. The goblin leader was hit with a spear. Kobold crew fired multiple crossbows at the merman vessel. One kobold was hit by another spear but the mer-ship was blown apart by the magic arrows of their giant crossbows. The vessel's mermen crew fell into the ocean or on the deck. The mermen, dressed in armor on their upper torso, were ugly male humanoids with dark fish bodies. Their heads were fitted with metal helmets, blue-green hair, brown teeth, and slits for eyes. Kobold leaped onto the fallen mermen on the deck and threw them overboard before any regained consciousness.

Traveler was already pulling the goblin leader off the deck to safety. The goblin yanked the spear out of his side and held the bleeding.

"That was not smart, goblin. Do you want to bleed to death before I get you to the infirmary?"

"For the pathetic creatures they are, they say that mermen show up at the sight of sinking ships. Are not some of their kind oracles?" the goblin asked.

The healer had no time to answer.

Traveler remembered his conversation with the drow cleric, Dr'raen. How the drow ridiculed him for saying that any land kraken was any danger at all when compared to its larger sea cousin. The human thought the darkness was of arriving storm clouds around them; then saw the single towering eye, many times the size of the entire vessel. The Iron Siren was now being ripped apart by the sea creature. Kobolds dove into the ocean for their lives. Traveler did not know if goblins or dire-wolves could swim, but was sure his own skills were far from adequate. Tunik threw the boy into the vast ocean as tentacles the size of the ship itself passed over them.

The kobolds had them tucked away in their magic pouches—giant water lilies. Each floating lily was large enough for four to five men. Traveler lay on his stomach, drenched. He looked around the ocean and saw kobolds, goblins, and dire-wolves on giant water lilies for as far as the eye could see. The young man turned to look back at the ship at the moment the kraken tossed the vessel into sky—the massive tentacles flailing and reaching, seemingly into the void of the heavens many, many miles above. What was left of the vessel broke into pieces.

"Our beautiful ship," Tunik said.

"Yes, captain," other kobolds said.

The giant water lilies moved the survivors from the titanic creature as its form slowly began to descend into the depths, and its giant tentacles crashed to the water's surface.

"We were too close to the other ships. They attracted the creature somehow and we were unlucky to be nearby."

"We survived, captain," a kobold said.

"Let us hope no merfolk or dark water fae are about," the captain said.

"Where will we drift to?" Traveler asked him.

"An island."

"Sirens?"

"Those islands are in the Sirenic Seas so no need to worry. I hope you got what you wanted from this series of voyages, human. I knew you were scheming all along."

"You are too smart for me, captain. But you have taught me so much. At last, how to escape the destruction of a kraken."

"Not much to learn there, human. Simply avoid the tentacles and the beak, dive, and pray. My beauty, my ship."

"You will build a better one, captain."

"Yes, we will, Mr. Traveler. It is what we kobolds do. Though the money for it will not be coming from these goblins."

PART SEVEN

THE FABLED MAGIC KINGDOM OF

ATLANTEA

The Return of Quest Master

CHAPTER FIFTEEN

Quest Master

The vessel sailed the very void of space. Sol-ren sat on his throne watching a floating circular mirror. The image was of the Pan-Earth above. It was not only a throne room but the captain's bridge of the space-faring ship.

"We will be over Atlantean territory soon, m'lord," one of the star elves in his court said. Many other elves stood in front of the magic watch-mirror.

Sol-ren said nothing. His face looked aged and his eyes tired.

"Tell the celestial elves we are in our sentry position."

"Yes, m'lord," a star elf said. Lit on his forehead were moving elfin symbols. "They will land their fleet within the hour, m'lord."

"M'lord," another star elf spoke up. "Our scheduled communication from the polymorph world is extremely overdue."

"By how long?" Sol-ren asked.

"Six hours, m'lord."

"Send a scouting party."

"M'lord, our normal portal is inactive."

Sol-ren turned to look at the elf. "Inactive?"

"M'lord, we cannot open the portal doorway because it is no longer where it is supposed to be. Our wizards say it is not there."

"Is it inactive or not there? Which one?"

"No longer there, m'lord."

"Then send a scouting party and warriors. Use another portal and land wherever you must."

"Yes, m'lord."

"See to it personally."

The elf nodded and excused himself from the throne command room.

Sol-ren's sleep was stirred in the late hours of the night, but when floating in the black void of the heavens, it is always night. He was never a deep sleeper so often even the slightest noise woke him. This time it was the marching of boots in the hallway outside his quarters. The naked elfess covered herself as his chief elfin aide opened the door and the elfin leaders strolled into his bed chamber. The candle lights flickered on, but not too bright.

"We beg forgiveness, m'lord, for the intrusion."

"What is it?"

"The world of the polymorphs, m'lord. We lost contact with the first party sent. We sent another but we lost contact with them as well."

"And?"

An elfin wizard stepped forward. "Lord, we sent many seeing eyes to the world. Before they could descend through the high clouds, all were ripped apart from flying creatures of no distinct form."

"The creatures have escaped?"

"We believe it to be far graver, m'lord. We believe the planet has been overrun by the creatures."

"Overrun!"

Sol-ren jumped up from his bed and grabbed his nearby robe from a table nearby. As he put it on his naked body, he wrapped the cloth belt tight.

"You are telling me that thousands of some of the best star elf warriors have been slaughtered and the planet is in the hands of these creatures. What of our vessels on the world? We can fly them from here."

"They are in flight, m'lord."

"How many?"

"All of them, m'lord."

"All?"

"Yes, m'lord."

"How many vessels is that?"

"The entire armada is one hundred thousand, m'lord."

Sol-ren felt light-headed and had to collect his thoughts.

"Where is our armada?"

"At the moment, m'lord, they are flying to us."

Sol-ren looked at him in shock.

"M'lord, should we contact the celestial elves?"

"Why? Are star elves not capable of handling our own affairs. Let me understand what you all have told me. We have lost the polymorph world. We have lost our armada. Our armada, in the hands of these creatures or unknown parties, are on a warpath to our fleet here above Pan-Earth?"

"Yes, m'lord."

"I want the entire war command woken."

"Already done, m'lord. They await your orders."

"My orders are to intercept the armada. If control cannot be established immediately, they are to destroy every vessel before they arrive here."

"Yes, m'lord!" the elves said.

"Go!"

The elves turned and briskly ran from the chamber. The one elfin wizard remained behind.

"What of the polymorph world, m'lord?"

"We will tend to them afterward. But these polymorphs are animals. They could not do this. They follow, not lead."

"M'lord, I did not want to say in front of the others."

The elf's attention turned to the elfess under the covers.

"Leave!"

The elfess wrapped herself in the covers and ran from the chamber. Sol-ren threw a magic chard of light, slamming the door after her.

"You know who is behind this?"

"We have many floating eyes around the world, m'lord. One of them viewed a vessel approach the far side of the world."

"When?"

"A month ago."

"And why was nothing done?"

"Something was done, m'lord. Our outpost kingdom sent a squad of the creatures to find the vessel and any occupants. The creatures returned to our base a week later but not alone. Thousands of those black goblin creatures were with them."

"Pookas?"

"Yes, m'lord. Thousands."

"Even those creatures do not possess the intellect to do this."

"Yes, m'lord."

"Then who? Who among our enemies did this? I want to know. If you do not know, I want a list. Do we not have the magic to tell us the race of every possible living thing in a place?"

"We used the magic, m'lord. Whomever it is, has the magic to block the spell."

"Whomever? One person?"

"Yes, m'lord. We believe it is only one person. It may be a human."

"Impossible. Humans know nothing of the void of the heavens, other worlds, let alone our secret world of the polymorphs. No. It must be another masquerading as a human. I want you to gather all our wizards. I want this single person captured, not killed. I must know if this is a wider plan against us."

Sol-ren paced back and forth in front of the watch-mirror in his throne command room. Elves ran in and out of the room with news or to get more information. His war wizards were assembled around his throne. Whether individually or in groups, they were casting spells.

"The fleet is about to make contact with the rogue armada," a star elf said.

"Let me see," Sol-Ren stopped in front of the watch-mirror.

The fleet vessels were smaller by half but faster than the approaching armada vessels. All looked similar to sea ships but covered decks. The ingenuity of celestial elfin design—vessels could travel the void of the heavens, through the sky of a world, sail its seas and oceans, or travel underneath its waters.

"The armada is not answering calls or slowing, m'lord. Do you wish us to board or destroy them?"

"Send a boarding party onto one. Tell them to get to the bridge and seize it."

"Yes, m'lord."

Sol-ren stared angrily at the watch-mirror. "What was that?"

All in the throne command room watched as the armada vessels opened fire on the fleet vessels. The fleet vessels were overwhelmed by starfire and destroyed.

Sol-ren looked at his wizards and men. "How could they fire?" he yelled. "Only I have the magic commands."

"M'lord!"

Sol-ren turned to see the armada vessels begin to explode, one after another. The elves stood helpless and in shock. Soon they were numb to their emotions. The disaster was beyond comprehension. Their void fleet that guarded their star elfin kingdoms and the armada that guarded the sky elves world of polymorphs were all destroyed.

Minutes became hours as the elves stood in the room staring at the watch-mirror.

"Lord, we are being contacted," a star elf said.

"The celestial elves?"

"No, m'lord. They did not identify themselves."

"Let me see."

A single scout ship from an armada vessel. Sol-ren waved his hand. The elves watched the vessel explode.

"Lord, did we not want to—"

"Want to what?" the star elf lord yelled. "Hear the voice of the one responsible for this horror. The cloud elves will take advantage of this. Or maybe night elves. The moon elves even. Whomever it was is dead too. That is all that matters."

"M'lord," one of the elfin wizards said. "Someone is aboard this vessel. An intruder."

Sol-ren reached and grabbed the wizard. "Take all the wizards and deal with them."

The wizards began to walk from the room.

"Don't walk! You are wizards! Teleport yourselves there."

A whirling doorway appeared in the throne room and the corridor of another level. The creatures spilled through. One of the wizards managed to collapse the portal doorway but he was the first killed. The creatures were transforming into a dizzying array of other forms as they attacked the elfin warriors and wizards. At least a dozen of the creatures got through and had already killed most of the elves and destroyed most of the throne command room, including the watch-mirror.

Sol-ren threw magic balls of starfire at them. One of the polymorphs turned into a phoenix and blasted the star elf with a wave of fire. A wizard draped his cloak over the lord and both elves reappeared elsewhere on the vessel.

"We must escape the vessel, m'lord," the wizard yelled.

"We have woman and children aboard!"

"We have no choice, m'lord."

Alarms sounded throughout the vessel. Sol-ren looked up at the ceiling.

"We are already here, m'lord. Take an escape vessel back to our floating castles outside Atlantea. I will remain and do what I can."

The wizard stopped speaking. A lone wolf-dog strolled down the corridor. The slender animal had a smooth coat, uncharacteristic of wolf dogs.

"Your wizard should attend to the woman and children. At least they should be able to escape. The Atlanteans will offer aid."

The speaker was invisible but Sol-ren recognized it. He looked at the wizard.

"Go. Ensure all who can escape to Atlantea can."

The wizard wanted to say something but instead ran, disappearing into invisibility.

Sol-ren turned back to stare at the wolf-dog at the end of the corridor. "You have your own creature, human. How long has it been? Twenty human years of so?"

A human male came out of invisibility. A hooded young man dressed commonly but cleanly, with two covered, sheathed swords strapped to his cloaked back. His dark hair was groomed short, and had no other hair on his face. Traveler.

Sol-ren smiled. "You have grown up too and learned a few fae tricks."

"I heard, Lord Sol-ren, that after our last encounter, that both the star and celestial elves were very upset with you. You and your entire kingdom banned from Atlantea. But you are a resourceful elf. You turned your demotion in rank on Pan-Earth to a promotion above in the heavens. Overseer of the conquered world of polymorphs.

"I am sorry to tell you this, Sol-ren, but my dog and I have turned the world back over to their natural owners. You sky elves will not be able to return to enslave any more shape-shifters for your amusement or wars. They have all the knowledge they need to defend that world from any outsiders. Losing the polymorph world, the flying Pan-Earth fleet, the flying star elf armada. Sol-ren, your lording days are over. Maybe the celestial elves will allow you to be a slave to some blind fae somewhere in Lands of Man."

Sol-ren's hands glowed bright yellow. "Is this between us? Or will your dog join in?"

Traveler pulled his main sword from his back. "Just me. I know how to use this now." He flicked the sheath off the sword and the star elf could see the translucent flame engulfing its blade.

Sol-ren created a magic sword of starfire. "You have come far, human. I guess I have no one to blame but myself. All I had to do was let you die at the hands of that land manticore."

"No, Sol-ren. All you had to do was not be the evil beast you are. You chose the path for us to be enemies when we could have been allies. I would have gladly stayed to learn the ways, the good ways, of star elves. But that is not what you wanted."

In the blink of an eye, Sol-ren had moved from his spot to Traveler, striking with his star magic sword. The blow was blocked by Traveler's sword with little effort—a piece of a Titan sword itself, said to be the combined power and essence of a real star itself.

Sol-ren stepped back. His star magic sword dropped to the ground, dimmed in intensity, then faded away. The star elf felt strange.

"I do believe you ran me through with your sword before you blocked my strike," the star elf said, almost slurring his words. "Humans are not supposed to be able to do that. I am in desperate need of...a healer."

"I am sorry. I am not a healer anymore. I am a quest master. I cannot help you."

Sol-ren collapsed to the floor. The blood of star elves was like milk to the human eye when not filled with its star magic. Sol-ren's body was soon at the center of a pool of milky white.

Traveler and the dog were gone. The alarms sounded as the entire vessel began to violently shake. The vessel had reached the upper atmosphere of Pan-Earth in the magical realm above Atlantea.

From below, within the fabled kingdom of Atlantea, fae, elementals, and others watched the skies. They smiled and cheered as a giant fireball fell to the earth, exploded, and became a shower of many falling stars, burning up as they fell. None knew the spectacle was indeed the end of a star elf empire, or what would follow.

The Fabled Quest Chronicles continues!

REVIEW REQUEST

Dear Reader,

I hope you enjoyed ***Quest Master (Prequel to the Fabled Quest Chronicles)***.

<u>Can You Write Me a Review?</u>

If you enjoyed ***Quest Master (Prequel to the Fabled Quest Chronicles)***, I'd greatly appreciate an honest review on one or more of the following sites:

Reviews are the best way for readers to discover good books. My writer's motto is simple: "Readers Rule!" Thanks so much.

Always writing,

Austin Dragon

JOIN THE CLUB!

Don't forget to Join My Exclusive **VIP Readers' Club**!

My fiction universe includes Epic Fantasy, Sci-Fi and more. Your benefits include free books, the latest announcements, special offers and fun giveaways.You can unsubscribe at any time.

Sign up Today and get FOUR of my full-length novels **FREE**! Join at http://www.austindragon.com

Always writing,

Austin Dragon

CONTINUE THE ADVENTURE

Get Your Next *Fabled Quest Chronicles* Books!

- ***Through Titan's Trail*** (Fabled Quest Chronicles, Book 1)
- ***In the Shadow of the Kings*** (Fabled Quest Chronicles, Book 2)
- ***Comes the War Wizards' Wrath*** (Fabled Quest Chronicles, Book 3)
- ***The Forest of Ancients*** (Fabled Quest Chronicles, Book 4)
- ***Siren Storms of Madness*** (Fabled Quest Chronicles, Book 5)
- ***Kingdom at Titan's End*** (Fabled Quest Chronicles, Book 6)

- ***Fabled Quest Chronicles Box Set*** (Books 1-3)
- ***Fabled Quest Chronicles Box Set 2*** (Books 4-6)

Prequels

- ***Quest Master*** (Prequel to the Fabled Quest Chronicles)

Also by Austin Dragon

See all my books in fantasy, science fiction, and horror:
http://www.austindragon.com/books

GLOSSARY

List of Races, Beasts, and Monsters of Myth and Magic

Axex - pronounced A-Z-E-X. They were popular in the Lands of Man before the griffins. They had the head of a hawk and a body of a very slim, sleek lion and were swift runners. Smaller ones are used as hunters and watch dogs; larger ones are used as steeds. There are also different feline species such as leopard axexs.

Basilisk - a creature with the head of a rooster, long serpentine tail and leather skin and wings, though it cannot fly. The size of a large chicken it can cause death in living things with a single glance. Its skin is highly poisonous to the touch.

Brownies - halfling sprites who look like old men with short curly dark hair and wear brown pointed conical caps and clothes. These fae are nocturnal, coming out at night to do their daily chores. They make their homes in enclosed dwellings or traveling wagons.

Carcolh (or Lou Carcolh) - a gigantic hybrid creature, both snail and snake. On its long, snake-like, slimy body is a gigantic snail-like shell larger than a two-story hut. Its head looks like a giant snail but it had a teethed, circular mouth like a lamprey encircled by tentacles. But its long tail was also covered with tentacles.

Centaur - one of the major races of fae who live in patriarchal societies. They are half-man, half-horse; having the torso of a man extending where the neck of a horse should be.

Cù-sìth - the name means "fairy dog" and it is as large as a small horse with a shaggy, green coat. It has pointy green ears and a long-curled tail. Some have a long tail rolled up in a coil on its back. Often, it has other animals such as birds and squirrels resting on its back. Forest fae, especially leshies, have them as watch dogs or guardians.

Cyclops - a sub-race of giants with a single eye in the center of their forehead. There are any different clans, both civilized and savage. Some are gifted builders, craftsmen, and merchants. Others are scholars and artisans. Rare ones are seers and oracles, able to see what cannot be seen with the normal eye or the future. There are also savage clans known for their ferocity and cannibalism.

Dire-cat - a large, black saber-toothed wolf-sized wild cat.

Dire wolf - a large black wolf used as steeds by goblins.

Doppelgänger - said to be a sub-race of day-walking trolls, the creatures take the identical form of other living humanoids to assume their identity, including their exact attire at transformation. Accounts conflict as to whether they also can magically assume a victim's memories. Most believe it is their observing a victim over time from invisibility to learn all their mannerisms before taking their victim's form. Contrary to human stories, they rarely kill victims; they simply move on to another, so as to not arouse suspicion and cause mischief and trouble for the victim upon their return.

<u>Drow</u> - or dark elf (not to be confused with a night elf) is a member of an elfin sub-race characterized by dark bluish skin, most often white hair—though some have black hair, and their eyes often have irises of a bright color, such as blue or purple. Drows wear only dark colors like black, dark blues, and dark purples. The original Drow sub-race had separated from high elves due to embracing dark magic. Drows abandoned the practice long ago but remain enemies to all elves, and most fae.

<u>Elf</u> - one of the major races of fae and the one most resembling humans in appearance. They are humanoids characterized by pointed ears, taller than the average human, and slim in build. They have fair to porcelain-like skin—though there are sub-races with darker skin. Their eyes can be one of many different colors, depending on their sub-race and clan. Their senses, strength, and stamina are far superior to humans. As with many fae, they can make themselves invisible through magic in their natural environment, can move at extreme speed whether running or fighting—almost seeming to jump from one point to another in the eyes of humans, and are very long lived. Along with centaurs, they are known as the top archers in Faë-Land. They fight with blade weapons never bludgeoning weapons, and bows, never crossbows.

Different sub-races of elves have additional physical and magical abilities.

<u>Sub-Races of Elves:</u>

<u>Drow</u> - or dark elf (not to be confused with a night elf) is a member of an elfin sub-race characterized by dark bluish skin, most often white hair—though some have black hair, and their eyes often have irises of a bright color, such as blue or purple. Drows wear only dark colors like black, dark blues, and dark purples. The original Drow sub-race had separated from high elves due to embracing dark magic. Drows abandoned the practice long ago but remain enemies to all elves, and most fae.

<u>Fairy Elf</u> - one of the flying elfin sub-races with greenish or bluish skin, the tips of their pointed ears are at least six inches tall, their foreheads have long antennae above each eye, and they have large insect wings, invisible to humans.

<u>Forest Elf</u> - one of the elfin sub-races of the large forest lands of Faë-Land.

<u>High Elf</u> - one of the elfin sub-race of tall, regal elves, exceptionally beautiful/handsome in appearance. High elves consider themselves the most royal and highest of all elves. They dwell exclusively in highly advanced and magical cities.

<u>Woodland Elf</u> - an elfin sub-race known as the best trackers in the forests with strong societies built around hunting. They have eyesight more powerful than eagles and magically can see the "after-presence" of prey they are tracking. There are two main divisions: Rustic—who live in wooded lands of modest hamlets, and Hunter— who fashion themselves after high elves and live in large tree cities.

Fairy - one of the major races of fae who live in matriarchal societies governed by queens. Fairies are often insect-like, but there are also bird-like, reptile-like, amphibian-like, mollusk-like, snail-like, and plant-like races. They are shape-shifters able to take the form of other animals, such as smaller mammals, birds, or insects. Like sprites, their different sub-races and tribes have differing magical powers. Like many fae, they possess the ability of "sizing" wherein they can magically increase or shrink their size to defend themselves. Fairies live and work with animal companions, most often birds or insects.

Giant - one of the major races of fae who live in patriarchal societies governed by kings and chiefs. The majority of the giant races are warriors, all possessing great strength, but others have kingdoms of diverse occupations. Giants can range in height from ten to one hundred feet.

Sub-Races of Giants:

Cyclops - a sub-race of giants with a single eye in the center of their forehead. There are any different clans, both civilized and savage. Some are gifted builders, craftsmen, and merchants. Others are scholars and artisans. Rare ones are seers and oracles, able to see what cannot be seen with the normal eye or the future. There are also savage clans known for their ferocity and cannibalism.

Grendel - sub race of evil shape-shifter and carnivorous giants.

Gnome - fae halfling sprites known for their perpetual happy-go-lucky personality, amiability, and love of dancing, singing and music. They often have beards but not always. They often look older, but there are baby-faced clans. They always wear hats, though gnomes exclusively wear pointy, often red, conical hats.

Gnomoid – there are many races of sprites similar to gnomes, though not as good-natured. They also wear hats but not the pointy conical ones of gnomes.

Goblin – one of the major races of dark fae that resemble a kind of elves in appearance. Their skin is green, their frame stout and muscular, their noses flat, and their pointy ears were larger. They are the mortal enemies of elves.

Griffin – a fantastic beast with the body, tail, and hind legs of a lion and golden yellow fur. Its head and foreleg talons are that of a giant eagle. The animal is known for its echoing roar. Griffins are often used by fae as royal steeds or guardians of treasure. Like hippogriffs, they have a fondness for eating horses of the Lands of Man.

Sub-Races of Griffins:

Elefantagriffs – are large griffins with the head of a feathered elephant.

Liongriffs – winged lion with forearms and talons of an eagle.

Owl griffins – are griffins with the head of an owl.

Tigergriffs – winged tiger with the forearms and talons of an eagle.

Zebragriffs – head of a zebra.

Haltija – a sub-race of sprites that guard, help, or protect something or somebody. Haltijas appear as frowning full-bearded halfling men with pointy hats.

They are nocturnal sprites like brownies, coming out at night for their daily tasks. They are ill-tempered, rude, surly, and hate being talked to directly. They are also shape-shifters. A clan of haltijas is called a väki and there are many different clans in Faë-Land. (See Väki)

Hieracosphinx - a wingless beast with has the head of a hawk and the body of a lion.

Hippogriff - a fantastic beast that has the hind half of a horse and the front half, including head and forelegs, of a giant eagle. It is known for its loud eagle shrieks. Like griffins, they have a fondness for eating horses of the Lands of Man.

Hobgoblin - the creature is about three feet in height. Their pointy ears are longer and thinner, sprouting from the sides of their heads. Their noses are hooked. Their teeth are long and sharp like piranha, and have beady little eyes. They wear dark clothes—tunics and trousers—and curled pointed shoes.

Il-Belliegha - often called an "arm monster" is a creature that appears as a monstrous arm with thick pulsating veins. It lives in deep dark wells and any large dark cracks or holes in caves or mountains. They prey on passersby by grabbing and pulling them into their lair never to be seen again.

Keythong - a beast, a slender griffin but without wings. Instead of wings, it has spines from its back and shoulders, often resembling an abstraction of the missing wings.

Kobold - a race of shape-shifting sprites who can take the form of an animal, fire, a human being, and a candle, or become invisible. In their humanoid form, they appear as figures the size of small children, little, wrinkled old men wearing caps. There are three major types of kobolds. Most commonly, the fae are house sprites of ambivalent nature. They sometimes perform domestic chores, but can play malicious tricks if insulted or neglected. Another type of kobold haunts underground places, such as mines. A third kind of kobold, the Klabautermann, lives aboard ships and helps sailors. Those that live in human homes wear the clothing of peasants; those who live in mines are hunched and ugly, and sometimes are said to have black skin. Kobolds who live on ships smoke pipes and wear sailor clothing.

Though harmless to the benevolent, when angered kobolds have been recorded as cutting victims to pieces and eating them.

Mine kobolds are expert miners and metalworkers, often drilling, hammering, and shoveling dirt to claim metals or precious stones. Evil ones are blamed for accidents, cave-ins, and rock slides that upon human or fae miners. A favorite kobold prank was to fool miners into taking worthless metal ore or gems, or, sometimes even, when smelted, could be deadly poisonous. Benevolent ones warned miners not go in a dangerous direction, led miners to veins of metal or richer ones.

Kraken (Sea) - a gigantic squid-like creature that attacks with multiple giant tentacles and has a beak-like mouth. Sizes of the creature vary but it is known to be the largest and most fearsome of hunters in oceans of the magical lands.

Leshy - known as guardians of the forest, they are male fae with white skin and hair and full beards of living grass and vines. They have bright green eyes and hoofed feet, and some have horns and tails. They are shape-shifters known for the ability to take the form of any animal or plant. They can shrink to the size of an insect or grow to the size of the tallest tree. They can imitate the voice of any human or humanoid, make the sound of any animal, and can scream horribly to frighten enemies. They often keep animals as companions, the favorite being a cù-sìth.

There are also dark leshies given to leading travelers astray, kidnapping, or making people sick.

Merman - Ugly male sea humanoids that look like a brown fish but with the head of a man—blue-green hair, unsightly teeth, and slits for eyes. They enjoy storms and being present at sinking ships. Despite their appearance, they can magically cure sickness and lift curses. Others are sages and oracles.

Mimics - are deadly guardian creatures created by magic that appear as a wide variety of inanimate objects wherever treasure is found. The objects spring to life to prey on treasure seekers by retaining their main form—a weapon or piece of furniture—but contorting and stretching parts of their form to attack as sharp stabbing or cutting objects, tentacles or mouths with sharp teeth.

Nisse - A sub-race of sprites who are very friendly and gregarious little people, knee-high, wearing bright green pointy hats as long as their bodies. They are never without a smile on their face. There are both men and women. The bearded men dress in standard dark tunics and trousers; the women dress in lighter colored dresses with their blond or brunette hair braided behind them. Other nisse wear red or orange hats too. They are believed to have shape-shifting abilities too.

Despite size, they have tremendous strength, like all sprites. Often, they are protectors of farmlands, livestock, and animals. They are easily offended by rudeness, laziness, and the mistreatment of animals.

Nix - are a race evil shape-shifting water nymphs who can appear in the form of other creatures and fond of drowning humans.

<u>Nymph</u> - one of the major races of fae who live in matriarchal societies. They are enchanting, beautiful women with long hair. They look human, but have an angelic glow. Human men are helpless to their powerful, magical attraction; fae men can also be susceptible to their enchantment.

<u>Phoenix</u> - a bright orange-feathered bird glowing and flickering in flames, with wings twelve feet wide or more. The elemental birds make its habitat in volcanoes, the Nether-Lands, and lands of earth and fire elementals.

<u>Phooka</u> - also known as pooka, púca, phouka, phooka, phooca, puca, orpúka. They are fae shape-shifters that always take the form of some humanoid animal or animal but always black in color. The malicious ones are violent and dangerous, taking the form of frightening black animals. The benevolent ones are given to mischief and harmless pranks, not unlike fairies, but they can be quite helpful and are only dangerous to evil beasts and beings. All phookas can take the form of dogs, foxes, wolves, cats, horses, goats, rabbits, birds, and much more to frighten and shock their enemies. They are especially fond of changing into distorted versions of those animals or a combination of more than one or changing into humanoid forms with animal features.

<u>Redcap</u> - are a sub-race of evil, murderous goblins. They appear as short, old-looking humanoid males with coarse, graying hair down their shoulder, long prominent teeth, skinny fingers ending in talons like eagles, large eyes of red, a fiery red color, grisly hair streaming down his shoulders. They wear iron boots, carry pikestaff weapons, and, more prominently, wear red caps on their heads, said to be red from soaking it in the blood of their victims.

Urisk – a benevolent fae that looks like a satyr or smaller stature, with a human torso and shaggy goat legs. Urisks were extremely introverted but also able fae guardians of the woodlands and especially of animals.

Väki – a clan of haltijas. Besides the tulen väki or väki of fire there are also väki of specific trees, forests, mountains, water, precious metals or gems, underground lands, etc.

ABOUT THE AUTHOR

Austin Dragon is the author of over 20 books in science fiction, fantasy, and classic horror. His works include the cyberpunk detective *LIQUID COOL* series, the epic fantasy *FABLED QUEST CHRONICLES*, the international epic *AFTER EDEN* Series, and the classic *SLEEPY HOLLOW HORRORS*. He is a native New Yorker but has called Los Angeles, California home for more than twenty years. Words to describe him, in no particular order: U.S. Army, English teacher, one-time resident of Paris, ex-political junkie, movie buff, Fortune 500 corporate recruiter, renaissance man, futurist, and dreamer.

He is currently working on new books and series in science fiction, fantasy, and classic horror!

Connect with Austin on social media at:

Website and blog: http://www.austindragon.com
Pinterest: http://www.pinterest.com/austindragon
Goodreads: https://www.goodreads.com/ADragon

See all my books at:
http://www.austindragon.com/books